Also by Eden Finley and Saxon James

Bromantic Puckboy

Also by Eden Finley and Saxon James

Puckboys

Egotistical Puckboy
Irresponsible Puckboy
Shameless Puckboy
Foolish Puckboy
Clueless Puckboy
Bromantic Puckboy
Forbidden Puckboy
Possessive Puckboy
Stubborn Puckboy
Charming Puckboy

BROMANTIC PUCKBOY

EDEN FINLEY & SAXON JAMES

canelo

First published in the United Kingdom in 2024 by Eden Finley and Saxon James

This edition published in the United Kingdom in 2026 by

Canelo, an imprint of
Canelo Digital Publishing Limited,
20 Vauxhall Bridge Road,
London SW1V 2SA
United Kingdom

A Penguin Random House Company
The authorised representative in the EEA is Dorling Kindersley Verlag GmbH.
Arnulfstr. 124, 80636 Munich, Germany

A CIP catalogue record for this book is available from the British Library.

ISBN 978 1 8359 8490 1

Printed and bound in Great Britain by Clays Ltd, Elcograf S.p.A.

Look for more great books at
www.canelo.co | www.dk.com

CHAPTER ONE

BILSON

"A-are you ... crying?" Aleksander Emerson asks beside me. He's one of the best teammates ever, and it's a shame he's not going to be there for me this season. In a weak moment, I decided it was time to leave Seattle once and for all, and as a free agent, I was shopped around to any team interested.

Nashville, here I come.

But that's not why I'm crying.

"Is it because you're not up there getting married?" Aleks whispers. "You know, not every wedding in Washington State has to be yours."

"It's so beautiful," I say.

Our linemate Dennan Katz stands at an altar, watching the love of his life as she walks down the aisle in all white.

"Don't get any ideas," Aleks says. "You don't need a fifth divorce."

Amen. Hence the wanting to get far, far away from Seattle. There are too many exes here, and when you have four ex-wives and countless former girlfriends, you realize Seattle is actually really, really, *really* small. Minuscule.

The reason I ended up signing with Nashville is because it was the team the farthest away from all my exes that was willing to offer me a good deal. Nashville needs help on their offensive lines, and I had one of the highest assist records in the league last season.

Moving to a new team isn't ideal—Emerson, Katz, and I helped take Seattle to the championship game this past year—but I need out.

"What can I say? I love love." Even with the number of exes I have, I still believe in love. For some unknown reason.

Love has ripped out my heart and put it in a blender countless times. It's as if my perpetual broken heart sees everyone I date as *the one*, and then I get so wrapped up in the possibility of finally finding true love that I ignore all the red flags telling me this *isn't* my person.

It's a real problem.

Which is why, since my last breakup, I've sworn off relationships. Which also means I've sworn off sex. Because I know me, and my pathetic neediness reads into every sexual encounter I have.

A therapist would say—and has said—that my need to be loved stems from a childhood of being neglected by my parents. I grew up as a privileged kid, but as my parents always liked to remind me, the only reason I was able to have the opportunities I had was because they worked. All. The. Time.

I barely saw them, they weren't affectionate, and they were such assholes to everyone around them, none of the nannies or housekeepers or butlers they hired stuck around long enough for me to get close to them.

It sounds like a whole lot of rich people problems, and I guess it is, but that doesn't mean the emotional scars are any less traumatic.

So, new state, new team, new town, new me. It worked for Aleks. He moved from San Jose to Seattle and found

Gabe. It could work for me too. I could find my Gabbie. You know, as long as I deal with all my baggage first.

I might crave love, but at this point in my life, I need to sort my shit out. I'm in my thirties now. Time to be a put-together human and all that other crap.

When Dennan and his new wife, Krystal, seal the marriage with a kiss, everyone cheers and whistles. I just watch them like a creeper because what they have, that spark in her eyes when she pulls back, the smile on his lips …

I sigh.

Aleks nudges my side. "I'll hand it to you, man. You haven't let any of your marriages make you bitter. One failed marriage was enough to turn me off for life."

"As if you and Gabe aren't practically married."

Aleks came out as pan after his marriage to his high school sweetheart fell apart, and his first season playing with Seattle, he fell for a firefighter. Who then introduced me to his coworker Rina. She was my most recent ex and the person who made me realize something.

With all my failed relationships, the common denominator is *me*.

Since that breakup, I've been hanging out with Aleks and his Collective friends that consist of all the queer dudes in the league. It's safe there. No women.

"Is it drinking time yet?" Gabe asks from the other side of Aleks. "I swear you've dragged me to five different weddings this summer."

"That's what happens with hockey players," I say. "Marriage and babies all take a back seat to the game. Once hockey season finishes, NHL wedding season begins."

Aleks taps my shoulder. "And this time, you weren't one of them. That's growth."

I'm not going to tell him that if she hadn't gotten scared off at the mere mention of living together so soon in our relationship, Rina could very well have been the next Mrs. Bilson. Thank fuck she has a good head on her shoulders and decided I'm too much work.

I know I am. I also know if I don't get my head out of the clouds and work on myself that I will never find what I'm looking for.

She'd told me when she broke up with me that love is like the fires she puts out. For it to grow and flourish, you need to stoke it and give it oxygen. Suffocating it will extinguish the flame.

She'd explained in one simple analogy why none of my relationships have worked out.

So, I'm working on me now. Can't say that it's easy or that I haven't checked out at least four different women at this wedding, Krystal's bridesmaids being two of them.

It's a sickness that I'm so damn desperate, but I'm trying here.

"Remember the wedding rule?" I ask Aleks and Gabe.

"Don't let you talk to any women," Aleks says. "How could we forget?"

"Yay," Gabe deadpans. "Another wedding where we get to babysit a grown-ass manwhore."

"Is that really any different than spending time with any of the guys in the Collective?" Aleks asks. "The only difference is, with them, you have to keep them from getting drunk and setting each other on fire."

"Fair point. Distracting Bilson with something shiny is much easier than trying to control that lot."

I cut in. "I know you're trying to offend me, but it's hard to be upset when it's the truth."

Gabe laughs. "I'm actually going to miss you, Cody."

I hold my heart. "Aww, for that, you can call me what everyone else on the team does."

"Ross Gellar?" Gabe asks.

I gasp. "Is that really what y'all call me behind my back?"

"No. Gabe's being an ornery asshole."

"You love my ornery asshole," Gabe argues.

Queer dudes talk about assholes a lot, I've noticed.

"Bilson. You can call me Bilson," I say before they start talking about all the gay sex they're going to have later. It doesn't bother me like it would with some other guys in the league, but I'm so hard up from refraining from sex that even thinking about it would make me horny. Gay sex, straight sex, any form of sex.

Urgh. It's already happening.

"I can't break my celibacy streak. Don't let me."

Aleks snorts. "You say that like a couple of months is long."

"It is!"

Aleks throws his arm around me. "It's official. You can't move to Tennessee. Who's going to keep you from having sex there?"

I freeze because of course I haven't thought of that.

"I think you broke him," Gabe snarks.

"Maybe you could ask your new bestie, Miles Olsen," Aleks says, knowing that's the last thing I'll be doing.

Miles Olsen is a cocky little dude-bro, who has ridden the goalie bench for Nashville or played in the AHL for most of his career. Until Czuchry kept playing on an injury and fucked his knee up for good. It was announced at the end of the season that he was retiring, and word has it that Miles will be taking over. So, this green rookie with a whole frat boy vibe will be my next goalie.

The man on my team all of us have to protect above any other on the ice.

I have nothing against the guy other than the way he'd smile at me after saving any shot on goal I'd try to get past him. There are some goalies that are easy to read on the ice, ones that you love going up against because you know how to score on them, but Miles is one that is impossible for me to penetrate.

At least I won't have to worry about that now we're on the same team.

Dennan and Krystal walk back down the aisle together, holding hands and hugging the guests seated at the edge as they congratulate them.

I'm so happy for my friend. "I don't think I've ever been to a wedding before where I didn't doubt the outcome. Look how in love they are."

Aleks squeezes my shoulder, but it's not in a playful way this time. "I think you're forgetting that marriage is more than the wedding. Anyone can fall out of love if they don't work at it."

I turn to him. "Are you saying I didn't work at any of my marriages?"

"No."

"Because all I did was work at them." Want them to stay. Stop them from leaving me.

"I know. But both parties need to put in the work."

"Please don't let me get stupid tonight."

"I got you."

"I thought you said he'd be easier to handle than the Collective," Gabe says from somewhere. "We turn our backs to go get off in the bathroom, and here he is, wasted off his face."

"I asked Gallagher to watch me while you were gone, and his idea of watch was to make me take shots. He said if I have alcohol in my mouth, I won't have room for some rando's tongue."

Aleks and Gabe look at each other with a defeated "he has a point" look.

"And I'm not that drunk."

"When we found you, you were hitting on one of the decorative ficuses," Aleks says.

"Gallagher said I should get all my flirting out on an inanimate object so I don't accidentally fall into a vagina."

Gabe presses his lips together like he's trying not to laugh.

"You're a lost cause," Aleks says and brings me into his side.

I must've been swaying or something because I feel steady in his arms. My head falls so it's on his shoulder, and with his big arm holding me up, it's the first time in a long time I've felt … stable? Like I'm not going to jump out of my skin?

I want to hold on to that feeling, but it doesn't last.

"Should I get you two a room or …?" Gabe asks.

I flip him off. "You get him all the time. Just let me use him as a standing post this once."

"Have fun with that, babe. I'm going to go get some cake." Gabe walks away, and Aleks calls after him.

"You're leaving me with him?"

"Don't worry. I'll have a piece for both of you too!"

"Your boyfriend is mean," I mutter.

"He is. But he wasn't lying when he said he'd miss you. So will I."

I lift my head. "You will?"

He nods. "You and Katz accepted me on your line, as your friend, no questions asked. When I started dating Gabe, you guys didn't blink an eye."

"Love is love, man."

He smiles. "You're an awesome friend. That's all I'm saying. And I'm really sorry your life isn't going the way you wanted it to."

"Nashville will be different." But even as I say the words, I have to ask, will it though?

Dennan appears out of nowhere, squishing all three of us together. "Group hug."

I push him off us. "You have a wife to cling to. Aleks is mine."

"And what does Gabe think of that?"

"I find it hilarious." Oh, Gabe's back. He shoves a fork full of frosting into his mouth.

Krystal steps up next to Dennan. "Dennan is going to miss you this season, Cody."

"Duh. Everyone will miss me. That's the point."

I'm either too drunk and am seeing things, or they all roll their eyes at me. That can't be right. I speak the truth.

"He even asked me to introduce my sister to you in the hopes you'd stay," Krystal says.

"Sister? You have a sister?" I perk up.

Aleks clears his throat. Oh. Right. Celibacy and all that jazz.

"No, thank you. I'm good. I have my hand. And Aleks and Gabe."

Gabe face-palms. "You have to hear how that sounds."

"How what sounds? I don't need a girlfriend to be happy when I can make myself happy. And when that doesn't work, I have you guys."

Everyone laughs, and that's when I do hear it.

"I mean to stop me from doing something stupid, not ... for that. They have each other for that. I have ..."

"Your hand?" Krystal asks, her eyes still shining at Dennan.

I clear my throat. "Yes. That. Exactly that."

"So, you don't want to meet my sister?" She glances over at her bridesmaids, and fuck, it's tempting. So tempting. Especially with me leaving. It would be the clean break I'd need. I could get off and forget about her tomorrow.

Only ... that's not me. Knowing me and my past history, I would probably fall in love with her, cancel my contract with Nashville, screw my career up, and it wouldn't work out anyway.

"No. I'm good on my own."

Now, if I could just get myself to believe that.

CHAPTER TWO

MILES

I sneak in the back door and wrap my arms around Mom from behind. "I'm nervous."

Without seeing her face, I know she's smiling at me in the way moms seem to have perfected. "I'm gonna be supportive because I love you, but I really don't know how I love you sometimes when you're such an idiot." She pats my hand.

I huff and pull back. "You're supposed to tell me everything will be okay. That I'm so talented and I've worked hard for this and everyone is going to love me."

She goes back to her iPad. "Why would I tell you all that when you're so good at it yourself?"

Dad laughs, and I swing around to glare at him.

"I don't hear you being supportive either."

"You're a goalie. That alone shows how supportive I've been. Do you know how many looks we get when we confess that our son is a ... a ... *crease keeper?*"

I scoff. "Goalies are the best."

"Did your rocks tell you that, buddy?"

"Don't you drag Stone and Seddy into this. At least *they* told me I was going to kill it today."

Mom hums, clearly not listening, and Dad throws his hands up. "A goalie, Lord. You gave us a goalie. What did we do to deserve this horror?"

"Why did I miss you both again?"

Mom doesn't miss a beat. "Because we're incredibly charming."

"Did you finish making your jewelry?" Dad asks.

I hold up the ziplock bag I'm clutching. "Got a baggy full of party favors." And definitely not something I was working on to keep my hands busy and mind off the huge year I have ahead.

"Someone's going to think you're talking about drugs," Mom says.

"That says more about them than me." I blow my folks a kiss before grabbing my gear from the back door and heading out to the car.

It's been a long three years. Longer, really, when I factor college into it. I've always been a family guy, super close with my parents and my siblings, cousins, aunts, and uncles. None of us had ever moved out of Nashville until I had the wild idea that going to college in Connecticut was a good idea. It was, because I met my frat brothers and had a hockey coach who saw a lot of potential in me, but it was a struggle not to throw in the towel. Homesickness is a very real thing, a thing dudes aren't supposed to have if you ask people round here, but my frat brothers, they got it. They're the main reason I stuck around.

Then my agent is the other.

He told me I could get a contract with Nashville, and while I've had interest from some other teams, I roughed it out with our farm team in Milwaukee for three years to get to where I am now.

Exactly where he told me I'd be.

Kinda.

My agent probably didn't envision me living with my parents, but when I'm already nervous about proving the team made the right choice with me and have no clue what this season will be like, moving back home was a no-brainer.

Optimal fam time while I'm at home while not stressing about having to look for a place on top of everything else.

My gut's in knots the whole drive to training camp. This is my team. I know them; I played with them multiple times last season, but that was only as a fill-in. The greenie stepping into the big man's pads.

This year, that number one is all mine, and I'll fight tooth and nail to keep it. All off-season, I've been working out, eating my body weight in pasta, and studying game tape until it made my eyes bleed. I haven't caught up with any of my frat brothers, only saw some of my teammates a handful of times, and other than a few family things I had to show up for—and the broship bracelets I handmade—I lived and breathed conditioning.

I've never been more ready.

I pull up in the parking lot at Ford Ice Center, feeling like a fraud compared to the fancy cars that are normally parked here. I'm proud of my truck, but it's no Merc, and that kinda thing gets in my head easily.

I open the group chat I have with my Sigma Beta Psi brothers.

I'm getting the doubts.

Dooms:
You deserve this. You got this. And if your team gives you shit, I'll fly down there and personally egg all their houses myself.

Their enthusiasm boosts my confidence. Even as more of my brothers weigh in, I close out of the message and jump from my truck, ready to own it. This year is gonna be frat as fuck.

There's no greater feeling than hauling my gear bag into the arena, knowing that I belong here. I'm bouncing. Excited. Gonna tackle the dudes I know in a hug and prepare any new ones for the Olsen era.

We're a team. We support each other. Ride or die. Stanley Cup or bottom of the barrel, we're all each other has.

Which is why I'm starting with these goddamn bracelets.

I bounce the ziplock bag in my hand as I walk, memorizing the hall and the smell of cleaning chemicals that do nothing to mask the decades of sweaty meatheads. This is the first day of the rest of my life. The moment I was born for.

The only time I hesitate is when I reach the players' lounge. I'm earlier than the coaches said, but that was on purpose. It'll help to get in, get settled, and then see my team one by one instead of all at once. I'm not expecting anyone else here yet, so when I walk in and find a guy I've gone face-to-face with a few times over the last year, my footsteps stall.

I'd forgotten about him.

Cody Bilson. Veteran player. Seattle superstar turned Nashville newbie.

I've admired the hell out of him for years, and saving all the goals he sent my way last year was one of my favorite moments of my career so far.

My smile spreads wide.

"Welcome!" I throw my arms wide. "Hope there's no hard feelings about handing you your ass last year."

He snorts and gets up to shake my hand, but I tug him in for a hug instead. Thankfully, he hugs back, zero awkwardness, and that's always a good sign to me. You can really tell a lot about a guy by the way he hugs. "Handed me my ass? Tell me again, which team made it to the Stanley Cup final?"

I look around the locker room. "Weird, I don't see the Cup with you. Oh wait, Seattle lost. Now you're with us, you might want to aim for more than a failing grade. You're working with the best goalie in the NHL, after all."

"Best? Might want to wait to actually play a few games before you go throwing those claims around, Rook."

"Why wait when it's inevitable?" I'm talking out of my ass, but it's easier to warm to people when they act confident. The last thing I want to do is go all rookie on someone with a career like Cody Bilson. Or fanboy. Nope. Nashville is my playground, and I'm never giving it up.

So I'll do what Robbie said and manifest my way to the record books.

"Oh, hey, I made you something," I say, dumping my gear bag and yanking open the ziplock. I fish around for the orange band with "MY DUDE CB" threaded on it, flanked by a star bead on either side. My teammates won't wear these, I know that, so we're not gonna talk about how long making the stupid things took me. No, the whole point of it is to get everyone relaxed and united right off the bat.

And so they know that I'm the kinda bro who makes other bros bracelets.

That part is important to me. Loads of my frat brothers are queer, and I'm not stupid; there are people in the league who are, too, and haven't come out for whatever reason. I'm not queer myself, but I sure as fuck love everyone the same. Sadly, that's not something I learned from my folks, and it's one of the reasons I'm so glad I did the whole college thing.

I pass Bilson his bracelet, waiting for the ribbing. The teasing. Maybe even him handing it back and telling me I'm an idiot.

He just *stares* at it though. For longer than is comfortable.

Then he glances up with the goofiest grin I've seen in my life and holds it out to me. "Help me put it on?"

Fuck yes.

Look at me and Cody Bilson being besties right off the bat.

CHAPTER THREE

BILSON

Miles Olsen? Complete opposite of what I was expecting. Sure, he's still got that fratty dude-bro vibe, but off the ice and up close, I get the impression he's faking his cockiness.

Would a guy who thinks he's the next best thing in hockey be giving out friendship bracelets?

Friendship bracelets. Are we in fifth grade?

Not going to lie though, it eased my mind about settling in with the new team. Made me feel welcome.

When Stoll, a veteran D-man who's been in the league about as long as I have, arrives and dumps his bag in the cubby next to mine, I notice he's also been Olsen'd. Though instead of MY DUDE CB, he has BIG D STOLL.

"Big D? Am I going to have to ask to move cubbies so I don't get a complex if we're naked near each other?"

"No one can compete with me, so someone has to do it." Stoll claps my shoulder. "Welcome to the team, old buddy."

"Thanks. That's one way to feel welcome."

Stoll smiles. "You can relax. Miles started calling me Big D last year as in big defenseman. I saved his ass on more than one occasion."

"Well, that makes me feel marginally better."

Stoll turns and folds his arms. "Now you tell the truth. Why did you sign with us when Seattle made it to the Stanley Cup game last season? We didn't even make the playoffs."

"Needed a change of scenery."

He whistles. "Bad breakup? I didn't even realize you'd gotten married again."

Having a reputation is *fun*. "Don't have to be married to have a bad breakup. But it's not only that. I needed out of that city where old Bilson was an idiot."

"Are you saying you're no longer an idiot?"

"Answering this is a trap, isn't it? Of course I'm still an idiot, but at least here I don't need to be reminded of past mistakes. I can start fresh. And hey, now I'm here, maybe this team will make the playoffs."

From across the way, I hear a deep laugh. A fratty laugh.

Both Stoll and I turn to where Miles is sitting on the bench in front of his cubby.

"Think that highly of yourself? From memory, how many goals did you get against me last year?"

He's doing it for show, I remind myself. At least, I think he is. So I use the brand-new information I have in my back pocket.

"How many times did Big D stop a goal for you last year?"

That makes his face fall, and now I feel like a jackass, but he recovers quickly and says, "Touché." Then he turns and gets back to paying attention to … is that rocks inside his cubby?

He pets one of them, and I look at Stoll to see if he's seeing what I'm seeing.

Stoll shrugs. "I'll take pet rocks and friendship bracelets over Czuchry's need to sage everything and urge us to put raw garlic up our butts any day."

"Goalies, man. They're an odd kind of species," I say.

"Heard that," Miles singsongs but doesn't turn to look at us.

As the room fills with more and more players, I watch as Miles hands out bracelet after bracelet. He's charming and easygoing, but I notice the breath of relief each time someone takes it from him. Like he's anticipating someone rejecting it.

It must be a rookie thing. Sure, I'm nervous about fitting in with the team, but that mostly has to do with gelling on the ice, getting our lines right, and kicking ass. He seems to genuinely want people to like him.

He's going to get eaten alive.

I've been in the league long enough to know that there are teammates who'll become your best friend and those who you'll have a professional relationship with only. Not everyone is going to love your personality, and as long as you keep it civil and respectful, it will all be okay.

For forwards, it helps if you're close with your linemates because you need to be in each other's heads. Same with D-men pairs. But as a goalie, Miles is kind of on his own.

I should take him under my wing, but I still don't know the guy well. Though I'm quickly realizing he's not as cocky as I first thought he was. He's young. Green.

I'll make sure to take it easy on him.

—

Fucking cocky little shithead. Screw taking it easy on him.

We've been running shooting drills, and I haven't gotten one past him. Not a single one.

And the more I try, the more frustrated I get and the cockier he gets.

I will not let this twenty-four-year-old baby get to me. I won't.

Yet, when I miss again and let out a hissed curse in frustration, all I get from him is a wink and an air-kiss.

I only need one. One score against him will make me feel better.

"Taking it easy on the new kid, huh, Bilson?" Finch asks.

"You can't tell through my gloves, but I'm flipping you off."

Finch doesn't look at all offended. He's the other winger on my line, so we need to be able to work together.

"It's like the guy can read me. Do I have a tell?"

"Statistically, you should've gotten one by him by now."

"Not helping," I say through gritted teeth.

"Does it really matter when he's on our team?"

Yes, I want to scream, even though it doesn't. It doesn't matter. I'd just like to not be bested by a rookie goalie who somehow knows where I'm going to put the puck every single time.

On my next shot, I tell myself not to think. Not to prepare. If I don't have a plan, he won't be able to read it on me. Still have no idea how the hell he does it, but I'm going to win.

Just. This. Once.

I shoot. Hold my breath. And then watch as the puck skims the top of his glove but keeps going, hitting the net.

"Yes. Fucking finally!"

Miles takes off his helmet and shakes out his sweaty blond hair that looks darker when it's wet. "Congrats, CB. One out of one hundred is a one percent success rate. Want me to call up the Writers' Association and tell them to start engraving your name on the Hart Trophy for this year?"

The team around us "Oohs" and laughs.

I skate up to Miles. "Just watch, Rook. Now I know how to get one past you. There's no stopping me."

"Bring it." Miles lifts his chin, pops his helmet back on, and challenges me with his blue, shining eyes.

So I do.

And the talented motherfucker stops every last shot.

I don't know whether to hate him or be impressed. Maybe it's both.

CHAPTER FOUR

MILES

"Say you're proud of me. Just once."

Stoll chuckles and shoves me from the side, almost sending me into the doorframe as we leave our last day of training camp. "You know what I miss about Czuchry? He didn't talk."

I humpf. "No, he poisoned my water with turmeric instead." It might have only been one time, but you don't forget attempted murder.

"Eh, turmeric is all right," Bilson says.

I whirl on him. "You actually like that stuff?"

"One of my ex-wives was really into the all-natural life."

"Maybe I need to ask for a trade."

"Good luck," Stoll says. "No one is going to want to be saddled with an unproven goalie who already has a cocky streak."

"No love." I throw my hands up. "No love from anyone."

But I'm talking out of my ass because we're through training camp—which I dominated—and half of my team are still wearing the bracelets I made them.

"Don't let a shot in first game, and I'll tell you I love you." Stoll's going to be eating his words.

"Annette and I have got this."

"Who's Annette?" Bilson looks my way. "One of your rocks?"

"Why would a *rock* be called Annette?" On what planet does that make sense?

"Then—" He face-palms. "Oh. A net."

"Yes."

"You named your posts?"

"Obviously."

"Next, you're going to be telling me you named your stick."

"Which one?" Who *doesn't* name their stick? "What am I talking about? They're *both* Cobra."

"There's a story there, and I don't want to know it." He turns to Stoll. "United Beerhouse?"

"See you there in ten."

The three of us split off for our cars before I think better of it. If I'm drinking, I don't want to be driving, and after a long-ass dry spell this off-season, I'd like a night of release before we get into our preseason games. My truck can wait here for the night. I redirect toward Stoll, but he's already pulling out, so I head for Bilson's car instead.

He hasn't turned it on, and when I get closer, I can tell it's because he's scrolling on his phone. He's so engrossed in his screen that when I pop open the passenger-side door, he jumps.

"Shit, Rook. What are you doing?"

"Getting a ride."

Bilson thankfully doesn't boot me out of his car—his very shiny, very *expensive* car. Exactly the kind of thing I'm going to be able to afford on my contract, and considering my meager salary in the AHL, I'm still struggling to believe this much money is real.

I wait for him to finish texting and toss his phone in the center console.

"How are you finding Nashville?" I ask.

"It's not as manly as I'd like."

"Umm ..."

He turns the car on. "Don't get me wrong, there are a lot of women. Practically everywhere. The grocery store. My hotel foyer. Even at the arena. I can't escape them."

My gaze rakes over his face as I try to figure out what he means by that. Too many women ... hangs out with Aleks Emerson's queer friends. The light in my brain clicks on. "Ohhh. Because you prefer men? That's cool with me, man."

"*What?*" Bilson yelps, just about breaking the sound barrier. "That's not what I'm saying."

"It's either that or you're a chauvinistic dick weed, so which is it?"

"Neither. I love women. Too much. That's the problem."

All his past divorces support that theory. "Must be hard at your age. Loving all the pretty young things and not being able to score."

"Fuck you, I score plenty."

"Yet to see evidence of that."

"What are you doing in my car again?"

I recline the seat and tuck my hands behind my head, getting comfy. "Catching a ride. Unlike some people in this car, I'm gonna get laid tonight."

Bilson's hands tighten on the wheel. "Have fun. I'm on a ... a celibacy kick."

"Sure you are, bro."

"No, really."

"Uh-huh." It's cute how desperately he's trying to sell it. "I really don't care if you strike out or not. My only concerns are my own dick."

"Cobra?"

I push down on my crotch. "Shh, don't summon him!" I swear to God, he rolls his eyes at me. Next time, I won't bother to give him the heads-up. "Look, I'm *just* saying that it makes sense, you know? You're not in your prime anymore, and when a girl sees you and then sees me, well ..."

His head whips around so fast he almost steers us off the road. "Wait. You think you're hotter than me?"

"Hotter, more charismatic, know what to do with my stick ..."

"You're a puppy compared to me. Women love a man with experience, who they don't have to coach in how to give them a climax."

I give him an exaggerated cringe. "Is that what happened with your ex-wives?" Emphasis on the plural. "Couldn't find the button?"

"Sex wasn't our issue."

"Just yours, then, huh?"

"You're very confident for a guy who only recently got off his training skates."

"At least I don't need a walking frame out there."

"These old jokes are fun," he says.

I sure think so.

"Next time, you can walk."

"Like you did?" I ask. "For three miles in the snow every day?"

"No one wants three of you that desperately."

"Ooh, dad jokes." The car slows as Bilson pulls up around the corner from the bar. "But if you really want to know which of us is hotter, there's an easy solution."

"What's that?" He switches off the car and looks at me.

"See who can get the most numbers tonight. It's going to be busy, and let's face it, none of our other teammates would give me a run for my money."

"Ha!" He points at me. "Even you think I'm good-looking."

"Duh, I'm not blind. Some people are into the Daddy look."

"I'm only thirty-one. At least I can grow a beard."

I automatically stroke my jaw because he has me there. Stubble is about the most I can manage before it looks like an untidy mess. "Beard or not, I'm easily hotter than you."

"No way."

"Admit it."

Bilson laughs. It's deep and husky, the kind of confident laugh that makes it obvious he's not threatened by me. "You're hot, but you've got nothing on me, Rook. I'll play your stupid game—maybe it'll shut you up for good."

"I doubt that." I unclip my seat belt so I can jump out. "I'm pretty fucking annoying when I win."

Then I hightail it inside to make sure I beat him to the bar. This game is stupid—and okay, juvenile, I can admit it—but it's fun to rile my teammates up. Stoll and Bilson are two of the most experienced players, and I don't want them to see me as a rookie forever. I want to meet them on their level and leave them with no doubt I can go toe to toe with them on and off the ice.

I have no idea what Bilson drinks, but I grab two beers and make my way to the table our teammates have overtaken. It's two days until our first preseason game, and we're sure as hell going to make the most of it because this season will be brutal. I refuse to think too deeply about it, but with Bilson filling in our weak side and a goalie who's not injured stepping up, well ... I knock on my head.

Will. Not. Think. About. It.

I'm only as good as my next game, and that's as far forward as I'm going to look.

I press into the space between Bilson and Jorgensen and hand over the beer.

Bilson takes it with a smile. "You old enough to be buying drinks?"

"It's either that or I pissed in a bottle to mess with you. How do you like your chances?"

"You know what, I think tonight is my lucky night." He takes a long swig. "And that hottie over there is making eyes at me."

I watch Bilson as he leaves the table and heads toward a leggy brunette. I'm such a nice guy I'll even let him have a head start.

"Think that'll be the new Mrs. Bilson?" Jorgensen sniggers.

"Nah, she's not blonde," Finch throws back. "Can't wife her if she's not blonde."

"We are a rare breed." I flick my hair, narrowly avoiding Finch's backhand.

"Put the flow away. Nobody here wants to lock down your ugly ass."

"Lucky for me the bar is full of pretty ladies. Future Mrs. Olsen, here I come!"

Bilson's moved on to his next target, and it isn't clear if he struck out with the first or if he's better than I gave him credit for, but that's the head start over. In the competition of rookie versus veteran, this round is going to the rookie. I might be able to save all the pucks he sends my way in training, but when it comes to anything else on the ice, he has me beat by a country mile.

He can have the ice … for now. The bar is mine.

The first woman I approach is gorgeous. She's really sweet, the type of woman my parents are begging me to bring home, and while we chat for a while and I get her number, there's no doubt in my mind that I won't use it. I'm not looking to settle down, though it's in the cards in the future, and there's no way she'd be into the kinda shit I am.

Bilson appears on my way to the bathroom, and he leans in as he passes me. "Three, motherfucker."

"There's no way."

"Keep underestimating me. You're making it too easy." He blows me a kiss and disappears into the crowd again.

I double up my efforts because I refuse to lose. I meant it when I said I was a cocky winner, and I'm not a great loser either. That's one of the bad things I learned from my frat brothers. We were all competitive to a fault—sports will do that to you—and the only time you accept a place other than first is never.

I get to three numbers and push harder. The fourth one is a struggle, but then lady number five walks over and slips a piece of paper into my pocket. I strike out as often as I score, but once I hit six, I let up.

Bilson's back with the team, and while it's tempting to keep going and really drive home how much better than him I am, I decide to call it a night. I already know which one I'm calling because she confirmed that she does, in fact, eat ass.

I drag a stool over beside Bilson and drop down onto it.

"Damn, it's a good night to be a winner."

He takes a long drink. "How many did you get?"

"Six."

I watch him slowly set his drink down.

"What's wrong?" I taunt. "Are you embarrassed I won, or is Alzheimer's kicking in?"

Bilson picks up his phone and is about to unlock it when he changes his mind. "Five."

I *crow* I'm so happy. "Five? Only *five*?"

"What's only five?" Stoll asks.

"Bilson's game." I break out into a dance, ending on the sprinkler that I pretend to spray all over Bilson. "Now, if y'all will excuse me, I'm gonna head off and claim my prize."

"Bilson didn't get five."

I gasp. "Liar! You only got one, didn't you?"

Jorgensen shakes his head. "He told us eight right before."

Eight?

Fucking *eight*?

Bilson shrugs. "Guess we'll never know."

I stare at him, trying to figure out if he's screwing with me. "Prove it. Show me the numbers."

"Nope."

"You have to. It was a bet."

He slowly takes another sip of his drink. "You know what? I don't think I will. You're just going to stew on it now, aren't you?"

"Stew? Me? Never. I won fair and square."

"Whatever you say, Olsen."

"Don't be an asshole. Show me."

"Nope."

Yeah, he's not getting out of it that easily. I go for his phone, but Bilson snatches it up before I get a hold on it. We wrestle over it for a second until I throw my weight against him—forgetting we're both on stools. I go toppling over, dragging him down with me, but no amount of bruised elbows and jarred hips are going to stop me from getting my answer.

The second I tug it out of his grip though, Bilson slaps it across the floor.

He tries to scramble after it, but I grab his ankle, fighting against him as I pull my way up his body until my legs are locked around his thighs, and my arm closes tight over his neck.

I snatch the phone up and hold it to his face.

"Say cheese."

Bilson grunts instead.

Close enough, the phone unlocks, and the second it does, I throw myself off him and run. I'm hollering and laughing as I tear through the crowd, madly trying to thumb through Bilson's notes app, where there's a new note for each number. I can feel him behind me. Gaining on me. Hunting me down like I'm opposition on the ice.

It just makes me run harder. Even when I count *nine* and could easily stop and admit defeat, I shove through the front doors. The bright streetlights lead my way through the people on the street, but before I've gotten a couple of steps, Bilson skids to a stop in front of me.

"Nine?" I act disgusted as I toss his phone back to him.

The asshole catches it with a smirk. "What can I say? Experience counts."

We're both panting lightly, and as much as I'd love to hold it against him, I can't. There's one thing still on my mind though. "Why'd you lie?"

"What?"

"You said five."

"Eh. I say a lot of things."

"Like lies?"

Bilson drags a hand over his face. "It doesn't matter because I'm not going to call any of them anyway. I *wasn't* lying when I said I'm on a celibacy kick. This is my fresh start."

"Your fresh start from what?"

He groans. "All my exes."

"You could stop marrying people, you know?"

"Of course! Why didn't I think of that? Stop marrying people—it's much easier than diving under a table every time I see them. Silly me!"

I stare at him. "I'm scared you're serious."

"Coming from the guy who talks to rocks."

"What? You don't talk to your pets?"

Bilson's face drops, and he looks miserable. "I don't have pets. Anymore."

"Oooh, did it die? See, I never have to worry about that with Stone or Seddy. They're my pals for life."

"He didn't *die*. My ex-wife kept him." Bilson expression sobers. "I miss his little face."

"That sucks, CB."

"I know."

"She won't give him back?"

Bilson does this adorable thing where he scrunches up his nose. "She said I work too much. Not like she can talk." He turns to steer me back inside. "Anyway, new start. New team. And new beer. Let me buy one for the winner."

I glance up at him in surprise. "Seriously?"

The smile he gives me is genuine. "Seriously." Then he *has* to add, "Doesn't matter what the team thinks. *We* know the truth."

CHAPTER FIVE

BILSON

The more time I spend with the team, the closer we get. I'm an easy guy to get along with; the only drama in my life is when it comes to relationships, so I'm gelling well.

Miles, on the other hand … He's choking on the ice, which makes him desperate to please the team off the ice. Since he was only the backup goalie for these guys last season, he stepped up when he had to and impressed everyone, but now we're heading into the regular season after losing every preseason game. I wish I could say it was because we're all sucking on the ice, but we aren't. Not totally anyway. There are the usual teething problems of a team welcoming newbies into the fold, but as a whole, we're not doing too badly.

I'm sure the last game ending with a 7-0 shutout is weighing on Miles's mind. Sure, we didn't score, and that's on us as offense, but we had so many shots on goal, and their goalie shut us down every time. The other team had way fewer chances to score, and Miles was like a sieve.

As we dress for our first regular game of the season, I can't help feeling sorry for the guy. He looks like he's going to vomit.

I cross the dressing room in my base layers and tap him on the shoulder.

He's holding his pet rocks, one in each hand, running his thumbs over them like he's patting them, and it might be weird for anyone else, but I'm realizing his weird quirks are a coping mechanism for him. At least, I think they are. I dunno, I'm not a shrink, but I've had my head shrunk enough to kind of understand.

He turns to me with something like fear in his eyes.

"Forget preseason. None of them counted." It's not the most reassuring thing I could say, but he needs out of his head. "I know it's not that easy to do, but if you go out there tonight with that rattling around in your brain, you're going to choke more."

"Anyone ever tell you that you're terrible at pep talks?"

I laugh. "Sorry. Just trying to help."

Miles lowers his gaze. "It's so much fucking pressure, you know?"

"Yeah, I get it."

"Do you? Like, if you screw up on the ice, the other team might score. If I screw up, it's pretty much a guarantee."

Damn. When he puts it like that …

"You know what I've learned in my many years playing?"

"Your many, many, many years? Go on."

I narrow my gaze. "I'll let you have that because you're shitting bricks, but the biggest lesson I've learned is to let losses go. Don't hold on to them. It will ruin you. This is a fresh start. A clean slate. Just remember that out there."

He nods. "I'll try."

"And hey, if that doesn't work, maybe go out there with the goal of not embarrassing us."

"That doesn't help. At all."

"Okay. So the clean slate thing. Do that. Do you have, like, a pregame ritual other than your rocks?"

Miles closes his hands over them. "Shh. They can hear you."

I roll my eyes. "Do you have any other ritual besides talking to your … pets?"

"No. Should I?"

"Doesn't have to be anything big, but for me, I like to start each game the same way. It centers me."

"What's your ritual?"

"I bring two fingers to my lips, kiss them twice, and then send them up to the hockey gods in the sky." I demonstrate.

"And people say goalies are weird."

I glance down at his pet rocks but say nothing.

"Fair point. Can I steal yours?"

"Sure. See if it works for you, or keep playing around until you find something that helps center your energy."

"I'd rather something that centered my point of gravity so I could be a wall against flying pucks."

"One step at a time, Rook."

"One step at a time," he murmurs.

We fist bump before I finish getting dressed, and then we get out on the ice for warm-ups.

I get down on the ice on my hands and knees, making sure my knees and hips are stretched out and flexible.

Stoll joins my side. "Saw you talking to Miles. You think he's going to choke again?"

I squeeze my eyes shut. "You did not say that on the sacred ice and jinx him."

"He can't hear me."

I glance over at Miles, who's getting a feel for the ice, skating side to side in quick succession. Then, he drops to his knees and bends all the way back so he's lying as flat as he can. I forget how much more flexible goalies are than us.

I have the urge to protect him. "It's his first season as a starting goalie. He's nervous."

"Let's hope he gets over those nerves quick. I'm too old to be diving in front of pucks."

"He's got this."

Just before we leave the ice for the preshow to begin, Miles catches up with me and grins.

At the same time, we raise our fingers to our lips, kiss them twice, and then point them to the sky.

Fucking hell, I hope it helps.

Once we get started, I should be focused on my own game, but for the first five minutes, all I'm focused on is Miles and praying he doesn't let one in. Every time Tampa gets possession, I hold my breath. And every time they take a shot on goal, I let out the biggest sigh of relief when he shuts that shit down.

If he makes it the entire first period without letting a puck past, I'll kiss his goddamn helmet. I almost feel like a proud parent.

But just as I think that, Tampa scores, and my nerves for him ramp up.

Okay, time to get my head out of his ass and up my own. Wait, that doesn't sound right.

Once I've got my head in the game, it only takes Finch and me a couple of minutes to even the score. When the buzzer for the period sounds, we're still tied.

We head down the chute, and Miles gets encouraging backslaps because that was an amazing period for him.

"Still got this?" I ask him.

"Feeling good. They got lucky. They won't be so lucky next period." He winks.

I really hope this is real confidence shining through and not overcompensating cockiness, but as we head back out there after the break, it doesn't matter if it's real or faking it until he makes it because he's true to his word.

For the entire game, he doesn't let another one in. And Tampa try. They try hard. They get more shots on goal than us, but like preseason where Miles had a rough couple of games, it's their goalie's turn.

It's how we walk away winning our first game of the season. Miles showed up when it counted, and now we get to walk away with the W.

When Miles skates up to me as we're leaving the ice, I throw my arms around him.

"You did good, Rook."

"I've decided I'm going to do that every game. It's so much easier than stressing about getting scored on."

I laugh. "Amazing game plan. So we can expect a shutout for every game this season?"

"Yup."

"It's good to aim high, but that might be too high."

"We'll see about that." He walks off with a spring in his step, and if it were statistically possible, I'd almost believe him.

I just hope that when his plan fails, he's able to get back up.

—

The fucking son of a bitch keeps it going for two more games. Three shutouts in a row. It's two more than I thought he'd be able to carry it on for and almost unheard of for a rookie to have that many in an entire season, let alone in a row. And even though he got scored on twice in the game after that, we still won by a single point.

We're all on a streak. It's the best start to a season Nashville has had in a long time, and everyone is buzzing. Buzzing, but not overcelebrating. We're not allowed to jinx a good thing.

But as we head for the airport for our first long road trip of the season, the good vibes aren't enough to perk up my mood.

I'm somber and full of dread.

Sure, I'm excited to see Emerson and Katz, but I'm not so excited to face off with them. My friends. My ex-teammates in a city full of ex-wives.

We're off to play Seattle, and I really wish it had been later in the season before I had to go back.

I get on the team plane and take a window seat, immediately putting on my noise-canceling headphones and disappearing into my own world. The only thing on my playlist is death metal because if I listen to any poppy love song, I might start crying. With my head on the window, my eyes closed, I try to drown out the sad voice in my head telling me I'm a failure. That's all that's left now when I think of Seattle.

My marriages. The Stanley Cup final that we lost last season.

Ugh. I am not this melancholy usually, and I hate when I get in this mood. It's been barely there since I moved to Nashville, and while that's been an adjustment, it's also been what I needed.

The seat next to me dips as someone throws their big body into it, but I ignore them. That is, until there's a tap on my shoulder.

I crack open an eye and turn my head. Miles is smiling at me like a puppy.

"We're a bitch?"

I frown. "What you call me?"

He cocks his head before reaching for my headphones and exposing one ear. "Swedish Fish?" He holds up a bag of candy.

"Oh. Sure. Maybe some sugar will give me some energy."

"Not feeling good?"

"Didn't sleep well," I mutter.

"Is it a sleep-deprived sex thing or a Seattle thing?"

"You know the answer to that. I'm still on my celibacy kick."

His eyes widen. "Still? Are your balls okay, man?"

There are snickers around us from those listening in.

"Completely fine, fuck you very much." I take some candy from him and pop them in my mouth, but before I can go back to my music, Miles lowers his voice.

"Is it facing your old team or facing your old city?"

"It's not so much the city but the people in it."

"Ah. The evil exes?"

That's the thing I probably hate most. I wish they were evil, but they aren't. "They're not evil."

"Anyone who steals someone else's pet is evil. End of story."

"Okay, yeah, that was an evil thing to do, but Hadley made a good point. I'm always gone. I can't look after a dog."

Miles throws his head back. "Aww, man, it was a dog? I thought it was like a cat or a hamster. Who the hell steals a dog?"

"She didn't steal it. Technically. She … wouldn't give him back."

"Same thing in my book."

Okay, now I'm sad again. "I really do miss that ugly fucker."

"Hey, whoa." Miles holds up his hands. "Even though she stole your dog, it's not okay to call a woman an ugly fucker."

I burst out laughing, and I think it's the first time in days—ever since being reminded of this game coming up—that I've genuinely laughed. "I meant the dog, dipshit. I don't miss her at all."

"Oh. Thank you for the distinction."

"Yeah, kinda important. I want to get in there, play the game, see Aleks and Dennan, and then fly to Edmonton. In and out real quick."

"Easy. I'd say it's like your sex life, but it's more than you're going to get anytime soon."

"Ugh. Don't remind me."

CHAPTER SIX

MILES

After sending a kiss to the heavens with Bilson, I prep my crease, stretch, and then have a word with Annette. This game isn't just a game. Bilson's going to be in his head enough as it is about the move, and I don't want him to start doubting it now.

"We've gotta do it for him," I explain. "You wouldn't want to make my CB sad now, would you?" Annette radiates affirmative vibes. "That'a girl." I give her a drink before filling my mouth with water too.

I feel like I'm finally warming up in my position. Preseason was a whole world of different to training camp, where I was saving straightforward goal after straightforward goal from my teammates that didn't prepare me for the tricky shit some of these other players are capable of.

There's a big difference between your instincts reacting under pressure and being prepared for what's coming.

It's unlucky for the opposition that I'm a fast learner.

"How are you feeling?" Stoll asks as he skates by.

"Like Seattle better be awake tonight. It's starting to get boring out here."

He moves off while I ignore the knots forming in my gut. It's another game. Another chance to prove myself. But all that pep talking ain't doing nothing for my brain because the silly fucker keeps reminding me how disappointed Bilson will be if we lose.

Nope. Not it. Not happening.

Apparently, Seattle isn't here to play around either.

Those assholes *are* awake tonight, and even when the first period ends with no points on the board, I'm beat. Annette's had my back, but I've had to work damn hard as well.

I catch up with Bilson as we're about to head out again. "I know he's your friend, but I really hate Emerson about now."

"Yeah, I think he and Katz are making it their personal mission to show me what I'm missing," he grumbles.

"Then let's show them everything you've gained." I hold up my glove for a fist bump, and he hesitates before bumping back.

"Don't embarrass me out there."

Not tonight. I take to the ice and leave the old man behind.

Annette's hyped up and hydrated, I'm ready to go, and this second period is when my guys will get points on the board.

Except we're barely five seconds into the period when Seattle has the puck and is bearing down on me. Katz passes to Emerson, who shoots it back to him so fast I'm sure Katz is about to take a shot. I'm in position, blood beating so loudly it's all I can hear. Katz lines up—

Then the puck is gone.

No.

I spin toward Emerson and cover as much of the goal as possible. The puck is a blur, coming right at me, and I throw out my glove, waiting for the hit that never comes.

The lamp lights up, and the home crowd goes wild.

I whirl on Annette. "What the *fuck* was that, babe?" I'm so mad I could kick something. I'm tempted to give her a warning tap with my stick, but I reel it in. That was as much my fault as hers.

Gritting my teeth, I water her down and force a drink myself, and then I tap her gently with my glove. "Sorry, Netty, I didn't mean it. I was mad, you know?"

Nothing.

"Aww, come on. Don't be like that."

I can feel her cold shoulder even over the chill of the ice.

She's such a brat sometimes. "Fine. Fine, it was all my fault. Better?"

She grudgingly accepts my apology, and I let out a breath of relief. The last thing I need is to be on bad terms with my posts.

Apparently, she's still pissy with me because a few minutes later, another shot goes whirling past, and Aleksander Emerson finger-guns me. I glare at him because I can't glare at Annette.

"All right. I get it," I snap at her. "I was an asshole. Can we move on now?"

She finally lets it go.

And while we might have messed up with those two goals, it's not like the rest of my team is doing all that well either. The wheels are slowly coming off, and my defense is nowhere to be seen. Seattle takes shot after shot, and it's lucky Annette is back on board because she saves as many attempts as I do.

The more Seattle dominates, the more Bilson screws up, and he gives away an easy penalty in the third. The power play might be Seattle's tipping point of confidence, though, because Finch sneaks one past them, making it 2-1, and we ride that score to the final buzzer.

I'm zapping with agitation. Still kinda pissed at Annette, not that I'll tell her that, and just all-around bummed that we couldn't get it together for Bilson's sake. I'd give up any of our other wins to have won tonight.

It feels like a long walk to the locker room, and Bilson beats me there. He's sitting in front of his cubby, still in full gear, dark hair a sweaty mess, and usually sweet eyes dull.

That won't do at all.

I throw myself down beside him, dying to get these pads off but wanting to make sure he's okay first, which is pretty fucking ridiculous, considering he's been in this position a thousand times more than me. Talking shit out is important though; it helps you get out of your head, and not enough of my teammates face their emotions like that.

"You good?"

"Yeah, just sucks." He yanks his jersey over his head. "Now I've gotta see Aleks and Dennan and hear about how that could have been me if I stayed."

"Yeah, but if you'd stayed, you wouldn't have gotten my awesome broship bracelet or had a rookie clinging to you like his life depends on it."

"You're right." Bilson hangs his head back. "What have I done?"

I laugh, feeling confident enough to leave him now he's at least making jokes.

We go through our usual cooldown and shower. Talk to the reporter circulating the locker room and listen to Coach reminding us that "Next time! Next time, we've got it!" I try really hard not to shoulder the blame of the loss when it was the whole team out there. The thing is, our forwards have each other. Our D-men have each other. They've got their lines and the people they work with side by side.

I'm the loner at the end. I meant what I said to Bilson. If they fuck up, they've got each other to pick up the slack and stop the worst from happening. If I fuck up, that's it. Having Annette beside me helps.

Stone and Seddy are right where I left them in my cubby, so I tuck them in my pocket and pack up my gear, ready to go back to the hotel before our early flight out tomorrow.

Bilson appears beside me. "Ready to go?"

I glance around to check he's talking to me. "Go where?"

"I need backup with Aleks and Dennan. I voted, you lost, so now you have to hold my hand and remind me I'm pretty."

I pretend to look him over. "Well, I can do *one* of those things."

"Just hurry up."

"Ahh, asking for a favor, then insulting me. How could I say no to that?"

"That question implies I'm giving you a choice here."

"What are you going to do? Kidnap me?"

"If it comes to that." He's so serious I almost believe him. "We're going to the bar where I met my ex-wife—"

"Which one—"

"And I *know* she's going to be there. She makes it a point not to go to games anymore, but she'd always meet her WAG friends afterward."

It's a struggle not to laugh. "And you can't meet them somewhere else?"

"You want me to ask the winning team of superstitious hockey players not to go to the bar we always drink at after we win a home game?"

He's got me there. "Then don't go."

Bilson looks stricken. "But it's the Queer Collective rules. We always meet up with each other."

"I thought that group was for queer dudes?" I look him over, but this time, I *actually* look, wondering. "You said you're not queer."

"I'm an honorary member!"

"I didn't know that was a thing."

He crosses his big arms and *pouts* at me. "If you want me to go alone, fine. I will. I'll get ribbed by my old teammates, and have to see my ex-wife, and mope over her not giving up Killer, and deal with a loss all on my own ..."

I blink at him.

His arms drop to the side. "Did my guilt trip work?"

"Nope, but nice try, bro. Lucky for you, I want to drown my sorrows and tell your old buddies how much I hate them. Lead the way."

Bilson punches the air and calls goodbye to the others while I follow him. He doesn't seem as down as I was expecting, which is a relief, and no one blamed me for the loss. It fucking sucks, but it could be worse.

Like seeing my ex-team *and* my ex-wife worse.

I tuck my hands into my pockets, thumb brushing Seddy's rough sandstone face. The rocks started as a bit of a joke, a fill-in for not getting to have pets of my own, but I've grown to love them. They're not a joke anymore. I can't imagine if someone took one of my babies and didn't give them back, so Bilson losing his *Killer* must have been horrible.

It plays on my mind the whole way to the bar.

CHAPTER SEVEN

BILSON

Aleks and Dennan stand from their corner seats when they see Miles and me approach.

"Sorry about the loss," Aleks says, and he almost sounds genuine. "Someone had to end your winning streak." He laughs and then hugs me.

"And here I was thinking you were trying to show me what I voluntarily gave up." I move on to Dennan for a hug.

"That too," Dennan says.

"You guys know this rock star, right?" I pull Miles forward.

Dennan's the first to shake his hand. "You had some great saves tonight."

Miles preens under the compliment. Of course he does. He's desperate for validation. Dennan and Miles talk hockey for a bit, but Aleks turns to me.

"How are you settling in in Nashville?"

"It's not like I've had time to explore the place, but the team is great."

"Yeah, I was not expecting you to turn up with Miles Olsen. Didn't you call him a cocky little shit last season?"

Somehow, even though the bar is noisy, Miles over-hears. "You called me what now?"

"If you're expecting me to deny calling you a cocky little shit, you know I won't. I've called you that to your face."

"But I didn't think you meant it!"

I almost feel sorry for him, but then he opens his mouth again.

"Oh, I get it. You were insecure because you've never been able to score on me."

"Duh. We hadn't spoken two words to each other. What else would I base my judgment on?"

Ugh. Now he's deliriously happy about that, but whatever, it's not a secret.

"I'm going to go buy you a drink. Maybe that will make you less intimidated by my talent."

I shove him toward the bar. "Fuck off, you cocky little shit."

"Sure thing, old man. I'll see if they have warm milk for your old, old bones."

"I'm so glad you found a friend on the same maturity level as you," Dennan says, and he might have a point. Maybe I get along with Miles so well because I have the emotional maturity of a twenty-four-year-old.

Case in point: when a group of blonde-haired women enter the bar, I don't need to look at their faces to know they're the WAGs or that my ex will be with them.

"Argh." I duck around Aleks to steal his spot in the very tight corner and slink down so she can't see me.

"I see that hasn't changed," Aleks says. "Still hiding from your exes?"

"It's so much easier in Nashville."

"Won't be for long," Dennan jokes.

"Nope. Still not dating. Or fucking."

They're both shocked by that, and I can't say I blame them. It has been a long time since I had sex, and while my dick might hate me, my willpower is still strong-ish.

"Can you two sit down so she doesn't look over here?"

They humor me and even shrink down with me. They're probably mocking me, but I don't care. The less attention over here, the better.

"What are you guys doing?" Miles asks as he puts two beers on the table.

"Shh," I say at the same time Aleks pulls Miles down with us. "Hadley is here."

Miles lifts his head. "Where?"

"With all the blonde women."

"Seriously, why are all NHL wives blonde? I'm gonna marry a brunette to mess up the aesthetics."

"My first wife was a brunette," I say and then add under my breath, "when I met her anyway."

"Which one is she?" Miles is still looking around.

I kick him under the table. "I didn't see her."

"Then how do you know she's here?" Miles asks.

"Because she would be."

"Surely she'd know you're here and wouldn't come out," Aleks says.

"She barely followed hockey to begin with. It's why I married her. I thought, 'This time, I won't marry a fan.' Didn't work out, obviously, but now she's friends with all the WAGs. She won't know I'm here. I guarantee it. She probably doesn't even know what team I play for now, only that I'm gone."

"Which one is she?" Miles whines now.

Aleks lifts his head. "The blonde in the tight pink dress."

"You're going to need to be more specific than that."

He looks again. "The bright pink."

I close my eyes tight. "Damn. Is it the one with the cutouts on the side? I love that dress. I will not look. I will not look."

"I have an idea," Miles says. In the next second, he's gone, and I watch in horror as he goes right up to my ex-wife.

"What is he doing?" I ask, stunned.

Aleks's brow scrunches. "It … looks like he's flirting?"

"Uh-oh." Dennan mocks. "Trouble in your bromance already?"

I take out my phone and message him:

> What the fuck are you doing?

He ignores it or has his phone on silent, I can't tell.

Miles's confident exterior apparently has game because it only takes one drink for us to watch in horror as he leaves with her. I don't have any feelings for her anymore—I realized really fast with her that I had repeated the same mistake I always did—and we were only married for a year, but watching as my teammate, my friend, walks out with her, it feels like a betrayal.

But then when I get a text message back thirty seconds later, I realize he's not an asshole. He's a goddamn idiot.

> I'm going to get your dog back.

"Hey, babe?" Aleks says into his phone while the two of us hide in the bushes across the street from my ex-wife's house the prenup agreement bought her. "I'm going to be home late. We have to rescue a rookie player from a cougar." There's a pause before he laughs. "No, not a literal cougar, but by the look of her, she does want to eat him alive."

"Shh." I softly backhand him. "If anyone sees us out here, we'll get arrested."

Dennan didn't come on this side excursion because his new wife was at the bar with the other WAGs, but Aleks said he didn't want to miss this mess.

Silly me thinking he was here for support.

Hadley doesn't close the blinds as she leads Miles into the bedroom, which is on the second floor. The lights are on, and my stomach churns. Is he going to hook up with her? How far is he willing to take this harebrained idea?

I don't want to watch that.

Hadley steps closer to Miles, but at about a foot away, Miles puts his hands on her hips and holds her steady.

"Oh fuck, they're going to kiss, aren't they?"

"Turn away if you don't want to see," Aleks says.

"It's like a car wreck. I can't not look at it."

When their lips touch, I screw up my face.

"Sorry, man," Aleks says. "Maybe your new bestie is actually a psychopath and wants you to be seeing this."

Just before I start to believe that, Miles breaks the kiss, says something, and then Hadley turns and walks into the bathroom, closing the door behind her.

Miles frantically takes out his phone and looks out into the darkness in our general vicinity. He knows we're here. My phone vibrates a second later.

51

Rookie:
Where's the dog?

CB:
She usually locks him away in the laundry room when she goes out or has company.

Rookie:
On it.

He turns and tiptoes out of the room, looking ridiculous, and it makes me laugh. He's trying to be light-footed, but we're fucking hockey players. We wouldn't know how to do anything lightly. But I'll give him props, he's quick.

My heart is in my throat, beating erratically, when my phone vibrates again.

Rookie:
I can't find a dog, only a rat-looking thing. It doesn't even have any fur.

CB:
That's him! Quick get out of there.

Rookie:
Come get him from the front door.

"We're moving," I say to Aleks.

We get up and run across the street, reaching the front just as Miles opens the door and hands me my baby. I have to hold in my shriek of excitement.

Killer starts licking me and going nuts. He lets out a yip, and I can't help it. "Aww" falls from my lips.

"Leave before she gets out of the shower," Miles says.

"You're going to stay?" I yell.

"Teammates should share everything. Is ex-wives not on that list?"

This is one of those times where I can't tell if he's being his weirdo goalie self or serious.

He grins. Okay weird goalie self.

The water upstairs shuts off.

His face falls. "Shit. She's out. Let's go." He slams the door shut, and she for sure knows now that she's been ditched. All three of us sprint across the street and jump into Aleks's car. He gets it started and speeds away before there's any sign of Hadley.

My heart is still racing, Miles is cackling in the back seat, but I'm happier than I've been in such a long time.

I have my Killer back.

"Are you sure that's even a dog?" Miles asks.

"He's a Chinese Crested and so freaking adorable." I hug the little guy, who struggles excitedly in my arms.

"If you say so," Miles says.

Aleks cuts in. "Hey, question. How are you going to smuggle that thing on the team plane? Aren't you guys on a weeklong road trip?"

Miles and I look at each other, neither of us with an answer.

He runs a hand through his blond hair. "I kinda didn't think that far ahead."

Aleks looks delighted. "You guys are fucked."

CHAPTER EIGHT

MILES

Still can't believe I stole my teammate a rat, and then he has the audacity to think *my* pets are weird. We snag the very back of the plane, our coaches up front, and I let Bilson drop into the row before I follow him. He's wearing a very baggy hoody and has Killer tucked inside the front pocket.

"If we can keep him quiet until we get into the air, there's nothing they'll be able to do then. It's not like they'll dump him in Edmonton or ship him back to Seattle," I say.

"I don't want to test that out." His hands are stuffed in the front of the hoodie, stroking the dograt, and with the way it's sitting over his lap ...

I glance down suggestively. "Enjoying yourself?"

He doesn't take the bait. "Of course I am. I have my widdle squish face back." He drops his voice as Killer's bug-eyed head pokes out. "My widdle bubby wubby is happy to be back with daddy waddy too, aren't you?"

"Tell me women call you daddy waddy in bed."

That finally gets Bilson's attention. "How the hell did I end up friends with the goalie? I bet your strange ass would love to be called that, wouldn't you?"

"Nah, I'm more, uh …" How do I tell him I'm a guy who loves being given direction and praise when I've done a good job? "Whatever the opposite of a Daddy is."

"A Mommy?"

I crack up laughing. "When it comes to fucking, I'm not the one in control."

"Huh." He looks shocked by that information. "You're such a cocky shit I thought you would have been all about showing off what you can do."

"Oh, I show off the goods all right, and they can use any part of me they like."

"So … how does that work?"

"You need me to explain sex to you?"

He scowls. "No, I mean … *anything* anything? Even …" His eyes dart down, and I know what he's getting at.

"Have I been pegged? Oh yeah. A few times."

"How the hell did you get to that point?"

I shrug. "A few of my frat brothers were dating dudes, said how good being fucked was. I wanted to try it, and I hit up a sorority sister I was friends with. Turns out they were right."

"Wow …"

"It's a whole new world out there, Grandpa." Then, because I really need to bring it up, I add, "You're lucky I didn't hook up with your ex. I would have taught her so much."

He sends a glare my way. "You *did* want to stay?"

I could keep messing with him, but Bilson's friendship is important, and I want to make sure there's no doubt. "No way. One of the things I learned from my brothers is we respect each other. It's the same with the team. You're all always going to be a thousand times more important to me than a hookup." The next part is hard to get out. "I don't know if you saw, but we did kiss. I swear it wasn't planned, but I really wanted to get your dog back, and I was scrambling to figure out how to shake her so I could sneak off."

"I saw."

I brace myself for him to yell at me.

"And it was all worth it to have this sweet, widdle angel back."

Killer's tongue lolls out as he pants happily, Bilson's large hand swamping his head with each pat.

I cross my arms and glare at the dograt. "You could say thank you. Just saying."

"Aww, is Rook feeling left out?" Bilson stops patting the mutant and scratches me behind the ears instead. "Who's a good boy? Who's a good boy?"

"Fuck off." I slap his hand away, embarrassed to admit how much I *like* the attention. Apparently, my standards are so low I'll take being told I've done a good job, even if it's patronizing.

And I'm being treated like an animal.

"Can't win," Bilson says.

Killer yaps in reply, and the quiet conversation around us dies. Stoll and Coach both look backward down the aisle, and I'm scared for a whole second that we've been busted when they turn back around.

Thankfully, the idea of a player bringing a dog on board is so wild Coach would assume he imagined the sound rather than the reality.

I let out a relieved breath, but then Killer yaps again.

This time, the noise gets more attention, and so I do the only thing I can think of: I bark.

More heads turn our way.

"What are you doing?" Finch asks.

"Trying out a new pregame ritual, what do you think?" I bark a few times, loudly, as Bilson coaxes Killer back into his pocket.

"I think you need to shut up. Stoll's trying to sleep."

"What's more important? Sleep or the W?"

No one answers. I bark again for good measure.

Coach looks torn between telling me to quit it, and scared if he does, we'll lose the next game.

"How long is this ritual of yours going to last?" he asks instead.

I glance at Bilson's lap, where Killer has settled again. "I think I'm done, but I can never really be sure. Sometimes the need to bark just takes over, you know?" I tap Jorgensen's shoulder, who's sitting in front of me. "You know what I'm talking about."

"Rookie, I drink a lot, and yet I can confidently say I've never had the urge."

There are sniggers up and down the plane, along with some muttered "fucking goalies."

But the attention is off us.

I hold up my fist between us, and Bilson taps it with his.

"You're barking mad, is what you are."

Somehow, he makes it sound like a compliment.

—

When we take out the win against Edmonton, instead of celebrating, Bilson says he's staying in with Killer. It's tempting to go out—I sorely want to get my dick wet since it's been ... too much math to math, but I don't.

Instead, I walk down the hall, bottle of vodka in hand, and use the key card I swiped from him earlier to barge into his room. He throws the blanket over his lap like I've busted him jacking off.

"Killer or beating off?" I ask. "This could be a drinking game."

He lifts the blanket back off his dograt. "Most people knock, asshole."

"Why would I knock when I have a key?"

"You have a …" He glances at his nightstand. "Sneaky shit."

"Why, thank you." I set the vodka down on the table and find two glasses, then duck back up the hall to fill the metal bucket with ice. When I'm back, Bilson is already taking up most of the small couch, so I shove him over and push into the space beside him. "We have a real problem."

"Problem?"

"Obviously." I pull out Stone and Seddy, giving them a quick nip of vodka before pouring me and Bilson a drink. "We *won* tonight."

"How is that a problem?"

"Because I made a new ritual. And then we won. By a fucking lot. So now, obviously, we are going to have to fucking *bark* before every fucking game."

"We?"

"Yes, we. It was your dograt that got us into this mess, and why would I do it solo when I can drag you into it with me?"

"I'm not barking."

"Kiss and bark, bro. We got this."

"We don't got this."

"Wow, no sense of teamwork." I take a burning sip of my drink.

"Why are you here? I thought me and my baby were going to have a quiet night in."

59

"Wow." I stare at him. "*Woooow*. Here I was, thinking you'd want company, and I'm already being ditched for the dog. I get it." I go to stand when Bilson tugs me back down again. We're so close that I almost land in his lap before he shoves me back off him.

"I meant that I thought you'd be out hooking up."

"You and me both. It's been soooo long."

"Why? You're not celibate."

"No, but you're a cockblock, CB. I was going to the night of the bet, and then you plowed me with alcohol. And then I was planning to in Seattle, and instead, I picked up your ex-wife and took home dograt."

Bilson laughs. "Doesn't explain what you're doing here now though."

It doesn't, does it? *Why* didn't I go out with the team? I'm friends with them. If we went to a sports bar, it wouldn't have been too hard to pick up, but ... I chose vodka and bromance instead.

The thing is, I miss this. The closeness with other guys. Not just friends but people I can talk to, be bromotional with, not have to always put on the cocky and confident act. Sometimes I want to be able to say when I'm having issues and know I've got a friend who'll listen.

My frat brothers will always be that; we have a bromotions night through the chat every week, but it's not the same. Sitting here, in person, it's just right.

Bilson might intimidate me with his long career and incredible skill, but he's an easy guy to be friends with.

Which is why I'm sitting on his stupid small couch, drinking vodka dry, wallowing about not hooking up when I could be doing exactly that. I could not fucking imagine trying to go celibate.

"When do you think your Amish streak will end?" I ask.

"You know nothing about the Amish, do you?"

"I know they wear those stupid hats. There's no way they're not virgins."

"Do me a favor and never say that shit ever to anyone out loud."

I pretend to think about it to rile him up. "Can't make any promises."

He ignores me. "It's getting so hard I swear I'm at half-mast the majority of the time, and when I'm not, it's because I'm jerking off in the shower."

"Wow, not even in bed? What happened to romance?"

"Shut up, Miles."

I pretend to gasp. "You first-named me. You're serious."

"I *am* serious." He presses down on his groin, and I follow the movement. "I'm starting to think I need to see a doctor about this."

"There's plenty of doctors in porn."

He groans and presses down harder.

"Okay, okay, very serious and sad." I take another sip as I think through his problem. He doesn't want to hook up because he's worried about falling in love and whatever, but there is no way he's that pathetic.

"I miss sex," he complains.

Okay, so he *is* that pathetic. "What about this? If you don't want to hook up because you don't trust yourself, you just need a wingman. Not to pick up but kick out. I can do that. My momma always taught me to be a gentleman and walk guests to the door."

His eyebrows knit, and I can tell he's thinking about it. "What ... you'd just hang around until I was done?"

"Maybe ... or you could text me. If we shared a room on the road, it'd be easier. Take a bed each ... threesome ..."

His eyes bug from his head.

It's hilarious. "I forgot you're an old man. Gotta take it easy on your missionary generation."

"First, I'm friends with Ezra Palaszczuk—I know moves you'd never be able to come up with. Second, we're the same fucking generation, you punk."

Says the guy who almost wet himself over the thought of a threesome.

Bilson drops his head back against the couch. "Ezra and Anton are so lucky."

"Why?"

"Because they have each other. Traveling, at home, it doesn't matter. They can fuck whenever they like."

"You'd sleep with a teammate?"

"W-what? Uh—what are you—Jesus, Rook. No. That's not what I ... I *mean* they don't have to worry about all the land mines that come with finding a stranger to get off with."

He's got a point there. Greek Row was great because the houses were all so close together, and with the number of parties we had, it wasn't much effort. I was a Sigma boy, for fuck's sake. We were hot property. It might be similar in the NHL, but I haven't even begun to experience that, and on the one night I have a chance to, I don't take it.

Having a partner here with me sounds pretty ideal.

I glance over at where Bilson is still slumped, staring at the ceiling, stubbled throat stretched back and Adam's apple bulging. Am I attracted to dudes? No. Did I wonder what the big deal was when all my brothers started coupling up? You betcha.

My gaze strays down to where, true to his word, Bilson's dick is partially tenting his shorts. Poor thing.

He needs to do something about that.

And so do I, considering I'm suffering from the same issue.

"My offer stands," I say. "If you need help to get off, I'm your guy."

He laughs loudly. "Add that to the list of things you're not allowed to say out loud again."

"That didn't come out right."

"Olsen." He pats my thigh, and it's a struggle not to shake him off. "If you want to hit on me, at least have the balls to do it properly."

CHAPTER NINE

BILSON

The rest of the road trip is a bit of a disaster. And by a bit, I mean a lot. Who knew it would be so difficult to hide a dog?

Between me and Miles barking to cover up Killer's yaps and leaving the poor boy in the hotel room while I'm at the arena, it's been easy to lose focus.

After our win in Edmonton, everything goes to hell. Calgary, we lose, Vancouver, lose.

I'm not saying the whole team relies on Miles and me, but when you're down a star forward and your goalie, the team's game is going to suffer.

Not to mention, I can't get Miles's offer for a three-some out of my head. Threesome with two women? My only concern would be being able to satisfy them both. Threesome with a woman and another man?

When I picture Miles kissing Hadley and my reaction to it, I can safely say not one part of me was into it, but if he were to kiss someone who wasn't my ex-wife? Watch him have sex with another woman like my very own live-porn kind of situation? Yeah, I could be down for that.

Joining in, getting off, having him send our hookup on her merry way …

Fuck, I am way too horny to be thinking about this.

When there's a knock on my hotel room door, I automatically think it's Miles, but then I remember the shithead keeps stealing keys to my room, so it wouldn't be him.

We're not due to leave the hotel for another hour, so it's not going to be a checkout reminder.

Which means I need to hide Killer.

I get off the bed, where he's been snuggling on my chest, and reluctantly hide him in the bathroom, where I have food and water for him.

Then I put on my easygoing smile and open the door. It fades when I'm staring at Lucia Martin, our team's PR rep.

She's a gorgeous woman, even with the scowl on her face.

"Hey, Chia." My voice squeaks. "What can I help you with?"

"Cut the crap, Bilson."

Uh-oh. "Umm, okay?"

"Where's the dog?"

My eyes shoot wide. "What dog?"

As if on cue, Killer barks.

Lucia cocks her head. "That one."

I try to laugh it off, but it comes out nervously. "That's Miles. Ever since the pregame ritual of barking became a thing, he just does it now."

"Ah-huh. Why don't you let Miles out of your bathroom, then?"

"He likes it in there. It's cozy. Did you know that he's only twenty-four and still lives with his parents? He doesn't like to sleep alone, you see. So he asks to sleep in my bathtub whenever we have a hotel that gives us one." Fuck, does this hotel have a bathtub? I can't remember.

Just when I think Lucia might believe me, Miles appears. "Ooh, fun PR meeting! What are we talking about?"

I close my eyes, and Lucia sighs.

"Let's have this talk inside, shall we?" she says, and I step aside to let her and Miles in.

"Am I in trouble?" Miles whispers as he passes me.

"We're both screwed."

We turn to Lucia, who is trying to look intimidating, but we both know she's too sweet for that. It's hard to be scared of a five-foot-nothing woman, but then again, she is Italian, so she's got an edge.

"The dog?"

"What dog?" Miles asks.

She stares him down. "I have to say, you two have the dumb jock part down pat." She crosses the room and opens the bathroom door.

Killer tries to escape, but Lucia grabs him and picks him up. The traitor loves everyone and immediately tries to lick her face.

She gives him a pat. "This adorable man is all over the hockey sites."

"H-he is?" Miles croaks.

We should've expected this. I'm surprised Hadley hasn't been blowing up my phone, asking where he is. Or at least telling me he was doggy-napped.

"He's my dog," I say. "We were ..."

"Liberating him from the clutches of a cougar," Miles finishes for me. Not what I was going to say at all, but anyway.

"That cougar being your twenty-eight-year-old ex-wife? And choose your words wisely, boys. If twenty-eight is old, I'm—"

"Why, you don't look a day over twenty-two, Chia," Miles says.

"Flirting is not going to get you out of this."

"Okay, fine. I asked Miles to go steal my dog back for me."

Out of the corner of my eyes, I see Miles's mouth drop, but he got my dog back for me; I'm not going to throw him under the bus and say it was all his idea.

"You didn't think to maybe ask Hadley first?"

I rub the back of my neck. "We didn't exactly end things on good terms, and I haven't spoken to her in six months."

"So you thought stealing her dog—"

"My dog. I had him before we got married."

"My point is," she continues, "that you didn't think to ask before you took him? It didn't take her long to figure out who Miles was, though you'd think as an ex-hockey wife, she would've known immediately."

"She never was into hockey," I mumble.

"Anyway, she's gone to the press, and now this big custody battle for the dog is all over your socials and those gossipy websites that always post photos of you with women and those tacky headlines about them being the next Mrs. Bilson."

"I don't want to give him back," I say.

"Then I'm really sorry to be the one to tell you this, but you're going to have to talk to Hadley. Get this shit fixed before I have to step in and fix it for you."

"Couldn't you just … fix it for us?" Miles gives her the most bashful smile I've ever seen.

"Nice try, newbie, but I'm not here to babysit grown-ass men."

I would argue that is exactly her job, but I don't. I'm smarter than that. Surprisingly, so is Miles.

"Keep me updated," Lucia sings as she glides toward the door, handing Killer over to me in the process. "And for fuck's sake, stop barking before every game. The commentators are going crazy with speculation."

"Easy done. It's not like it's worked the last few games anyway," Miles says.

Lucia walks away, but I swear I see the twitch of her lips before she turns her head.

Once she's gone, the door closed behind her, Miles turns to me. "I think I'm in love with her."

"Jesus, you really do have a thing for dominance. All she did was chew us out."

Miles shrugs. "What can I say? It's hot."

The flashing images of Miles and Lucia hooking up are uninvited, but they happen anyway, and while I would never cross those lines with someone who worked for the franchise, I think I have my answer to whether or not I'd be into it.

But could I seriously contemplate it? How does one go about asking their new best friend if he'd fuck someone with me? Then again, he brought it up so casually he probably wouldn't even blink. Just be shocked that someone "as old as me" would want to.

I almost want to do it now to prove him wrong.

But first … I need to make a call.

–

"You could have asked me," Hadley says.

"No, I couldn't. When I left, you said you wouldn't let me take Killer."

"Because I was angry."

"So, you didn't want him?"

"I do. I love Killer as much as you do, but ... I wanted to punish you at the same time."

"What are you saying?" Hope blooms in my gut.

She hesitates a moment. "He's your dog. You should get to keep him. But I want updates, and you need to hire a dog-sitter for when you're away, and—"

"Done. Done, done, done. I'll do anything."

"Yeah, I think you've already proven that by sending your goalie to hit on me. A goalie, Cody? Even I know not to trust a goalie."

I burst into laughter as I glance over at Miles, who's sitting on the edge of my bed and watching me intensely. "The dog-napping was actually his idea."

"Ah. Everything makes sense now."

"Thank you, Had. You have no idea how much this means to me."

"Contrary to what all those puck bunny sites say, I'm not a monster."

"I know. But ... we didn't exactly leave things on the best of terms, and—"

"Breakups are hard. I'm over it."

I wish I could say the same. While I'm over her and not in love with her anymore, and I've fallen for other women since her ... all of my divorces remind me of how broken I really am deep down.

"Good," I say. "You deserve happiness."

"So do you."

We end the call, and I turn to Miles.

He bounces his ass on my bed. "What did she say?"

"She said you're weird."

69

"Pfft. Tell me something the world doesn't already know."

Even though his cockiness over his talent is a front, I can tell that when he agrees with stuff like that—that he's weird—he's being genuine. How can a twenty-four-year-old be so damn confident in his own skin?

Miles knows what he wants, knows what he likes, and even though he has his quirks, his need to be accepted, his search to fit in, never changes who he is.

He's loyal, empathetic, and doesn't cloud his emotions with toxic masculinity crap like a lot of hockey players do.

"Do we get to keep our baby?" Miles picks up Killer, who's been chewing on a pig's ear I bought him.

Killer immediately turns his attention to Miles, licking his face instead.

"Ugh. Our baby has bad breath."

"I'm sorry, *our* baby?"

"I stole him. I figure I should at least get some parental rights."

"Yeah, I don't think that's how kidnapping works."

"Come on. He loves Daddy Two."

"Killer loves everyone."

"Aww, he's taking after Daddy One. Hey, how many wives has Killer had?"

I shake my head. "You're such a little shit."

"You need a new insult, old man."

"So do you. And if you really want to share custody of Killer, he's due to go outside to do his business."

I expect him to hand the dog back immediately, but instead, he jumps up, says, "I'm on it," and disappears with Killer and the leash I bought him.

When will this kid stop surprising me?

CHAPTER TEN

MILES

That's it. I can't stand it anymore. The bromance is all well and good, but tonight, I need to cut the strings and get laid.

We're finally home from our rocky away trip, and I swear to fucking God, the wind is starting to get me up at this point. Maybe Bilson is contagious because I haven't been this hard up since I was a stupid freshman trying to hold down my spot on West Haven's hockey team.

So I ignore Bilson's message about what I'm doing on our night off and get ready for a night out.

"You're looking … inappropriate," Mom says the second I walk in the back door. I've got my own studio I had built behind the main house, but since my schedule is so erratic, I never bother to buy my own food and mooch off them instead, but that also means I'm open to opinions when I step foot in the main house.

"And you're beautiful as ever." I learned early on with Mom, you catch more flies with honey than vinegar. I won't point out that a tank top is hardly inappropriate. She smiles. "There's casserole in the fridge."

I *love* her casserole. The whole time I'm shoveling it down though, I can feel her eyes on me. "Yes?" I ask around a mouthful.

"I hope you're being a good boy to all those girls you … spend the night with."

My face immediately heats. "Don't say good boy. Please. Not in that sentence."

"Miles, I didn't raise you to be one of those sporting types who disrespect women and have a different one in their bed each night."

"No worries there, Ma. I haven't had anyone in my bed since I moved back home."

She casts a skeptical look over me.

"I'm serious!"

"Now that you're getting all rich and famous, I don't want you falling into anyone's traps. There are some sweet girls out there, baby, and the faster you settle down—"

Settle *down*? Jesus fuck, I'm not Bilson. "Noted."

"And make sure you use protection—"

"Ma! I'm a grown-ass man."

She steps forward and picks up a cloth that she uses to dab at my mouth. "Yet you still can't feed yourself."

I give her a scathing look—that mustn't be too scathing, considering she laughs—and rinse my bowl.

She holds her hands up in surrender. "I'm allowed to worry about you."

"Yeah, me. Not my dick."

"Don't be crass."

"Then nose out, woman."

Unfortunately, Dad takes that moment to enter. "What did you say to your mother?"

"Nothing. Not a thing." I plant a quick kiss on her forehead as I head for the door. "Love you both, don't wait up!"

I'm just climbing into my truck when my phone starts to ring. I answer without checking the screen and mentally curse when a familiar, deep voice comes down the line.

"You didn't write back."

"Ah …" I turn my car on. "Write back to what?"

"You have read receipts on, dumbass."

"Fuck." He caught me. I pull my truck onto the driveway and onto the road. "Sorry, I wasn't completely sure on my plans, but now I've decided to head out."

"Oh." There's something weird in the way he says the word. "Like, out *out*?"

"Yep. Time to put an end to the dry spell."

"Uh, so, that's sort of something that I kinda …"

"Yeah?"

"Can I come?" he blurts.

Guess that means the dry spell is over, then. I don't blame him. He gave it a good go, but the body wants what the body wants, and I've seen Bilson's *troubles* way too many times this week. Being half-hard in the locker room is *not* a good look, so like hell I'm going to deny him.

"Sure. Want me to pick you up?"

"Just give me the name of the place, and I'll meet you there."

Even better. It takes me twenty minutes to get to the bar on the outskirts of downtown, and Bilson is already there waiting out the front. I've gotta hand it to him, the old guy's got game. He looks good in his button-up, which is the kind of thing my mom probably hoped I wore out instead of a barely there tank top.

I pretend to look around as I approach him. "Sorry, I'm looking for my guy, CB, have you seen him? My height, crotchety as fuck. Definitely doesn't have this panty-drencher look going on that you do."

Bilson tosses his head back on a laugh. "Is that a compliment I hear?"

I know I'm supposed to say something back, but I'm thrown when his eyes meet mine and he looks like a totally different person. He's done something with his dark hair that makes his strong features stand out, and I might tease, but he really does look good.

I need to get laid.

It takes me a second to shake the stupidness off. "Let's go in."

He sticks close behind me on the way inside, and since it's still relatively early, we sneak two stools at the bar.

When he slides in next to me, I can't help narrowing another gaze at his face. "Why do you look different tonight?" Sure, his hair isn't the usual shaggy, damp mess I'm used to seeing, but there's something else.

One large hand comes up to rub his jaw. "Skipped shaving yesterday."

That's it. His usually light stubble is thicker. Darker. It makes his jaw stand out more.

"Maybe I should skip shaving."

"Why? You want to show off that baby fuzz?"

I scoff. "Wait until playoffs. Then you'll see a real bear—"

His hand slaps over my mouth, suddenly a thousand percent closer than before. "What the hell is wrong with you?"

I flick my tongue over his palm, making him flinch away.

"Gross."

"Never had any complaints." I throw in a wink to up my douchebag rating. Then, my gaze catches on something that I'm *not* expecting to see. "Apparently, I'm not getting any complaints from you either."

"Shut up." He shifts closer to the bar. "If anyone finds out you got my dick hard ..."

"You'll what?" I lean toward him. "Tell me again how straight you are."

"I *am* straight. This wasn't you. It was ... was ... your tongue. You know how horny I am."

Taking pity on him, I catch the bartender's attention and order us two drinks. "Lucky that all ends tonight."

"Yes. Umm. About that."

There's that weird tone again. I spin on my stool to face him, trying to read whatever this awkwardness is off his face.

"I want to point out first that this was your idea." He clears his throat. "I'm really, really bad with women. Form connections super fast."

"What in the four divorces are you talking about?" I gasp, pretending to be shocked.

Bilson slaps me about the head.

As he should, frankly.

"What I'm trying to say, if you'd shut your big mouth, is that I want to take you up on your offer."

Something deep and low in my gut is suddenly very interested in this conversation. I narrow my eyes. "Which offer? You want me to walk your hookups to the door, or ..."

His eyes get bigger and rounder, and that's when I catch on.

My grin eats my face. "You want a *threesome*?"

"Shut up," he hisses, looking around.

"Okay, okay." I lower my voice. "But to clarify, we're talking you, someone else, and *me*, right?" I'm way too entertained by the thought.

"If you were fucking with me—"

"No." The word bursts from me too quickly. "I mean, nah, man, it's cool. If that's what you need, I'm your guy." I hold up my fist between us, and after a couple of seconds, Bilson taps it with his. "I've got you," I assure him, inhaling sharply. "Not like I've never had a three-some before."

He gives me a dry look. "Of course you have."

"First time with a guy though."

His eyes clash with mine again, and something like nerves passes over me. We both take a moment, registering what exactly it is we're agreeing to before he quickly redirects his stare to the dance floor behind us.

I'm not chickenshit though, and I force myself to look—really look. He's got a faint bruise on his cheek, just above where his coarse stubble starts. The strong line of his jaw. His thick neck. Pecs hugged tight by his shirt.

If we do this, I'm going to see him naked outside of the team showers with a billion other dicks around. He'll be hard. I'll be hard. Will that be weird? Bilson is all man. Solid chest sprinkled with hair. Deep abs. Tree trunk thighs. The thing about threesomes is that they're all about give and take.

How much am I willing to give?

How much am I willing to *take*?

I lick my suddenly dry lips, my nerves stronger than before, and pull my gaze from his torso.

He's already watching me, smug look in his eyes. "You checking me out, Rook?"

"Just making sure you're not going to feel too emasculated when we're side by side."

He lifts an arm and flexes his bicep tight against his shirt. "I was scared you'd have the same problem."

I laugh to let some of my nerves out. "Threesome. Okay."

"Yep."

"Before we find someone, I guess we have to set ground rules," I say, trying to get my confidence back.

"Ground rules?"

"Well, threesomes are all different, aren't they? Obviously, once it's over, whoever we choose isn't going to stick around, but—"

"Will *we* post-sex spoon, you mean? Hmm ... Why don't we play it by ear?"

I stare at him because that was *so* not what I was going to say. Instead of making things weird—weirder—I go along. "Noted. But *also*. During. We need to figure that out."

He screws up his face, like he's trying to picture something. "I figured it'd be ... spit roast. Or something. Right? Is that how it works?"

"Dude, it can be whatever we want it to be. Just throwing it out there, I won't say no to being fucked."

"By *me*?"

It's hilarious that's where his thoughts go. "I was thinking more of a train situation. Choo choo! All aboard."

"Like ... I do her, and she does you?"

"Bingo."

"Huh." The word comes out on a heavy exhale.

"But it'd mean we were pretty close, so I guess it depends how you feel about that. Like, what if we bump balls? Or during warm-up, how close do we get? Do we kiss? Touch? What if our dicks get a little too friendly, you know what I mean?" Even I'm not sure how I'd feel having my dick brush up against Bilson's, but I'm not turned *off*, so that helps.

Bilson drops his red face into his hands. "Is it bad that I'm too turned on to think about it? I don't care. I just want to come."

I'm having the same issue. My dick is hard as a rock.

"Then I guess all that's left is finding someone to be the meat in our sandwich."

"You choose," he says.

I puff out a breath. "I think we both need a minute to calm down. It's not going to be a fast find."

"Good to know you're as into this as I am."

"It's going to be an experience, that's for sure."

Or, it would be if we could find someone to take home. The first woman I approach is a hard pass; the second is vaguely interested until I mention the two of us, and then she's out.

"This seemed like a good idea to begin with," Bilson says.

I'm not ready to give up on the idea. I'd say it's because I'm such a good friend that I don't want his dick to fall off from lack of use, but if I'm honest … if I'm really, really honest … I'm curious what it will be like.

I tug Bilson on the dance floor behind me and approach a leggy girl with black hair. She's got toned arms and is more solid-looking than the razor-thin woman beside her, and sure, maybe I'm stereotyping, but *this* woman seems more my type.

I approach her, and then when I'm close enough, I duck my mouth near her ear. "Wanna dance?"

"Sure do."

The woman turns to face me, and I wrap my arms around her waist.

Her gaze is confident as it meets mine, sharpening when she presses closer and feels my hard cock against her hip. "Exciting night?"

"Something like that." I catch sight of Bilson over her shoulder. "Can my friend dance with us?"

The instant she smiles, eyes giving away that she knows exactly where this is going, relief washes through me. "He better."

Pure lust hits my veins as I grab the front of Bilson's shirt and pull him against us. My hands are crushed between her back and his front, and it catches me totally off guard when, instead of touching her, his hands land on my hips. His hold tightens, and he pulls me closer until she's tight between us, and my dick is so damn hard I might pass out.

"So," the woman says. "What are you guys proposing?"

"You, me, and him," I say immediately.

Her smile gets wider. "And what do you guys want to do to me?"

"My buddy here wants to fuck you."

She laughs, wrapping a hand behind her to grip Bilson's hair. "And you, sweetie?"

Like I can feel Bilson's dark stare on me, watching for how I'm going to play this, I glance up. "I want *you* to fuck *me*."

The woman immediately stops dancing. "Oh. Umm … yeah. Sorry. I'm not into … *that*." Then she ducks out under our arms and disappears into the crowd.

My mouth—and excitement—drops as I watch her leave. "God goddamn damn it." My forehead drops onto his shoulder I'm so defeated. We were *this* close, and I had to go and ruin it. "I'm sorry. I'll find someone else. I …"

His hands are still on my hips.

Slowly, I lift my head to find Bilson still watching me. "What?"

"This isn't going to work." He steps away from me.

"Surely there's one woman who'll be interested. We have to—"

"Keep asking random women to come home with us? How many do we have to proposition before word gets out that the two newbies to Nashville are trying to have threesomes all over the place? I don't want to be on Lucia's radar for that. She's an amazing person but scary as hell."

"You're right."

Bilson's lips hitch. "I think it's the universe's way of making sure I remain alone. Alone and horny. Want to get out of here?"

"Oh, so because you have to be horny and alone, so do I?"

Leaving is the last thing I want to do. I'm so hard I could cry, and if I'd gone with a standard spit-roast offer like Bilson said, we'd probably be on our way to making that happen. But it's been forever. And I really, really want something in my ass again.

Why aren't more women into that?

"Well." He swallows roughly. I watch the deep dip of his Adam's apple before it bobs back up again. "What if …" The words hang in the air, the possibility of anything, as he shifts like he wants to move closer but doesn't.

"What if, what?" My voice cracks.

Bilson closes in on me, and his hands find my waist once again. "You, uh, want to be fucked."

"Yes."

"And, I mean, it would be a release without the risk."

"Are you ... do mean ... we have a threesome without the third?"

"Yes? No? We're both hard up, I can't have sex with a woman without getting attached, and you've already said you like ... *it* ... Maybe ... if we close our eyes ..."

It's lucky he is hanging on to me because the room goes all unsteady, and shockingly, it's *not* because I hate the idea. I think of being fucked by a silicone strap-on and try to picture taking an actual dick in my ass instead. Skin. Balls. Deep, rumbling noises in my ear. Thick arms wrapped around me.

I shudder. Pleasantly.

"You really think having sex with a man would be different? Emotion-wise? You aren't scared of falling for me?" I'm taunting him, testing him. I'm up for this if he is, but the worry of it changing things between us or screwing with the team dynamic is at the forefront of my mind.

Bilson laughs. "You're too much of a cocky little shit for me to fall for you."

I swallow hard. "As long as it won't get emotionally confusing, I'm in. But, uh, lights off, maybe?" I'm terrified. Excited. Confused. Body inching closer to his.

We're both clearly too horny to think straight.

That's obviously what's happening when Bilson's gaze dips to my lips.

When my breathing picks up.

When his hand slides around to squeeze my ass and pure fucking ecstasy floods me.

"Are we really doing this?" he murmurs.

"We are. Right now."

CHAPTER ELEVEN

BILSON

In the moment, on that dance floor, this seemed like a brilliant solution. To avoid falling for the wrong woman, I'd get my release from a man.

But the closer we get back to my place, the more I begin to doubt our decision. We haven't spoken a word on the drive other than for me to direct Miles to my house. I'd caught a rideshare to meet him earlier because I was hoping the night would end with us both in here. Of course, that plan also had a woman being with us.

This though ... This might work out even better.

"It's this one up here on the right." I point.

Miles pulls his truck into the driveway and throws it in park, but for all his eagerness in the club, he hesitates now. "Are you sure you're okay with this, old man? I know your generation thinks sexuality is a big deal, and—"

"This has nothing to do with sexuality and everything to do with needing to get off with something other than my hand."

"Aww, you know how to make a boy feel special."

I side-eye him, trying to figure out if he's being serious or not.

"I'm fucking with you. It's just sex."

Exactly. I've never had just sex before because sex and lust are so easy to confuse with love. But when it comes to Miles, the risk of falling is taken out because even though I might be open to having sex with a man, I don't see myself ever settling down with one. I've never given it much thought before—having sex with or dating a man—but I do know as I look at Miles, his wild blond hair in his face, his cocky smirk on his lips, all I feel is friendship.

I nod. "Just sex." Miles goes to get out of the car when I grab his arm. "And we don't let it mess with hockey or the team."

"Duh."

"Okay." We get out of the truck, and he follows me to the front door.

My hands shake as I unlock my house, and the second we're standing in the foyer, I hesitate to close the door, as if thinking once it's shut, there's no going back.

Is this something I want? My cock is already on board, but it's been so long since it's seen any action it would be happy with anything other than my hand at this point.

"You going to close that, or do you want all your neighbors to see?" Miles snarks.

The anticipation thrumming in my veins bubbles over, and I slam the door shut and move in on him, pinning him against the wall with my forearm across his chest.

Miles's eyes widen, and his lips part. His chest rises and falls rapidly, and the mixture of shock and heat in his gaze is surprisingly hot. Really hot.

But I don't know what the rules are.

We agreed on lights off, close our eyes, and pretend it's not a dude we're fucking, but already I can tell that won't work.

Miles is big, his chest wide and hard. His grunt when I press against him is masculine and deep. And when he rasps, "Are we going to do this here or in the bedroom?" there's no way I can pretend I'm not having sex with a teammate. A friend.

If I can push past that, I'll be fine.

"Bedroom." My voice is thick and gravelly.

I pull off him and lead the way, thankful Killer is already in the laundry room for the night, refusing to look back at him to make sure he's following.

He is though. Because as soon as I enter my bedroom, I go to flick on the lights when his hand comes down on mine.

"No lights. Remember?"

I might not be able to keep pretending he's someone else, but apparently, he's not there yet. That's okay with me because the more we can keep detached, the better it will be for the team.

I drop my hand. "Right."

"You got lube?"

"Umm, somewhere." I know the movers unpacked all my shit for me, but where would they have put the sex stuff? "I'll go find it."

"And condoms."

"Scared I'm going to get you pregnant?" I quip. My joke eases some of the tension in the room.

"Aww, were you of the generation where sex education only taught you about how to avoid pregnancies? No wonder everyone over the age of thirty has HPV."

"Fuck you."

"That's the point we're trying to get to, yes."

"Fine. You look in my drawers. I'll check the bathroom." I head for my attached bathroom and turn on the light.

Miles shuffles around the room, opening and closing drawers while I check the vanity.

"Oh, hello," Miles says. I turn to find him holding lube in one hand and the unopened sex toy Dennan bought me after my last divorce. The *pocket pussy*. He told me I'd be needing it.

I actually forgot I had it.

"This looks fun."

"Have at it. My old teammate gave it to me, so I never used it because I thought I'd only be able to think about him the whole time."

"We could pretend to have that threesome after all. It's not gay if it's in a three-way. Or so I've heard."

I burst out laughing. "No, of course not. Nothing gay going on here."

Technically, sex between two straight-identifying men would be bisexual behavior, and yes, I know how much of an oxymoron that it, but I'm holding on to any justification I can because I'm so desperate to stick my dick in someone.

"So we're set, then?" He pulls a box of condoms out of the drawer next.

"Looks like it."

Yet, we both continue to stand there. Not moving. With an entire king bed between us.

"Okay, this is awkward," he eventually says. "It seemed like an awesome idea at the club, but now ..."

"Now it's too real?"

He shakes his head. "Now it's too ... serious. Sex is supposed to be fun."

I huff. "I'm nervous. I've never, you know, with a dude, and even if it is only sex, even if we could guarantee nothing would change tomorrow, I don't want to fuck up what we have. You're completely different to what I was expecting, and this is the last thing I thought would be happening."

"How about we start small?"

"How?"

"We've seen each other naked already, so we may as well start there."

And we have. Countless times. Of course, in a locker room, it's instinctual not to look or make a big deal out of it, but if we look at this whole situation similarly, it won't be a problem to get naked in front of someone I have before.

I begin undressing with my button-down, and while I do that, Miles reaches back and takes off his tank top.

Shirtless. Easy.

Miles moves on to his pants, and I follow him, but he's going commando, and I'm not, so I make it a point not to look at his junk or in his general vicinity until I get my underwear off too.

I'm pulling them down my legs when he asks, "Favorite sex position?"

I almost trip over myself.

He laughs. "Need a hand with that?"

"No," I grumble.

"You going to answer the question?"

"You're asking what my favorite position is, really?"

"I like it when a girl's on top, personally. Taking control. Tits bouncing up and down in front of my face." Miles picks up the lube and squirts some into his hand, and I can't tell if this confident act of his is for show like it is on the ice or if he's actually this confident when it comes to sex.

He reaches behind him, and I can only assume he's prepping his hole.

Heat rushes through me.

Maybe the few years between us really is the difference between the purity culture generation and the sexually free generation. Where gender, sexuality, or body parts aren't a factor in chemistry.

I step closer to the bed and hold out my hand for him to throw me the box of condoms. Even though this situation is weird and awkward as fuck, I'm still hard.

He throws them to me across the bed. "Your turn."

If he's using this as a distraction technique, it's working. Because while I grab a condom and open it up, I'm not thinking about what we're about to do. I'm thinking about what I like in bed, but that's not exactly a simple question.

"All of them?"

"You have to have a favorite, but please don't say missionary. I'll be so disappointed in you."

"There's nothing wrong with missionary."

"And you wonder why you've been divorced four times." His face drops. "Shit. I probably shouldn't bring that up, should I?"

I shrug. "I'd dispute it if it weren't so true. Though, sex was never the issue in any of my marriages. And fine, I'll answer your stupid question. Missionary is good for when you want that eye contact. It's intimate. Doggy style is good for when you want to get off fast. Her on top is good for after a game when your muscles are all achy and you want her to do the work. Reverse cowgirl is probably my least favorite because it's so impersonal."

Miles stops what he's doing and stares at me. Cocks his head. Keeps staring.

"What?" I ask.

"Sex is emotional for you, huh? Like you get all the bonding hormones that come with it."

I've never thought of it in the sense that it's the hormones released during sex that fucks with my brain and tells me I'm in love, but that definitely is my problem. "Why else do you think I've stayed away from sleeping with anyone?"

Miles goes back to what he's doing. "In that case, we'll keep this as impersonal as possible. On your back, CB. I'm gonna reverse cowgirl the cum out of you."

"Now who's the romantic one?"

"Excuse me. I'm *bromantic*, thank you very much. Bros give each other brogasms all the time. Just ask my old frat buddies."

Even though he's ridiculous, I do as he says and get on the bed on my back.

"What's a worse idea?" I ask. "Having sex with a teammate or someone who says brogasms?" I stroke myself a few times.

"Lucky for you, you get both." Miles's knees hit the bed, and then he throws a leg over my waist so he's facing my feet. "I got myself mostly ready, but I might need a bit more prep. Your dick is bigger than any strap-on I've ever used."

"Woohoo, above average for the win."

"Don't know if that's a good thing in this situation," Miles points out.

"Anal is the only time a man will lie about how small his dick is. Instead of adding inches, they take them off."

Miles laughs. "Truth."

When I left the bathroom, I didn't turn the light out, so there's enough light in here for me to find the lube he's left on the bed so I can cover myself and my fingers with it.

From this angle, when I use two digits and push my way inside his hole, it doesn't feel any different than if I were with a woman this way. My cock is aching, and his ass is so tight we might be here a while before I can work myself inside him.

I get my fingers past his tight ring of muscle, and he sinks onto them. His body racks with shivers, and then he takes over, controlling how deep my fingers go by moving his hips.

While he fucks my fingers, I stroke my dick, trying to give it some goddamn relief. Some friction. Something to make it stop yelling at me from neglect.

"Oh, yeah. Right there." Miles's hips move faster. "This is why I love this."

Once he's moving more easily, I add a third finger slowly, but soon, he's taking that too.

His breathing is heavy, the sounds he makes are downright sinful, and if he's not careful, I could come from watching him sink down on my fingers over and over again.

"Oh God. I'm ready. Give it to me."

I pull my fingers free and line up my cock, but before I push inside him, I have to double-check. "Are you sure?"

"*Now* you ask that? Hurry up and fuck me."

And with that, I lift my hips and sink inside my teammate.

We've either just messed everything up between us or made it a whole lot better. I haven't decided yet.

CHAPTER TWELVE

MILES

I am so goddamn *full*. My ass is stretched wide around Bilson's cock, and I'm immediately kicking myself for wimping out every time and going with a smaller strap-on.

This? This is …

Bilson's hips withdraw and snap up, forcing the most ridiculous moan from my chest. There's a slight sting, but mostly, the feeling of fullness engulfs me, and it's such a fucking turn-on to be split open like this. His fat cock passes over that spot that sends me wild, and it's like a come-to-Jesus moment, right here in Bilson's bed.

I swear from this moment forward to take nothing but butt busters every time.

That's enough thinking about Bilson.

We agreed to lights out, and that didn't happen, so I slam my eyes closed instead. I might have a dick in my ass, but I meant what I said to him: this is sex. No need to make things weird between us.

I'm just a man, sitting on a very, *very* realistic strap-on, begging it to pound my brains out.

With the ache fading, I start to move, building up a rhythm as I bounce on his cock. My dick bobs in front of me, hard as steel and begging for relief, but I refuse to touch myself. Refuse to give in to the need burning in my balls because if this is the only time I'm gonna have a dick in my ass, I'm making this last as long as possible.

Which I'm scared won't actually be that long. For so long, I've been trying to find that high of the first time I was pegged, and nothing hit the same way. It felt good, of course—I wasn't lying when I said I love it, but it's hard to find a hookup who wants to try that out, let alone knows what they're doing.

And Bilson? Holy *damn*, he knows what he's doing.

"Ah, shit ..." His breathing is getting gravelly. "So *tight*, Rook."

The deep rumble of his voice slides through me, each low sound tingling in my ears, slipping down my neck, and shivering along my spine. My whole body is tuned into those harsh sounds, and having my eyes closed is making everything so much worse ... or better. My body claims better, but I'm trying hard to forget it's my teammate I'm screwing and rapidly failing at that task.

Might as well let go and lean in hard.

I'm being fucked by a *man*.

I'm sitting on Bilson's cock, and I'm pretty confident this is the best sex of my life. I don't know how to feel about that, so I distract myself instead. If we're doing this, I want the full experience.

My eyes flutter open, taking in his muscular, hairy legs splayed across the bed, his big feet planted on the mattress. Curiosity burns through me as my gaze travels over his calves, up his thighs ... just one peek. Just for interest's sake.

Fuck. My dick is in the way.

I grunt out my frustration at not being able to see his balls. Now I've had the thought, it won't leave me, this obsession buzzing in my bloodstream, making me hotter than I was even in the club.

My legs spread wider, and then I lean forward and plant my hands on the bed.

Bilson's thrusts hitch, then freeze. "*Nrg.*"

"What?"

"Nearly came."

My laugh is half-hearted at best. "Don't give up on me that easy, old man."

"Can you blame a guy? The second you leaned forward, I had a front-row view of me sliding into your ass." He exhales hard. "So, so hot."

Just hearing how tortured he sounds thrills me. I give him a minute, waiting for him to be ready again, and tilt my head down to see.

Bam.

There's the money shot. His tight balls nestled beneath mine make my heart rate speed up. It's so unexpectedly hot I reach down and cup us both.

Bilson shudders under me. "What are you doing?"

"Whatever feels good." I roll us together, running my fingers over us both, and while it's not the same stimulation as being pounded, there's something beyond sexy about feeling a pair of balls against my own.

"In that case ..." Bilson's large hands land on my waist before sliding down to rest over my hips. His fingers curve around, teasingly close to my dick, and then he thrusts again. It's slower this time but harder. He presses deep, taking his time, and I imagine that he's watching every move and being turned on by the sight.

The slower pace lets me feel him. All of him. The girth, the length, the ridge of his tip every time he pulls almost all the way out. It's agony. Sweet, sweet agony. My hands bunch in his blankets as I try to hold still and take it.

My patience doesn't last long though. He sinks inside again, making every nerve in my ass scream for more. My head tosses back on a whimper, and when he pulls out, I follow him, desperately seeking that deliciously full stretch.

Maybe tomorrow, I'll be embarrassed by how desperate I am for his cock, but right now, all I need is to feel it ruin me.

"That's the best you've got, old man?" A smile trembles my lips. "You sure sex was never a problem in your marriages? I'm getting bored over here."

Before I notice him move, Bilson wraps an arm around my neck and pulls me back against him. My knees are still on the bed, and I'm arched right back, plastered against his chest, his heaving panting filling my ear.

"Anyone ever told you that you're a cocky little shit-head?"

"No one important."

He chuckles, hand on my hip tightening in warning. "You're going to regret saying that."

My dick throbs. "Prove it."

"Prepare to have your mind blown, Rook."

"My guy ... I would *love* to have you try."

Surprisingly, he doesn't start fucking me right away. Instead, he lets go of my hip and searches for something. I can't turn my head—he's still got me locked in tight, and my curiosity is burning.

Then something wraps down over my cock.

I groan. "Pussy pocket."

"I got it ready while you were riding me."

"No fair. Now I'm the one about to come."

"You're going to need to give me more time with your ass first." His hand tightens around the toy, and the silicone hugs me deliciously. He's filled it with lube, and between that and him being buried inside me, it's all too much.

"No time like the present."

Bilson thrusts up into me at the same time as he uses the sex toy to stroke me. I try to move against him, but even with all my flexibility, he's got me pinned, and it's awkward, so he ends up doing most of the work. It can't be easy with my weight against him, but he's not a star forward for nothing.

"You know," he says by my ear. "Our first game during warm-ups, I saw you in this exact position. Bent right back like this. I never clued in to how hot it is until now."

"This is nothing. You should see me with my legs behind my head."

A low rumble fills his chest.

"That's the only good reason for missionary."

"I wanna see."

"Nope. I'm being your good little cowboy. Impersonal. Fucking in the dark. All that crap."

"Good point." His grunts get deeper, less restrained. Mine are no better. I'm pressing back into him as much as I can, wanting more, wanting to be filled, to be owned. To be pounded within an inch of my life.

"Tell me my hole's the best you've ever had." The words fall out before I can stop them, but my brain's swimming in a lust haze.

"No competition. So good, Miles. So, so good."

My balls tighten with every word. "Tell me I'm a slut for you."

He pauses for all of a fraction of a second, making my heart stop that I've gone and ruined it.

Then, his deep growl fills my ear. "You're such a fucking slut for my cock."

Oh holy shit.

He jerks me off hard and fast with the toy, relentless thrusts pegging my prostate and making me go cross-eyed. I'm total jelly. Bilson is in complete control, and I'm not so much approaching the edge as being thrown off it. His hard chest against my back, those heavy noises in my ear, large bicep against my throat, and when I reach behind me, hands sliding down his sides, there's all hard angles there too.

It shouldn't turn me on.

It fucking does.

My head drops back as his teeth sink into my ear. The pain shoots to my balls, and finally, the delirious pleasure releases. I come so hard into the fake pussy that my hips buck with each pulse.

"*Fuck.*" Bilson grabs my hips, and it only takes a few pumps before he follows me over.

We're both sweaty and panting as we come down from the high.

The incredible, incredible high.

I swipe my sweaty hair back from my forehead, and bit by bit, what happened creeps into my consciousness.

We just had sex.

I slept with a teammate.

And I'm still lying on top of him.

Talk about going from the fire and straight into the ice.

What the hell did we do?

CHAPTER THIRTEEN

BILSON

Boneless. Sated. A little … embarrassed?

No, that's not the right word. I'm not embarrassed about what we did, but now that it's over and neither of us is moving, with every second that ticks by, the awkwardness grows.

I'm still inside him, for fuck's sake, but I can barely move. And if I do shift and kind of kick him off me, will he take it the wrong way?

"Can't. Move," he gets out.

When I laugh, he de-straddles me. But he only gets as far as flopping onto his stomach with his head turned away from me.

"Oops. Your duvet is probably covered in cum now."

"Eh. It's smelled of worse before." I refuse to look at him, and for a moment, I think he's the same, but slowly, he lifts up on his elbows and stares down at me.

"I don't want to know. You all good if I use your bathroom to clean up and then get out of here?"

I make the mistake of making eye contact. He averts his gaze immediately.

"Go for it." I want a shower too. I'm sticky from the lube, I need to ditch the condom, but we're both so wooden and stiff that I wait for him to get up and close the bathroom door before I move.

I swing my legs over the side of the bed, deal with the condom and tie it off, but dump it on the floor to get rid of later after Miles is gone.

I don't regret what we did, and I didn't think fucking a guy could feel that way, but there's something uneasy in my gut that has nothing to do with the sex and everything to do with now.

Miles kept it as impersonal as he could, which I'm grateful for, but it makes it come with a side of guilt? Like using him that way was wrong. Though I can't deny the way he loved being called names was hot.

I knew having sex with a man would be different, but it's in ways I never imagined. I thought the hard body, the muscles, the obvious differences in anatomy would be what I'd focus on, but that part didn't even register.

I was raised to treat women respectfully inside and outside of the bedroom. That might be why I've always connected sex with love. But with Miles … him asking me to degrade him like that …

Fuck, my cock perks up, wanting to do it again.

The shower turns off, and I'm still naked, so I quickly jump up and pull out a pair of sweats from my drawer. Which is ridiculous now that I think about it because in two days, we'll be back in our locker room, seeing each other naked again.

He comes out only wearing a towel, steam billowing out of my bathroom after him, and I hold my breath.

Here's the part where we either pretend nothing happened, play it off like it's no big deal, or turn into mortal enemies who never speak to each other ever again.

Which will be difficult when we're on the same hockey team.

His eyes meet mine. "What? No sandwiches? No sustenance? Worst one-night stand ever."

"Is that a thing?"

"Orgasms and sandwiches should be a thing."

"Don't you mean brogasms?"

Miles fist pumps. "Yes. It's catching on."

"Sure. Let's go around telling the team that's what we get up to." My tone is dry, obviously sarcastic, but he either misses it or wants to double-check I'm not being serious.

"We're not … like, telling anyone about this, right?"

"Hell no."

"And we're still good?"

That's the big question, isn't it? "I am if you are. That should get me through to All-Stars week at least."

He rubs his chin. "I was hoping to be more impressive than that, but I guess I'll have to take it."

"You're good at … taking things." Am I testing how far we can push this? Yes. I need boundaries.

I'm thankful he doesn't recoil but preens. "I'm the best you'll ever have. I've ruined you for all the pussies in all the world."

"Oh, there's that cocky side coming out to play again."

"Always." He moves across the room and picks his clothes up off the ground but glances at me as if to tell me to turn away so he can get dressed.

Okay, so it's weird between us now but not ruined.

I can live with that.

"I'll leave you to it, then." I turn on my heel and leave the bedroom, having no idea where to fucking go in my own house.

I settle for the kitchen and pour myself a glass of water, but before I can drink from it, Miles appears out of nowhere and takes it from me.

"Thanks."

"Sure. Help yourself."

"What, you can have your dick inside me but can't share your water?" He side-eyes me, and I think he's doing what I was back in the bedroom: testing the boundaries.

I should wince or be turned off by him saying that, but I so am not. Pretty sure my need for more sex just jumped forward to Christmas instead of All-Stars.

"Is that going to be your comeback for everything now?" I ask.

"Sure is ... you know, when it's only us anyway."

"Want to pinky swear on this?" I'm half joking.

He holds out his pinky finger, and I link mine with his. After we shake on it and he pulls away, he kisses his two fingers and then points them to the sky. "New pregame ritual. It'll be like our little secret."

The thought of doing that in front of an arena full of people sends a shiver through me. To have a sign between us that so blatantly screams we had sex, without anyone knowing what it means ... my only fear is starting each and every game with a hard-on from now on.

–

Even though we left shit on good terms, the next time I walk into the arena, I'm on edge.

I wish I could say this feeling made the whole sex thing not worth it, but it really doesn't. If anything, I'm so on edge because I can't stop thinking about the way he rode me. How he was so needy for my cock.

Fuck, fuck, fuck. Get that out of your head, Cody.

We're only here this morning for a skate to keep warm for our game tonight, so technically, we don't even need to interact. Would it be weird if we didn't? Ever since the beginning of preseason, Miles and I have gravitated toward each other. There've been jokes about bromances and what-the-fuck-ever, so if we avoided each other, would the rest of the team pick up on it?

Am I overthinking this already?

He's not in the locker room when I get there, so I go straight to my cubby and start stripping off.

Maybe I can get dressed and out on the ice before he even arrives.

Then I hear, "Hey, old man," and I don't have to turn around to know it's him.

The other guys in the locker room do snicker though.

"What? Can't hear you," I sing.

He yells across the room now. "You so old you need hearing aids, pops?"

Thank God nothing's changed on that front.

But there is something that has changed between us, or at least from my side, and that's that I notice him a hell of a lot more.

Across the locker room, on the ice, during his stretches … it's like my eyes find him wherever he is, and every fluid move, every leg splits, I notice. And when he's on the ground on his knees and leans backward until he's lying on the ice? I have to force myself to look away.

It'll be fine. Completely fine. In a week or so, we'll have put the whole thing behind us, and I'll stop remembering how hot the sex was.

It's all good.

Even if it means not making eye contact with him for a while. Or showering at a different time than him in the locker room. I'll avoid everything that reminds me of his naked body, of him taking my cock like a champ.

On the outside, we may be able to play it off like we're the same two guys we were last week, but on the inside, he's worming his way under my skin and into my brain.

Like a tapeworm.

A slutty tapeworm.

And now I'm not even making any sense.

When we're told to hit the showers, I hang back at my cubby for a bit while he disappears into the steamy part of the locker room.

I slowly get my gear off and am still sitting there in my base layers when Miles returns.

"Is someone a wittle sore fwom all the skating? Old bones and all that."

"I might be old, but not as old as the old person jokes."

"Good one."

I stand, about to head for my own shower when Coach walks in. "Bilson. Olsen. PR wants to see you after you're dressed."

Miles and I look at each other, all playfulness gone and faces stoic.

My thoughts immediately jump to the women we propositioned about having a threesome and that one of them recognized us.

"Is this because I keep calling CB old?" Miles asks.

"I said PR, not HR, though I won't be surprised if that call's next."

Oh, fuck.

The only solace is that we never actually did have a threesome, so it's not like anyone can say we did.

Right?

We might be in actual trouble here.

CHAPTER FOURTEEN

MILES

Bilson looks like he's shitting bricks. I wait for him while he showers, watch him as he gets dressed, and note just how stiff he's holding his shoulders the entire time. I've got Stone in one hand and Seddy in the other. Running my thumbs over their smooth surface always helps keep me grounded.

I'm trying not to think too deeply about why Lucia wants to see us because we haven't done anything PR needs to worry about. Nothing. Not a thing.

My stomach knotting calls me a big fat liar.

We can't even talk about it until we're finally out of the locker room.

"Do you always dress as slow as a geriatric ninety-year-old?" I ask as soon as we step out into the hall, and I tuck Stone and Seddy into my pockets.

Bilson throws a look over his shoulder before leaning closer as we walk. "Shut up. We need to get our story straight."

I snort. "Straight."

"*Miles.*"

His serious tone makes me even more nervous, and it really drives home how much I hate hearing him sound like that. "Sorry. I'm stressed too."

"You really seem it."

"Fuck off."

"Mature."

"No, that's you, remember?"

Bilson throws me a cutting glare. "Can't help yourself, can you?"

"That is what got us into this mess." It's hard not to lash out and kick something, but it's even harder to admit that *I'm* the drama. If it wasn't for me suggesting Bilson and I even try to hook up with someone together, we wouldn't be on the walk of doom.

"What are you talking about?"

The genuine confusion in his tone makes me glance up, because hello? Does he really not know what's happening here? "Lucia. My future wife. There's really only one thing the two of us would be in trouble for together—well, now that we've got the dog situation fixed—and that one thing was all my idea." I blink and realize something. "As was the dog. And the barking." A long sigh falls from my lips. "Maybe we need to go in there and tell her that you're cutting me loose. That the CB and Rook days are over, our bromance has ended. Someone will write tragic poems about us one day."

"Eww, I hope not. Yeah, they might have been your ideas, but I'm the one who went along with them like a dumbass." Bilson holds up his fist between us, and the familiarity of the action sends something warm and light through the borderline panic. "Whatever happens, we've got each other's backs."

I tap his fist. "Right. Yes."

"Besides, we haven't actually done anything. Yeah, we might have hit up a few women for, uh, some *fun*, but so far as anyone knows, we didn't go through with it."

"What do you mean so far as anyone knows? We *didn't* go through with it. Period."

He brushes me off. "You know what I mean."

"Yeah." I drop my voice. "We had other fun instead."

An aborted cough-type choke starts and cuts off in his chest. "And again. Shut up, Miles."

"This whole first-name thing really isn't working for me, *Cody*."

"I'm stressed, and you're not helping."

Okay, that is something I feel legitimately bad about. We're supposed to be friends, and if Lucia tears us a new one—hell, if the story gets out there about us—no matter what he says, I'm largely to blame. And that makes me want to kick myself because I'm protective of CB.

My nerves creep higher the closer we get to Lucia's office. I swear they make it so far away from the locker room so that on the walk, we really get a chance to think back on what we've done. Because I think. A *lot*.

Even with Bilson in trouble though, I'm finding it hard to regret any part of what happened.

Maybe that makes me an asshole or a shitty friend, but I've jacked off to the memory of him behind me way too many times to count, and it's embarrassing to admit my own damn teammate is the reason Cobra's down for the count. Constantly.

I should probably ask the team to run some blood tests on me because I'm clearly unwell to be thinking about dick so. Fucking. Much.

That thought immediately evaporates when we reach Lucia's door.

"You go first," I say, because I'm a big, brave hockey player.

"She's your future wife."

"If you don't marry her first."

He smirks at me. "Didn't realize that option was on the table."

"Isn't it always with you?"

But before Bilson can react, I knock and twist the handle, and before the door can open all the way, I duck behind Bilson's large frame.

"Thanks for coming," Lucia calls.

She sounds happy, but I crane my neck over Bilson's shoulder to be sure. From what I can tell, she's in her sitting area instead of at her desk, looking at papers, and doesn't seem all that interested in us.

Which is an amazing sign.

When Lucia starts talking right away, she's mad.

When she all but ignores you, she's deep in her work, and you don't happen to be her problem of the hour.

"Lucy!" I step out from behind Bilson and dial the charm up to a thousand.

"Nope."

"But I'm so happy to see you."

She still doesn't look up from the paper she's reading. I exchange a glance with Bilson, who shrugs.

"You wanted to see us?" he asks, like the professional he is.

And it makes me want to face-palm like the frat boy *I* am.

He broke the cardinal rule: never face the problem head-on. Butter up the problem and bring it breakfast in the morning.

"What Cody means is—"

Lucia taps the chair across from her with her foot. "I'm almost done here."

Almost done is good. I *almost* know why the hell I'm here and how much trouble I'm actually in. We both take the sleek, modern chairs, and when I look over at Bilson, he's already looking my way.

He lifts his eyebrows, almost like he's asking if I'm okay. I upnod, and his expression turns dry.

And would you look at us? Communicating without words. If that's what dude sex will do to a man, we need to organize a team-wide gang bang. Telepathy on the ice would make us unbeatable. The downside to that is I'd have to fuck Stoll and Finch, and while I'll do almost anything for the W, I think I've found my line.

Interesting that I won't have sex with them for *hockey*, but I'll have sex with Bilson for something fun to do.

Ha! Yeah. Not touching that thought with a twenty-foot pole.

When Lucia looks up, she smiles, and while I wouldn't put it past her to be into torture and punishment, I doubt she'd bring that into a professional setting. So smile equals good ... right?

I try to be my charismatic self. "You're looking fierce today."

"Relax, the dog problem has gone away. You're not in my bad books anymore. Unless there's something you're not telling me?"

Well, that's a trap. I jump in before Bilson can go being all professional again. "Why, I never! We're the goodest good boys on the team. Total angels. I am offended you'd assume otherwise."

"Miles, you seduced Cody's ex-wife to steal their family pet. Good boy is not something I'd ever say about you."

Bilson did though.

So good, Miles. So, so good.

Lust shoots through me, and I almost goddamn whimper.

Argh. No. Not thinking about it. *Still* not thinking about it. If we want everything to be normal between us, the only way to do that is to choke my dick over it at night and turn it into a joke during the day. That's how brogasms work, dammit.

"Didn't mention you wouldn't say it about me though, did you?" Bilson asks, crossing his beefy arms and throwing me a smug look.

"I'm not playing this game," she fires back. It's somehow the perfect mix of kind and direct that makes me want to send her heart hands. "As the new guys on the team, I wanted to organize a feature on how you're settling in. Nashville have had a rocky few years, but while we might not have had the strongest start to the season, we're still in a much better position than we've seen since we made it to the finals seven years ago. We're seeing some good publicity, and I'd like to capitalize on it."

"What does having new guys have to do with it?" Bilson asks.

"It's a two-pronged attack. First, you're obviously going to talk about how amazing and welcoming the team is—"

Especially me, I think. Unfortunately, my short laugh isn't as internal as my thoughts.

"You disagree?" Lucia asks.

"What? No." I scramble around for something to cover that reaction when Seddy nudges my thigh. I quickly pull him out and rest him in my palm. "My boy said something funny."

She opens her mouth, pauses, then shakes her head and turns to Bilson instead. "*You* will tell the reporter how much you love it here."

"Got it."

"And then you both need to play up your friendship."

"We do?"

Her smile turns sweet, which sends the heebie-jeebies through me. Maybe not future wife material after all. "Everyone loves a good bromance. There have been a few over the years, and it really gets fans involved. You two are perfect contenders. First, you're both idiots—"

"Hey!" I protest.

"And if any other stunts like the dog thing get out, we can blame it on the bromance."

"Sounds like a Harley Valentine song," Bilson mutters.

Lucia ignores us both. "People will forgive you for anything if they're invested enough. So that's what we need to do. That pregame ritual of yours already has people talking. We want more things like that. Got it?"

While this does sound like an awesome idea for the team, I can't help but worry about what would happen if the women we hit on saw the bromance story everywhere.

I bare my teeth and send a sorry look Bilson's way, and then I raise my hand. "Ah ... Luce?"

"Put your hand down. We're not in class."

"Right. Yes. Obviously." I clear my throat. "I'm loving this idea. You're so clever and pretty and smart."

"Oh no."

"But we should probably tell you ..." I throw another look Bilson's way and find his mouth hanging open. "We went out together the other night and hit up some women about a threesome, and now I'm super worried that one

109

of them might come forward and say something and ruin this whole plan."

I see the exact moment Lucia regrets all her life choices leading up to this moment. Instead of the reaming I expect, she only manages a long exhale, then jots down a note on her tablet. "You boys are not the first, nor will you be the last." Then, like she can't help herself, she pins me with a look. "Honestly, what is it with you jocky dude-bros that you all want to get naked with each other?"

I manage a small breath of relief, assuming this means we're not in trouble. "Have you seen my abs? Bilson only has so much self-restraint."

His slap to the back of my head is not completely unexpected.

"I forbid either of you from mentioning that detail in your interview."

"My abs or the threesomes?"

"Dear God, get out."

I jump from my seat like my ass is on fire, Bilson not far behind me. I'm preparing for him to get pissy with me or call me an idiot or tear me a new one for giving up our secret.

Instead, the second the doors are closed, he breaks down into laughter. "What the hell is wrong with you?"

I pluck the broship bracelet he's still wearing. "What the hell is wrong with *you*? You're in an official bromance with me now. You really should learn to pick your friends better."

Bilson steps forward, right into my personal space, then slips his hand into my pocket. My breath catches in my chest as my entire body freezes up at the proximity, and my damn stupid cock gives a twitch in my pants.

He slides his hand out again and lifts Stone to our eye level. I finally remember how to breathe.

"What do you think?" he asks Stone. "Should I pick my friends better?" Bilson tilts his head like he's listening, and I can't help my smile. "Yeah, I agree." Our eyes meet. "I'm pretty comfortable with my choices."

That stupid, happy warmth fills my gut again as I take Stone back. "Better be careful, CB. You go around talking to rocks like that and people might think you're weird."

CHAPTER FIFTEEN

BILSON

I'm thankful Miles is able to move forward like nothing ever happened because I need someone by my side for this interview. It's not a well-kept secret that the media and I have never seen eye to eye. They like to splash my four divorces all over the place and make it out like I'm some kind of playboy when the opposite is true.

My marriages weren't a reflection of how many women I've been with but how starved I've been for love for so long.

Hopefully, with Miles here for the interview too, they might stick to actual hockey questions.

"Thanks for meeting with me," Langford Trest says. "Shall we jump right in?"

I glance next to me at Miles, who looks a little green. This is probably his first big article he'll be part of. His first write-up where what he says matters. It's understandable that he's nervous.

"Let's do it," I say, my issues with reporters getting pushed to the back of my mind.

I've lived this life a long time. While Miles has been playing in the AHL, it's a whole other puck game now he's in the big leagues to stay.

Langford must see Miles's nerves because he says, "Don't worry. I'll start easy. How are you two settling in with the team?"

"They've been great," I say. "And it's like we clicked immediately on the ice."

"My guy CB here was the thing Nashville needed to take us to the next level."

I try not to wince. Not at the nickname but the way his words could be misconstrued. "What he means is there was a place for an experienced winger to help the already amazing team, and we're already going strong."

Langford looks at his notes. "Preseason was a bit of a mess though?"

Miles hangs his head, but I know how to handle this.

"Preseason is always a mess, no matter what team you're on. After a summer off, some of the guys come back with extra weight. Teams have to integrate new players, new staff a lot of the time. It's always a learning curve, and that's why none of those games count for standing." I grip Miles's shoulder. "This guy showed up when it counted, and in his first month of being in the NHL, he managed three consecutive shutouts. I'm not sure any other goalie has done that right out of the gate. He's an amazing player and one to watch."

"That's big praise." Langford turns to Miles. "How does that make you feel?"

Miles seems to relax. "It's a bit surreal. The first day I walked into that locker room as starting goalie, Cody was there. It was intimidating walking up to this guy who I had admired since I was in high school—"

"I'm not that old," I grumble.

Langford laughs, but Miles keeps going.

"But he welcomed me easily, even though he was also new and has never gotten one past me during a game before. He was still nice."

"I can get one past you," I argue.

"Practice doesn't count. Statistically, you're bound to get one there."

There's the cocky little shit I know. But this is better than dealing with nervous Miles.

"This is great stuff," Langford says. He's recording the interview but is also making notes at the same time, and he writes something down.

"Miles here is really superstitious," I say. "He has lucky rocks, he talks to the goals, and everyone on the team just accepts his weird quirks." I can feel the heat of Miles's glare.

Langford doesn't look shocked. "I've heard that about goalies."

"It can't be too weird. This one"—Miles thumbs in my direction—"had a conversation with my pet rocks the other day. And the pregame ritual was his idea."

"So the rumors of your bromance are true, then?" Langford asks, and even though we were expecting this line of questioning, I tense anyway. Because when I think bromance, I think brogasms, and when I think brogasms, I picture Miles riding my cock.

Nope, nope. Not here.

Friendship. Bromance. Just friends and teammates.

"CB obviously took a shine to me because I'm at his maturity level in age." Miles wraps his arm around my shoulders, and it's the last thing he should do.

I shift and lean forward, hoping to cover my growing hard-on in my pants. "I actually took a shine to him because he's like Bambi. All young and doe-eyed."

"Aww, you think I'm as cute as a baby deer?"

My head swivels, and I glare at him.

As if realizing he's openly flirting, he tries to cover. "I'll take it. I am cute. Everybody thinks so."

"You're also conceited," I add.

"Aren't all hockey players?" Langford asks.

"Hey." I try to protest but can't. "Okay, fair point."

"Let's get down to some stats and career highlights," Langford says and starts peppering Miles with questions about his time in the AHL.

I sit stoically, listening as Miles says how grateful he is that Nashville signed him, even though their farm team is away from home blah, blah, blah, loves Tennessee, blah. But all I'm really thinking about is the question I know is coming. The one I knew would be a big focus of my move.

"And Cody, you were on the Stanley Cup runner-up team last season but opened yourself up as a free agent. I guess what everyone wants to know is why?"

Because I have too many exes in Seattle is the completely wrong answer here, I know that, but I've got nothing else.

"I heard it's because he got sick of winning," Miles says, and I snort. But hey, it's an actual angle I can take.

"I wanted to prove to my old linemates Katz and Emerson that I was the winning factor in Seattle."

They're so going to call me after this interview comes out.

"So you're confident with you on the team, Nashville will make it to the playoffs?" Langford asks, and I know it's a journalistic trap.

"Nope. Teamwork will get us to the playoffs. I'm just one hell of a team player."

"It's true," Miles says. "He's all about taking one for the team."

I want to argue that no, that's Miles, but I don't.

When Langford finally says he's wrapping things up, I let out a loud breath in relief. But it's too premature because as Langford stands to walk away, he turns back at the last second. "Oh, one more thing. What's with this rumor about you two stealing a dog?"

"We didn't steal him," Miles says, and I reach over and grip his arm to get him to stop talking, but he doesn't. "It was *his* dog."

"So there is a dog?"

I try to smile. "Didn't the team's PR manager give you guidelines on what can and can't be asked?"

Langford jots something else down. "Never mind. I've got all I need."

I hang my head, and once he's gone, I turn to Miles. "Lucia is going to kill us."

—

By some miracle, when the article comes out a couple of days later, there's no mention of the damn dog. Now Miles and I can stop avoiding Lucia and maybe start winning some games.

The last two have been disasters.

I wasn't lying when I said that Miles will be a great goalie, but right now, he's too unpredictable. He has amazing games and then shit games, and then there are nights where he does well, but it's still not good enough. And that's what the last couple of games have been for him.

Me, on the other hand, I've been playing like a drunk cow on skates.

All of that will change tonight now I know the article reads as Lucia wanted. Our snark was left, the playful banter, but it reads as teammates being teammates and not two people who have made each other come.

I know I said I'd be good for another few months without sex, but constantly being around Miles only makes me want another round with him. All the sexual frustration that was building inside me after my last breakup is already back, and it hasn't even been one month yet.

We said it was only going to be that once. That he did it so I wouldn't get attached, and he was as horny as I was. But the problem with that now is he's right there. Every day. Across the locker room from me. On the team bus, plane, in the same hotel only a few doors away …

He's quickly becoming my best friend on the team— possibly outside of it too—but I worry I'm even connecting sex to broship now.

Do I even like Miles as a person? Or did the sex cloud my judgment? Have I always been this way, and how the fuck did I get so messed up?

"Hey." His voice makes me jump as he sits next to me on the plane. We're off for another road trip, though this is only a quick one to Tampa, and then we're back tomorrow.

"Hey."

"Did you see the article? No mention of Killer anywhere. Who's looking after our baby while we're gone?" Yes, he's still calling Killer *our* baby.

"I found a place that will come to my house and feed him and walk him twice a day."

"But he's alone for the rest of the time? Who's going to snuggle him to sleep? Who—"

Of course he'd be worried about that. "He doesn't even let me snuggle him to sleep. He's good. I promise."

"We should find someone who'll take him overnight at their house. I would suggest them staying at yours, but having randoms in your house isn't cool."

"Yet, you've been to my house."

"That joke is about as old as you are."

"Same with that one."

Stoll turns from the seat in front of us. "When did you two become an old married couple?"

Probably about the moment I stuck my dick in him. Luckily, I don't say that out loud. Miles doesn't seem to have a filter though.

"Ever since our bromance article came out. Did you read it? Everyone loves us."

Stoll laughs. "Whatever you say, Rook." He turns back around.

Miles frowns.

"What's up?"

He lowers his voice. "He called me Rook."

"That's your name now," I say.

"No, it's your name for me. And I … I like that it's ours."

Even though that sends a spike of lust or warmth or what-the-fuck-ever through me, I ignore it. "Damn. We really are the old married couple."

"Aww, I'm wife number five!" Miles practically yells, except the "I'm" part was much quieter than the rest of it, so naturally, the noise on the whole plane stops.

"Please tell me you're not getting married again," Finch says, who'd only just climbed on and is halfway down the aisle.

"I'm not! I'm never getting married again. Guarantee it."

"Let's place our bets," Stoll says. "Next woman he bangs will be Mrs. Bilson number five."

Some things never change.

While the team makes bets on my future love life, I turn to Miles.

"You're going to pay for that, by the way."

"Don't promise me with a good time."

I hate that my mind immediately goes to sex. Only question is, does he mean it, or is he messing with me?

CHAPTER SIXTEEN

MILES

So apparently, I like teasing Bilson. I keep telling myself to pull back, not to be weird, don't make him uncomfortable, and yet every time I open my mouth, it ... comes out. Like an obsession. A stupid, dumb, unfiltered obsession.

I'm no better than Killer, really. A yappy dog begging for attention.

I get it from him too. The idiotic smiles, the "rookie" barbs, the shoving and jostling and waiting for me after practice if I drag my feet getting ready. He helps me drown my sorrows after a shitty game and celebrate the wins.

It's been exactly five weeks since our hookup. Things are exactly as they've always been between us, and I think we've safely made it past the risk of awkwardness.

Only problem is, things are *exactly* like they were five weeks ago. Bilson's problem is back, and every time I notice that hole-wrecker waking up, it's like a siren call for Cobra, and he rears his head in interest.

I should go out and hook up, but I don't want to.

The thing is, now I know what his dick feels like, I'm not so sure I can be satisfied with another strap-on. Sure, strap-ons are some people's preference, but it's very obvious to me and my dick that it's not mine.

Which really should make me question some things, but I don't.

If I don't think about sexuality, it doesn't exist. There's no harm in fantasizing about Bilson. I have zero problems with people being queer, I have zero problems with a man fucking me, but I can't be *not* straight. My parents are very much the "I don't hate queer people, I just don't agree with their lifestyle" types, and it kills me to think that anything could come between us.

I'm close with my family. I love being close with them.

So taking a dick once—and who knows, maybe twice—isn't going to change a thing.

I rip up my brake as I pull into Bilson's driveway. It's late, and he might be asleep, but I've been tossing and turning for an hour now and couldn't drift off, so if I have to be awake, so does he.

I'm pretty sure that's in the bromance fine print.

I jump out and approach his front door, wondering why I've never had the forethought to swipe a key to his place like I do when we're on the road. It's quiet on the street, so I try not to knock too loudly and wake everyone up. Just loud enough to wake *him* up.

My first knock does nothing, but the second sets off the alarm.

And by alarm, I mean Killer. His cute bark comes rapid-fire as I hear him barrel along the hall to reach the door, and after only a few moments, Bilson pulls it open.

He's all squinty-eyed and messy dark hair, pajama pants riding low on his hips. Before I can stop them, my eyes drop to his slightly furry chest, and I have to tug them away again.

Bad, eyes. Very naughty.

"How is it that the second I knew someone was at my door, I was certain it was you?"

"Wishful thinking?" I stoop down to pick up Killer. The dograt immediately starts licking my face and shaking in excitement. "Let's go."

"Go where?"

"I dunno. Somewhere."

"You came around at …" He pats his pocket and searches for his phone.

I pull mine out. "Twelve thirty."

He scuffs a hand through his already messy hair. "After midnight with no plan and woke me up to go 'somewhere'?"

"Yes."

He laughs. "Let me put on a shirt."

"And underwear."

"How did you …" He looks down to where his dick print is tenting his pajamas. "Fucking hell."

"My thoughts exactly."

He closes the door on me, so I wrap Killer in my hoodie, and we go and wait for him in the car. He shows up five minutes later, beanie pulled down almost to his eyes, looking all kinds of adorable.

"Cold, huh?"

"Tired. Get me coffee."

"Yes, sir."

He leans forward to turn up the heat, and Killer jumps from my lap to his. "We're taking Killer?"

"Duh. He's family."

"I lost the dog in my marriage. Don't tell me I'm going to lose him in my bromance too."

I back out of the drive. "Easy solution. Never brosplit from me, and there's no issue."

We go through a drive-through first to get the old man coffee, and then I jump on the long road out of town to one of my friends' properties. We've gone four-wheel driving there countless times before, and even though the house is all but abandoned, I know the code to the padlock, and I'm itching to do some donuts.

Bilson drinks in silence for a while, Killer sleeping in his lap.

"Wanna know where we're going?" I ask.

"Nope."

That wasn't the answer I was expecting. "Why not?"

"Because we're going there anyway, and knowing you, it'll either be something ridiculous or … no. My money's on ridiculous. I can't wait."

My lips purse. "I'm trying to decide whether to be proud or offended you can count on me for dumbassery."

"Definitely proud. It's one of the things I like best about you."

"My ass is the other, isn't it?" I know I shouldn't say it, but I just really, really wanted to.

"Surprisingly, not even top three."

"*Wow.*" I gasp, reaching down to pat the side of my butt cheek. "Don't listen, baby. He's a liar. Thinks puppies are ugly and hates chocolate. You can't trust someone like that."

"And now you're talking to your butt."

"The fact you're still surprised by things like this says more about you than me."

He goes to argue but changes his mind. "You're right. I should embrace the coo-coo. But if you'd let me speak: while your ass is undoubtedly the best I've ever had and ranks super high in best asses I've seen, it's still outranked."

Okay, that sounds more promising. "Outranked by …"

"Of course you'd want to know."

"I'm a whore for compliments."

"Among other things," he whispers so low I almost miss it. The gravelly edge to his voice gets me all the way hard, and I curse mentally that I can't move on. "Top three goes: loyalty, sense of humor, ridiculousness."

It's bittersweet knowing loyalty came in at number one. I'm so fucking glad he knows I'd have his back no matter what, but it just reminds me of my frat days and how much I loved them. How much I learned about the kind of person I want to be. Maybe one day, I'll look back on my days with the team and feel the same.

"Bromotions."

"What?"

I'm not even sure why I'm telling him this. "It's something my frat buddies and I used to do. Sit down and talk about our emotions and how we feel about things and support each other. I haven't had that in a long time." I take another quick look at him, but there's nothing cocky in it this time. "I'm pretty sure I could tell you anything, and you wouldn't be a dick about it. So ... like, thanks. For giving me that back, I guess."

He's quiet for a minute, and I don't want to look at him and have some stupid expression prove me wrong. "I don't think I've ever really had that. So thanks for that, too, and shit."

My grin is out of control when I look at him, and while I might love these kinds of talks, my mouth does that thing where it takes over again. "So. Best you've ever had?"

He groans. "Of course you weren't going to let that go."

"Be honest, you've never actually had anal before, have you? I'm the *only* one you've ever had."

"I've done anal." He sniggers. "Once."

"Yes." I punch the air. "Best of two for the win."

"You should feel proud. She had a great ass."

And while I do feel pride, there's something else there. Something I don't like. So I play it off and ignore it like I do with everything to do with Bilson. "It was ex-wife number three, wasn't it?"

"I'll never tell. Some of us know how to leave sex in the bedroom."

I hide saying *boring* behind a cough.

"Wasn't so boring when I was calling you a good boy, was I?"

My jaw hits the footwell. "Why is hearing you talk about it *so* hot?"

He cracks up laughing, smile still on his face when it dies off and he says, "It was a pretty mind-blowing night."

The way he says it, with a tinge of *something* in his voice, tells me this is my opening. My moment to suggest that maybe it didn't have to be the only night. We could fuck again—we've already proved we can get past it and move on.

But I pull up to my friend's property and still haven't said a word.

Because I'm chickenshit.

Once can be blown off as two teammates helping each other out. What does twice equal? At that point, we might as well go for the hat trick. Will fucking more make it easier to bounce back from … or harder?

Sex is just sex.

But Bilson isn't just anybody.

This stupid bromance might be overhyped and fan-driven, but when it comes right down to it, we've bonded like I never have with a teammate before.

I get out and free the padlock, then push open the gate. When I get back in my truck, I decide to ignore the stupid thoughts. No conversation worth having happens after 1:00 a.m.

"You ready?" I ask.

"For what?"

"Hold on to Killer."

Then I put my foot on the gas. We tear through the field, kicking up grass, and when I hit the center, I stamp on the brake and yank my steering wheel to the side.

The holler Bilson lets out as mud and dirt fly past the window is music to my goddamn ears. My *whoop* joins his as we drift to a stop.

Then we go again.

CHAPTER SEVENTEEN

BILSON

I can't remember the last time I let go and had this much fun. Killer's had a big night too, yapping away while trying to see outside the window as Miles does donuts. I can only assume he's yelling at Miles to be more careful.

It tires him out, and now, as we drive home at close to 3:00 a.m., Killer settles on my lap and goes to sleep.

"Poor guy is tuckered out," Miles says.

"What about you? Did you burn off your excess energy enough to go to sleep yet? I don't know if you've noticed this, but I'm no spring chicken; I need sufficient sleep to be as awesome as I am."

"Damn. I'd hate to see you on no sleep if this is as awesome as you get."

"Fuck you." I laugh.

"Nah. We already played that game."

And there he goes bringing it up again. I can't tell if he does it to test me or if he's hinting at wanting to do it again, and I think I'm too scared to ask. Mainly because if it's the first, calling him on it might make things weird. If it's option number two, wanting another go, there's no way I'm going to turn it down.

It's taken us this long to get comfortable with it—to joke about it—and while there have been moments of awkwardness about our hookup, I'd say we moved past it pretty unscathed. Team dynamics haven't changed. We're still the same as we have been out on the ice. Our games haven't been noticeably affected.

If we do go there again, will that change? Or will we sink into more comfort surrounding it?

Miles pulls into my street and then into my driveway, but his hand lingers on the keys in the ignition.

We idle for a few seconds before he looks over at me.

"Hypothetically," I say at the exact same time he lets out, "I'm still not tired."

I smile. "Of course you aren't."

Whether he realizes he's doing it or not, those big puppy eyes of his are almost impossible to say no to.

"Are you really not tired, or are you using that as an excuse to come inside?" I ask.

"Actually, I was kind of hoping to use it as an excuse for you to ... *come inside.*"

It takes a second to register what he's saying. "Smooth, Rook."

"I like to think so."

I want to say yes. It's on the tip of my tongue. But I can't seem to get it out.

Miles holds up his hand. "You can say no, and we'll pretend I didn't bring it up, but—"

"I can't stop thinking about it," I blurt.

He looks relieved.

"But at the same time, we got away with it the first time. We're still friends. The team doesn't know. No one knows. Which brings me back to my hypothetical question. If we were to go there again, what's to stop us from doing it again and again and again? By which point, the more we do it, the riskier it becomes. We get sloppy and make a comment in front of someone else. We mix the physical with emotional, which I'm fucking known for. I can't keep feelings out of sex, and I love you as a friend, but I don't want to fall *in* love with you. No offense."

"You're getting ahead of yourself there, aren't you?"

"Have you met me? It's what I do. I don't go around marrying everyone for the hell of it. I'm known to fall hard and fast. The last thing I need is another divorce."

He pulls back. "Now we're getting married? Dude, chill."

I run a hand over my head. "I'm not saying that, but I'm scared of letting this situation get out of my control."

"Cody, look at me."

Cody. Not CB. Not Bilson. Cody. I shift in my seat and turn to him.

"When you see me, what do you see? What am I to you?"

"A friend. A teammate."

He nods slowly. "Good. What else?"

"Someone I want to stick my dick in?"

"Is that it?"

I look at him. Really look at him. From his floppy blond hair to his bright eyes and easy smile that gives him that cocky edge. "I see someone who has the ability to make our careers implode if what we did ever gets out."

Miles finally turns off the car. "Okay, one, you give sex way too much credit. There are queer dudes in the league. You're friends with all of them. Their careers didn't take a hit when they came out or when any of them announced they were a couple." He holds up his hand. "And I'm not saying we're a couple or will be or anything like that. Just that if a little sex between teammates got out there, it wouldn't be a big deal for you, personally or professionally. Argument number two: not once did you say in there that when you look at me, you see the potential of falling in love. You're more worried about the scandal of us sleeping together than the risk of falling for me. I can be your friend. Your teammate. And the person you stick your dick into."

When he puts it like that ... I can't deny that the majority of my thoughts have been around what fucking Miles would do to the team.

"And just so we're clear here, when I look at you, I see someone whose career I've admired for a long time. I wouldn't want to do anything that would mess that up."

"What else do you see?" I throw his question back at him, hoping he doesn't psychoanalyze me too deeply.

He doesn't disappoint. "A giant walking, talking strap-on. I can't stop thinking about your dick."

I want to laugh, but I can't. I'm too turned on. I open the door. "Go to my bedroom and get yourself ready while I put Killer in the laundry room."

"Poor guy probably thinks we're punishing him."

"Would you prefer he watched from his place on my pillow?"

Miles shudders. "Fair point. That would be much more traumatic for him. You, laundry room. Me, bedroom."

It's practically a race to the front door, and Miles even holds Killer for me so I can fetch my keys out of my tight pocket, only made tighter by my cock trying to escape my jeans.

His hand lands suddenly on my forearm. "We're still not telling anyone though. Right?"

"Right." I'll agree to anything right now.

As soon as the door's open, Killer's back in my arms, and Miles is stripping off his clothes as he walks down the hallway to my bedroom.

Killer whines as he watches Miles walk away, and I begin to worry that Killer has adopted Miles as much as Miles has adopted him.

"Traitor." I put Killer in the laundry room, where he has food and a bed set up. I top up his water and give him a treat to occupy him until he falls back asleep.

He'll be fine in there. It's like his den. His safe space. While he prefers to sleep on my pillow next to me, he doesn't hate being put in the laundry room.

By the time he's settled, I head toward my bedroom, stripping off my jacket, shoes and socks, and my shirt as I go.

I'm so not prepared for the sight I walk in on.

Miles Olsen, naked on my bed on his hands and knees with one of his hands reaching behind him and prepping his hole for me. The light is completely on, not just a sliver of it coming from the bathroom like last time.

I don't think he's noticed me yet. He has his eyes closed, and as he fingers himself, he lets out a noise that makes my cock leak.

The first time, it was lights off and as impersonal as possible, but I can't deny the way his deep masculine sounds cemented in my brain.

I reach for the light switch to turn it off but hesitate because I'm under no delusion about Miles. I wasn't the first time we did this either. We might have pretended we were imagining someone else, a woman, but I wasn't.

I drop my hand and finish getting undressed while I watch Miles get himself ready. He still hasn't acknow-ledged me, but he has to know I'm here.

"Good enough. Hurry up and get over here so you can fill me up."

Yep. He knows I've been watching him this whole time.

I approach the bed and spot the condom next to the bottle of lube.

Miles has his ass in the air as he leans forward on his elbows, his long, muscular body before me. I don't waste any time in suiting up or lathering myself in lube, but apparently, I'm still too slow for him.

"Come on, CB. Fuck me already."

"You're so fucking desperate," I rasp.

"So, so desperate."

I step up behind him but make sure I enter him slowly. I don't trust that he's prepped himself enough with how impatient he's being. His ass is so tight, and I can only work myself in about halfway.

"Breathe," I say.

"I'm good. I'm good." He doesn't sound good.

I pull out of him.

"No, wait." He tries to reach behind him for me.

"I'm not going anywhere." I grab more lube and cover my fingers in it.

I press my fingers inside him, searching for that spot that drove him crazy last time. He relaxes for me, lets me in, and this time, when I pull out of him, he makes a needy noise at the back of his throat.

I replace my fingers with my cock and slide in a lot easier now. We both let out a moan, and this is what it's about.

This is the point of what we're doing. It has nothing to do with hockey, with being friends, or anything else. It's about getting off.

It only takes a few thrusts for him to start trembling.

His ass surrounds my cock. So hot. So tight.

As soon as he's adjusted completely to my size, I can't hold back. He feels too good.

My hands bite into his skin, gripping his hips and pulling him back to meet my every thrust.

There's no way I can last long when his body takes me so easily, but with how he's trembling, begging for more without words, I get the feeling I won't have to last long. I only have to last longer than him.

"You gonna come for me, Rook?"

Miles whimpers, breathy and desperate, and then reaches for his cock, frantically jerking himself off.

The muscles in his back tighten, his ass squeezes around my dick, and warmth floods my entire body.

"I'm coming," he cries.

That's what I need.

He grunts and pushes back. I'm balls-deep inside of him and can't hold back anymore. While he writhes and breathes through his orgasm, I unleash, and it only takes a few more thrusts before I follow him over the edge.

Pleasure spreads through my body, a ripple that turns into a wave. I don't let him go until I'm completely empty. The second I soften my hold, Miles collapses on top of my bed, and it takes all my strength to stay standing and not fall on top of him.

My vision blurs, and breathing is hard, but fucking hell, that was amazing.

I stumble my way into the bathroom and deal with the condom and then throw on a fresh pair of boxers to go get us bottles of water from the fridge.

Before I can head back to the bedroom though, Miles steps out in his underwear and follows the trail of clothes he left on his way in.

"Water?" I hold out the bottle.

"Thanks." He uncaps it and takes a sip and then throws on his pants and shirt.

"You heading home?" I stupidly ask. Of course he's heading home. This isn't a slumber party.

"Yep. Just in time to get about four hours of sleep before we have to be at the practice rink."

"We're going to hate ourselves."

Miles smiles at me. "Nah. Can't hate something that makes us feel that good. I'll see you in the morning."

As easy as that, Miles leaves as if we didn't just fuck each other's brains out.

Maybe this could work after all.

CHAPTER EIGHTEEN

MILES

The knock on my front door sounds dramatically loud. After our last home game, another sweet-as-pie shutout, I had a brilliant idea. I worked out who could dog-sit Killer while we're gone tomorrow.

Only now it's happening, my palms are clammier than they have any right to be.

"Expecting someone?" Mom asks as I jump from the couch. I've been hanging around inside like a bad smell for the last half an hour, and I know she can tell something's up.

"Yeah, one of my teammates."

"You mean we're finally cool enough to meet one?" Dad shouts as I go to let Bilson in. I leave them behind in the living room and step into the hall to head for the front door.

This was a stupid, very bad idea.

It will be good for Killer, I remind myself. When did I fall for that little dograt?

"Hey," I say, opening one side of the French front doors. Bilson's standing on the front stoop, all handsome with his dark hair neatly styled and Killer huddled adorably in his arms.

"You sure about this?" His forehead creases with the question, which is what I need to play confident.

"Totally. Look how big this block is. Killer will love it here." Tall trees, orangey and losing their leaves, hug the property.

He casts a doubtful glance around. "And your parents?"

"Ehh. I'm sure it will be fine—they took me in, didn't they?"

"But you're their kid."

I steal Killer and lean into the tongue attack, his little butt shaking faster than the rest of him. "And you're basically their grandson. Aren't you? Aren't you, widdle dograt?"

"Stop calling him that." It's about the thousandth time those words have left him, and I'm sure it's more of a reflex than anything by this point.

"He doesn't care."

"Oh, yeah? Next time I see Seddy, I'm going to tell him quartz is clearly more impressive than riverstone."

My whole damn mouth drops. "You wouldn't."

Bilson leans in close, eyes gleaming with evil victory. "Oh, but I would."

That husky tone should be illegal at two in the afternoon, standing outside my parents' place. I swallow roughly and take a step back from him. "No more dograt."

"Better. Now, let's ambush your parents."

"I prefer persuade over ambush."

"Prefer what you want; you're doing the talking. And making it clear this is all your idea."

Fine by me. I lead Bilson through the house into the large living area. There are wooden ceiling beams that match the polished floor and a slate fireplace next to huge glass doors that lead to a large deck outside.

"This is incredible," Bilson says.

He's right. Mom and Dad worked hard to have this house designed and built.

"Who's this?" Mom calls from her place on the sofa.

"Cody, this is my mom and dad. Mom and Dad, this is …" I trail off as I'm hit with the complete awkwardness of the situation. A chill creeps through me, and I quickly redirect, holding up the furless creature in my arms. "Killer. This is Killer."

Neither of them says anything for a moment.

"What … what is it?" Dad asks.

The tension leaves me. "He's a dogr—ah, a dog."

"You sure?" Dad leans forward and eyes Killer in concern.

"He's a Chinese Crested," Bilson jumps in. "Super friendly."

And like Killer knows what Bilson has said, the wriggly little thing squirms from my arms, drops to the ground, and pelts at Dad, long ear fur flapping.

Dad barely has a second to react before Killer jumps into his lap and starts yapping happily for attention.

"Why is there a dog in here?" Mom asks.

I can feel Bilson's unease from here.

"Look at him." I put on my most pleading, baby voice. "So much love to give. And there's only so much me and CB can do. We're away again tomorrow, and this barbarian"—I point right at Bilson—"has been locking him in the laundry room and having someone stop over a couple of times a day. My heart is bleeding for him. *Bleeding*."

"Absolutely not," Dad says, trying and failing to keep Killer from slobbering all over his face. Bilson really does spoil him.

"The laundry room, Dad. Have a heart."

Mom speaks up. "Miles is right. The poor dog can't be holed away all that time."

I whirl to her, excited to have an ally. "You are so wise. And pretty. And clever."

Bilson actually scoffs from behind me. I throw up a finger at him, which earns me *the look* from Mom.

"In my house? Really?"

"Sorry. Sorry. Back to the dog and how right I am."

She turns to Dad. "This is better than the time he brought five pigs home and tried to hide them in his bedroom."

Dad still doesn't look convinced.

"And the time we found him stuck hanging from the deck."

"I'm sorry," Bilson cuts in, sounding like he's trying not to laugh. "He what now?"

Dad's *gotcha* smile is immediate. "Thought it would be cute to hang a squirrel feeder from the tree outside. Didn't get out of his hockey gear first though, did he? Ended up hanging by one of the straps."

Bilson turns to me with glee. "Tell me you didn't try to climb into a tree *in your full pads*?"

"I thought it would be better to get it out of the way before I went up to shower."

"Why didn't you shower in the locker rooms?"

"I was twelve and self-conscious. I didn't look like this back then. Why are we talking about this? Killer is the subject of today's meeting."

"I dunno, I'm pretty happy with the detour we're taking."

Dad sighs. "We have more stories than we can get through in one afternoon. Never had any problems with the others—it was all Miles. Should'a known when he was five and decided he'd only play in goals. His coach at the time tried to rotate out the players to give everyone a turn, and the first time he tried to put Miles in defense, he clung tight to those goals and screamed his head off."

I give Dad a dry look, so Mom takes over.

"The next practice, he covered the pads and helmet in maple syrup so no one else got to use them."

I shrug, trying to play off my childish antics. As the youngest of four, I was very possessive of anything I saw as mine. "Even back then, I knew I was the best. Just trying to do the team a solid."

"Well, that answers my question about whether you've always been a cocky brat," Bilson says. He turns to Mom. "I told him you wouldn't be okay with me foisting my dog off on you. I'm so sorry I put you in this position."

He's talking with a tone I've never heard from him before. It's so … charming. Gross.

"He really, really doesn't mind the laundry room. It's small, but he's small, so it's fine."

Bilson's laundry room is so *not* small. That asshole is playing them.

And it works.

"No, really, it's fine," Mom says.

Dad huffs. "Can't be leaving the thing alone."

Satisfied he's done his job, Killer hops down off Dad's lap and curls up at his feet.

"And now we run before they can change their minds," I tell Bilson, grabbing his sleeve and tugging him toward the door. "We'll be back for him soon! I'm gonna show CB my pad."

"If he tells you he has girls back there every night, he's lying," Dad calls after us.

Ergh.

It's not until we're out of the house and crossing to my small place that I'm able to be almost normal again. "That was weird."

Bilson laughs. "I loved it."

"You're not the one who was being picked on."

"Exactly. I wish we'd given them time to pick on you some more. Baby Miles sounds adorable. And dumb as bricks."

"You're gonna say nothing's changed, aren't you?"

"Why, when you said it for me?"

Asshole. I unlock my door and lead him inside, that self-conscious feeling settling over me again. It's a pain in the ass, and I wish it'd fuck off already. Ignoring it is hard to do when it's making my movements stiff and awkward.

I sit on the trunk at the end of my bed, and Bilson's eyes linger on it.

"That looks like it's the perfect height to ..."

Damn, he's right. "Well, now I won't even be able to walk into my bedroom without picturing it. Thanks for that."

"We could try it. I bet I could be fast."

And as much as I'd love that, as much as I've been craving another pounding from him, my good mood crashes.

"Yeah, not a good idea."

"Oh." He actually backs up a step. "No, you're right. Twice was enough. Sorry. I don't know what I was thinking."

"Calm down," I say, managing a smile at his rambling. "Twice definitely wasn't enough. I just mean we can't do that stuff here."

He tucks his hands in his pockets, head tilted to the side. "I'm not following."

"My parents."

"Worried they'll walk in on us? We'll put a tie on the doorknob."

But the more he tries to make me feel better, the more it has the opposite effect. "They wouldn't approve. Of all that."

"All that?"

How does he still not get it? "The gayness," I explain. "I love them, but they have some pretty outdated views on shit, and the worst part is that they don't even realize they're outdated. They think they're all progressive and loving when they say things like 'love the sinner but not the sin' after I told them about some of my frat buddies getting together."

Bilson crosses the room and sits on the trunk next to me. "That's why you don't want us telling anyone."

"Exactly."

"I don't get it. I didn't think anyone thought that way anymore."

If only it was that simple. "A *lot* of people still think that way. Maybe not in Seattle, and Nashville is mostly okay, but venture out a bit, and the sad part is my folks really do look progressive by comparison."

"I'm sorry, Miles."

"Don't be. It's not like I'm …" Like I'm what? Queer? So what, I like sex. Does it matter whether it's a woman or a dude on the other end of the thing fucking me? It doesn't change anything.

It can't.

We're quiet for a moment, and I hate that the tension is so thick.

"They really will take good care of Killer."

"I believe you."

"And I meant what I said." I wait for Bilson to look at me. "Twice wasn't enough. We might not be able to have sex here, but we're doing it again. Agreed?" I hold up my pinky finger, and Bilson bites back a laugh.

He links his finger around mine. "Can't wait."

CHAPTER NINETEEN

BILSON

My phone goes off in the visitor cubby while I'm getting into my pads. When I look at it, I can't help letting out an "Aww."

"Staring at a photo of me? I *am* cute," Miles says next to me.

"Nah, my baby." I show him the text from his mom, where there's a photo of Killer asleep on Miles's dad's chest.

"Jesus. Maybe it wasn't a good idea to have them babysit *our* baby. We'll never get him back."

"I'm still confused as to when exactly Killer became our baby."

"When I stole him for you. Duh."

"Wait," Stoll says on the other side. "You guys still have that dog?"

"It's my dog," I say.

"Our dog," Miles corrects.

There's no winning with him.

"Looks like you adopted an extra puppy." Stoll nods at Miles.

Miles shoots me a sly look. "You hear that? Stoll thinks I'm cute too."

"Did I say that? I might hate puppies. You don't know."

143

"What kind of monster hates puppies?" Miles does the sign of the cross.

We're interrupted by Coach entering and trying to rile us up for the game with a pep talk and a ridiculous war cry he makes us do.

Coaches, man. Some of them are even weirder than goalies.

We're in Colorado for the first of four away games, and I'm pumped. Especially knowing Killer won't be alone for the next ten days. Miles was right. Having a dog-sitter check in on him twice a day for that long would be mean.

Without having to worry about my baby, I hit the ice with nothing but the W on my mind.

Some nights, I go out there with a clear mind, and everything clicks. Other nights, it feels like my brain and my body aren't connected, and I can't put one in the net no matter how hard I try.

Usually when that happens, I try to take a back seat, play both defense and offense and hope for an assist, but I can't even pull that together tonight.

Colorado gets so many more shots on goal than we do, and we're lucky that Miles is on his game. Unlike me.

It's one of those frustrating nights where there's no score for the entire first period, but both sides are fighting hard for it, so we're exhausted by the time we head into the second.

It doesn't get much better when we get back out there, but at least we're increasing our chances. Even if we miss. Every. Damn. Time.

Halfway through the period, Connor Kikishkin intercepts a pass between Finch and me. I'd be impressed by the fluidity of the play if he didn't cross the blue line like he's going to shoot it but passes to his sniper of a younger brother, Easton, instead. Miles has no chance against Easton Kikishkin in a perfect position.

The lamp lights up, and it takes all my strength not to break my stick on the ice. I'm not pissed at Miles—that was an unstoppable shot—but I am pissed the Kiki brothers outplayed me.

That goal was on Finch and me for not anticipating the kind of move the brothers are known for.

Once the first goal is in the bag, it's as if Nashville deflates and Colorado becomes more confident. They try riskier plays and pull them off, and we can't strip them of the puck, no matter how much we try.

And try we do.

It's a frustrating struggle, so when we close out the second period 3-zip, I want to scream.

During the break, we hydrate, shove down some carbs, and sulk.

Three nothing. It's not impossible to turn this around, but it's unlikely.

Miles has his head in his hands, his hair stuck to his neck from sweat.

"It's not your fault," I say.

"I know."

I turn my head. "Do you though?"

"Logically, I know that. Colorado is all up in my crease, and you're all playing shit. I'm on my own out there. But I still let those three in."

"No, you're right about us playing like shit. We should have your back, but they're all over our asses."

"This isn't done yet," Coach says.

We're trying to keep our spirits up, but it's next to impossible.

"We got this," I say to Miles, even though I don't completely believe it. "I'll do everything I can to make sure they stay out of your crease."

"Good." He lowers his voice. "There's only one man I want in my crease."

I'd worry that one of the guys was listening, but they're not. We're all too depressed.

I nudge him with my shoulder and laugh.

Before we know it, the break is already over, and we have to head back out there.

The record is eight, I think to myself. We only need half that.

Easy.

Fucking easy.

And for the first few minutes, I believe we can do it. We take control of the puck. We own it and don't let Colorado get possession. But after getting shut down on every damn attempt on goal, we get frustrated again.

Frustrated hockey players are sloppy hockey players.

So when big brother Kiki strips me of the puck, I know it's all but over. No matter how hard I chase little Kiki and our defense try to trip him, he's too fast.

So fast he can't even control himself, and instead of stopping, he somehow trips himself and ends up slamming into Miles and taking out the whole goal.

Seeing Miles hit the ice makes me snap.

I catch up to them as they're getting back on their skates, but I don't stop. All I see is red. Frustration from the game fills me with adrenaline and rage. My promise to have Miles's back has been blown to hell.

I collide with Easton, and we hit the boards. The sound is so loud I'm surprised neither of us drop to the ice. Instead, I pin him.

"Come after my goalie again. I fucking dare you."

I'm suddenly hit from behind. Easton's big brother, Connor.

"You hit my fucking brother, you have to deal with me."

Hockey fights. Fun times.

I generally don't engage. But sometimes, a situation calls for it. Picking a fight with one of the biggest defensemen in the league? *Yeah, not smart, Bilson.*

But here we are.

Our gloves are gone, and I'm just trying to get in any punch I can while staying on my skates.

The fucker hits me so hard my helmet flies off my head, but I get a good punch in too. Or I think I do until he barely flinches and is on me again.

I swear the fight lasts an eternity, and I'm tempted to drop to the ice to end it, but I'm too proud for that.

I am thankful when Stoll pulls me back and Easton does the same for his brother.

I'm not so thankful when both Connor and I are thrown in the sin bin for major penalties, Easton for a minor, and then I have to watch from the sidelines as Easton is released and immediately goes out there and scores another fucking goal.

I never had beef with them before, but now I can officially say I hate the Kiki brothers.

CHAPTER TWENTY

MILES

The Kiki brothers are pains in my pads. The second-ever game I was called up for last year, I was overconfident from my amazing NHL debut.

Those assholes caught me unaware and handed me my ass. I'd never been so embarrassed walking off the ice.

This time though, I'm walking off the ice happy.

Which is ridiculous because I'm pissed at the loss, annoyed we couldn't put a single point on the board and Colorado got four of them past me. The difference between last year and tonight, though, is that I know the rest of my team sucked as much as I did.

We reach the locker room, where I dodge reporters to cool down and shower. I drag the process out, wanting to be ready right as we're grabbing our gear and heading out to the bus. Jorgensen tries to motivate us a couple of times, then stops trying, and the rest of the team are kinda *bleh*.

Especially Bilson.

That major penalty was … something.

Hot. It was hot, Miles.

I'd barely worked out what had happened when Bilson shot past and took Easton out. My heart had jumped into my damn throat for a second after that hit, and then the adrenaline, the pressure of the game, and Bilson's raw anger and strength were all too much for me to process.

It's no wonder I let Easton's easy goal past me. Being distracted on the ice is a no go, but being distracted by a misbehaving dick makes things impossible.

So yeah.

That last goal was all on me. The others were because my teammates had an off night. They've forgiven me plenty, so I'm happy to give them this one.

On the bus, I take my usual seat next to Bilson, but we don't talk. Something's up with him, but I'm scared that if I open my mouth, "I'm horny" will fall out, and my whole team doesn't need to know.

Just Bilson.

"Anyone heading out?" Stoll asks, almost like an after-thought.

A few guys murmur about an early night, and some others mention the hotel bar.

Bilson sighs. "I'm good for one or two."

My hand comes down on his thigh. "Dude, you got a major penalty tonight. Don't you think you should sleep it off?" My fingers dig into his muscle in warning.

"Ah, yeah. You're right. Penalty. Very bad."

Finch snickers. "You really are married. Listen to Rookie, the old ball and chain."

"If I'm anything as hot as your wife, Finch, I'll take that as a compliment."

"Fuck off, Rook."

I lean forward and thump him in the arm. "Don't call me Rook."

"What?"

"You heard me."

He turns around, confusion rightfully marring his face. "But you're our rookie."

"Call me rookie, then. Or Olsen. Or shithead, I don't care. Just don't call me Rook."

I'm sure half the bus has thought I've lost my mind, while the other half already assumed.

"Too easy, shithead."

"That's better."

Bilson is shaking with silent laughter beside me. "Weirdo."

I check the guys across from us aren't watching and blow him a kiss.

—

Another night, another stolen card, another bucket of ice. Only this time, we won't be drinking.

I let myself into Bilson's room and find him lying on his bed, arms tucked behind his head like he was waiting for me.

"I thought I was a naughty boy who had to go to his room?"

"I don't think I said those words." I kick the door closed behind me and approach the bed, where I set the bucket of ice on the nightstand and then disappear into the bathroom for a washcloth. When I get back, Bilson's kicked his legs over the side and is watching me.

He's got a split eyebrow that's already been cleaned up, but all under his eye, the skin is splotchy purple and swollen.

"How do you look hotter all busted up?" I ask, filling the washcloth with ice. "It should be a criminal offense."

His teasing smile finally makes an appearance. "Hot, huh?"

"I don't get it either. Somehow, dried blood in your eyebrow makes me want to jump your bones."

Bilson's sharp eyes watch me as I step closer, nudging his knees open with my own until there's enough space between his legs for me to stand. Then I tilt his head up with my free hand and press the ice to his face with the other.

"You got into a fight for me," I tease him.

Bilson huffs. "No one touches my goalie."

"Your goalie ... or me?"

His glare is adorable.

"I'll warn you that one of those options comes with a very sincere thank you that I think you'll like, so choose wisely."

Bilson's big hands land on my hips. "You gonna let me fuck you if I say that I saw red over him potentially hurting you by being careless?"

My bones melt. Now, that's what I call bromantic.

"Maybe," I hedge. While it sounds like a great idea, there's this need in my gut to make tonight about him. To maybe try ... something else.

"No one touches my Rook," he finally says.

I step closer. "Such a big, strong protector. Defending me like that out there."

His gravelly hum perks up my cock as his hands slip to rest on my ass. The last two times we've done this have been as hands-off as possible. No eye contact, no talking about anything other than the logistics. The awkwardness was thick pre- and post-sex, but this time, I'm not as nervous. I can't tell if he feels the same, but he doesn't look away when I pin him in my stare, faces only inches apart, and say, "You know ... one of my holes is getting jealous that the other gets all the action."

It takes him a second, but the moment he catches on, his eyes darken and drop to my lips. "Jealous?"

"Uh-huh. My mouth wants a go of your cock." It's not even about thanking him either, as much as I might play it off that way. Him fucking me is out of this world, but the thought of all that girth stretching out my lips, using my mouth, just for his pleasure ... *urgh*. My dick is so hard.

"You're so greedy for it. It turns me on like crazy."

I toss the makeshift cold pack aside, then drop to my knees, tugging down Bilson's fly. His dick presses forward like a fucking jack-in-the-box, trapped in his boxers, and seeing how hard he is goes straight to my head.

I've never touched his cock. He's never touched mine—other than with a fake pussy as a barrier. My heart is goddamn hammering, and my hands are clammy, but even with all the nerves, I'm excited.

My teasing is gone when I drag my gaze away and look up at him. "You want me to suck your cock, CB?"

A long "Yessss" hisses past his teeth.

Holy shit, it's happening.

I grab his boxers, and Bilson lifts his hips so I can drag those and his pants down his legs. Then I'm faced with the sight of thick, hairy thighs, heavy balls, and a long cock, reddened at the tip, vein standing out angrily on the underside.

Bilson must take my hesitation for doubt instead of sheer lust because he shifts. "You don't have to. If you've changed your mind."

Fuck that. I lean forward, confidently keeping eye contact, and suck his tip into my mouth.

How's that for doubt?

I'm not sure what I'm expecting, but Bilson's eyes flutter a second before mine do, and I might have been scared about starting and not liking it, but that worry is gone.

I reach down and press between my legs to get my dick to settle, then pull off him.

"I wanna warn you that this might just be the best head you've ever gotten, so try not to propose, okay?"

He barks a laugh and cards a hand through my hair, pushing my face down again. "Just suck it already."

"Ah, say more things like that." I spit into my hand and wrap it around him, then suck him back down again. I have no idea what I'm doing, but I know what feels good on me, so I try to go with that. Smooth strokes right down to his balls, tongue flicking against the tiny spot on the underside of his cock right before his tip flares out. The only problem is this is way harder than it looks.

Coordinating all that at once? No way. Deep-throating? Forget about it. My jaw is stretched wide and tongue working overtime, but whenever his tip nudges my throat, I gag.

It's starting to frustrate me. I want to make this good, damn it. Want to be the best.

"So good. Like that, Miles, so fucking good."

A thrill runs through me. I don't know if he could pick up on my annoyance and is reassuring me or if he really means it, but my body doesn't care. My cock is begging for more.

He increases the pressure on the back of my head as his hips give tiny thrusts. The grunts he's trying to hold back are delicious, and I'm so desperate to pull my cock out and jerk off, but I'm trying to hold off, trying to focus on him and making him come.

The way he's using my mouth, fucking my face, has my whole body on fire. It doesn't have any right to be

153

this hot, and the only thing that could make it better is hearing him talk dirty to me.

The noises he's making are incredible though. I'm not complaining. Especially not when he gets a little rougher, pulls my hair a little tighter. I keep jerking him, resigned that if I can't give the best blowjob, it will have to be the sloppiest.

"Yes ... So hot. You're such a—" He cuts off, and I hate it. I need him to keep talking. Need to hear those husky words, the ones he can barely control.

I moan around him, looking up to find him watching. Pupils blown wide, jaw tense, both terrifyingly turned on and so shiveringly sexy. I don't want to take him out of my mouth, don't want to stop sucking, so I try to tell him with my eyes. Keep going. Keep talking. Where the hell is that mind-reading power gone when I need it?

"You want me to say it, don't you?"

I can barely breathe, let alone manage a sound, but he gets it.

He gives my hair a sharp tug. "You're such a slut for my cock, aren't you?"

Fuck.

I scramble for my dick. All those thoughts about making him come first? Gone. I need to touch myself, and I need to do it now.

It's pure relief when I wrap my hand around myself and jack off. My hand is dry, and the precum helps, but there's no way in hell I'm freeing Bilson's cock to add some spit, so I deal.

His salty taste hits my tongue, making me groan and double down my efforts on him. I'm taking him deeper now, still not as deep as I want, but those tiny thrusts have gotten faster, harder, less controlled.

"Love seeing my cock in your mouth. You belong on your knees for me." He's panting. "Shit, Rook. I'm so close. So, so close. Gonna be a good little slut and take my cum?"

I fucking whimper. Tremble. Too turned on to think through the question or even care at this point. I can't fill my throat with his dick, so I'll do it with his cum instead. If the choice is between stopping or keeping him in my mouth for longer, I'll take whichever option lets me keep going.

Bilson lets out a loud curse, and before I'm ready, his cum hits the back of my throat. I hurry to try and swallow as much as I can, but he seems to be coming forever until he finally relaxes his hold, body going boneless.

I stand and spit a mixture of spit and cum into my hand, finally giving me the smooth glide I need. With one hand planted on his thigh, I beat myself off hard and fast, gaze pinging between his softening cock and those deep abs. His round pecs, the light chest hair. My jaw aches, a pleasant reminder of what happened, and I'm tipping so close to the edge I know this is going to be a good one.

I'm close.

So close.

My hold on him tightens.

"Come on me."

The request is so sudden and unexpected it sets me off. Ropes of cum paint him from his chest to his cock, and I ride my way through my orgasm, mesmerized by the sight.

It takes way too long for me to come down from it, and I slump forward, completely boneless, trying to catch myself. As the high ebbs and I check back in, I realize

I'm lying on him. Legs twisted, skin against skin, dicks practically kissing.

I quickly roll off onto the bed.

Bilson's head drops my way as he takes a second to check me out. "You look fucking wrecked."

Then he breaks down into laughter, and I follow him. Tension officially broken.

CHAPTER TWENTY-ONE

BILSON

Something's ... happening. I can't pinpoint what it is, but I think it starts with D. And it's not my dick. Or Miles's. Or maybe it is.

But my gut is telling me I'm in serious *denial*. I think Miles has been there a lot longer than me, but that's not my place to point out to him that he might be less straight than he thought he was.

Sure, he's all sex is sex, and he can detach sex from emotions unlike I can, and I'm under no delusion that he feels more for me than our bromance or whatever, but ... I think we both have to face facts that what we're doing isn't detaching.

After Miles gave me one of the best blowjobs of my life and we recovered, he got up and left, going back to his own hotel room, and that's when it all clicked for me.

Sure, it's taken a whole night of tossing and turning, my brain searching for that answer. The label that makes sense. All the while, my denial keeps trying to push it away, but now, in the bright light of morning, it's clear.

I'm not straight.

Either that, or I'm so desperate to be loved that my clinginess has no gender preference. Hoo boy, my therapist will probably want to analyze that for multiple sessions.

Because while I can acknowledge that I'm sexually attracted to females and now males, there's one big difference when it comes to Miles.

When I look at him, I don't have grand ideas of marriage, babies, and that happily ever after I've been chasing in all the wrong places. I'm not getting ahead of myself.

Is it because I really do only see him as a friend, even though I want to fuck all of his holes any which way he'll let me? Or is it because I'm sexually attracted to him but romantically not? Is it because I know that he would never want to disappoint his parents by acknowledging he's bi or pan or however he wants to identify, so I know there is no future?

With all my past wives, girlfriends, anyone I've had remote interest in, my imagination has always gotten away from me. I think they're the one, so I lean into it, make mistakes, and then realize I'm stuck in a sucky situation where I chose the wrong person.

I don't have that with Miles because he's not available to choose.

Ugh, this is messing with my head, but I can't say it's in a bad way. It's frustrating that I can't put my feelings into something coherent or find a label that makes me go yes! That's me! But at the same time, admitting to myself that sleeping with my teammate repeatedly isn't straight behavior, a weight has lifted.

I don't have the need to come out or even tell anyone. Not even Aleks or any of the other Collective guys who adopted me as an honorary member. Ooh, I could join for real now if I wanted to. But just letting it out internally makes me feel better about what we're doing.

Like it wouldn't be a big deal if it did get out. For me, anyway.

I know for Miles, it's different.

I saw how disappointed he was in his parents. The way they interacted around asking them to babysit Killer while we're away, it was obvious that they're extremely close. And maybe that's why he's never been with another guy before me. Maybe growing up in the type of household where he's taught it's wrong has repressed all his attraction to men.

Either way, I could overanalyze both of us for an eternity, but I have to get up and pack to get back out on the road. Next stop is Dallas.

There's a knock at my door, and I know it's Miles. Even his knock has that weird, upbeat energy he has about him.

Though it is weird, he's not using his key.

I open up and cock my head. "Lost the key?"

He steps inside with two coffees and hands one over to me. "Left it in here last night."

"Rookie move. How can you stalk me if you forget important things like that?"

"Eh, you let me in anyway. I think you like it when I stalk you."

"What can I say? You're like Killer. I can't say no to the big puppy eyes." I pinch his cheek, and he swats my hand away.

"Are you not even packed yet? Ooh, Barry is going to hate you."

"Nah. Everyone loves me. Even equipment managers. I have charm."

He looks me over. "Unfortunately, I can't refute that. You have four ex-victims—I mean wives—to prove it."

For some reason, acknowledging that I'm … queer? Not straight? Bi? Doesn't matter what I am. By acknowledging that I don't have to pretend that Miles is a woman or that we're not fucking, I have a newfound confidence.

I put my finger through the belt loop in his pants and pull him toward me. His big body presses against mine, and he grunts.

We're still holding our coffees, and I wish I'd made us put them down before I did this.

"Are you saying my charm doesn't affect you?" I rumble.

My gaze is locked on his lips. The whole time we've been fooling around, we've never once kissed.

I want to see if the stubble I felt around my cock last night feels the same on my mouth.

Miles swallows hard but steps back and takes a sip of his coffee. I can't say I'm not disappointed, but I get it.

His lips quirk. "My ass and mouth might have fallen for your charm, but my brain hasn't caught up."

Fair enough. And maybe I am wrong about him. Maybe he's still able to keep what we're doing in bed separate from everything else. I have to respect that and let him come to the same conclusion I have in his own time.

So, I go the only route I can. Snark. "It figures your body is smarter than your brain."

He mock gasps. "Just for that, I'm not going to help you pack." He throws himself in the chair next to the really small table and sips his coffee again.

"Like you were going to in the first place."

He smiles behind his cup. "True, but now I can pretend I was going to."

And this is probably my favorite thing about Miles Olsen. We can have these intense moments, these split seconds in time where we have something real, that threatens the very friendship these moments are built on, but in the next second, he shakes away the awkwardness, says something stupid and/or insulting, and everything goes back to the way it was beforehand.

I no longer fear ruining our friendship with physical stuff because I'm confident that Miles has my back.

Just like I have his.

–

Dallas is a fight where we scrape in a win 5-4. It was a great game because it was high scoring for both sides, so the crowd loved it. You know, until Finch put one in the net with only seconds left on the clock, taking the win away from the home team.

The sex Miles and I had after that high was amazing. Still impersonal but mind-blowing. Apparently, we've let go of all pretenses that we're only doing it when we're desperately horny and have no other options. Now we do it when we're celebrating. Or commiserating, it seems. Because after that, we flew to LA, lost spectacularly, had more amazing sex, and now tonight, we're playing against Anaheim.

It's our first back-to-back of the season, and we're still tired from last night's loss, but after tonight, we get to go home in the morning, and I can't wait to see my Killer.

But first, I have to decide if I'm going to meet Oskar Voyjik after the game or not. The guys in the Collective have been welcoming of me—think it's funny I wanted to join them so I could stay away from women—but now that I'm learning these new things about myself, I'm not so sure I'll be able to keep my mouth shut. Not around someone who would understand and maybe offer an ear.

At least I'm not close with Oskar, and the whole Collective rules bullshit doesn't actually apply to me, so I do have the choice on whether or not to ask him if we can catch up.

I could ask Miles if he wanted to go with me, but even I know that's unlikely.

I push it to the back of my mind and try to focus on hockey.

Anaheim is having a similar season to us. We have really high highs but really embarrassing lows, so tonight's game will be interesting.

Every time we hit the ice, we're told to visualize the win and ignore all the things going against us. Like that we're the visiting team, and statistically, away games are lost more than they are won. Or that we played a brutal game last night against LA, so we're coming off a loss and the exhaustion from a game.

Hockey is terrorizing on our bodies. Some players have been known to drop eight pounds per game because of the way we push ourselves out there—goalies even more than that.

I fucking love it, but at the same time, it can become too much sometimes.

Sometimes, you go into a game expecting the loss.

And tonight is one of those nights for me.

The game starts off rocky. We're all moving slow, we're missing simple passes, and Anaheim is refreshed and looking like spring chickens out there.

Oskar is a great defenseman, but his hits are terrifying.

He seems to know when is the perfect time to bodycheck me into the boards, right before I'm about to pass so he can get away with it legally.

He's frustratingly talented.

In between plays, he skates up to me. "You coming for a drink after this?"

I glance at Miles. "Maybe. I'll see what the rest of my team is doing."

"Ooh, are you no longer avoiding women? Are you getting married again? Who is she this time?"

I'd shove him if the refs wouldn't think I'm trying to fight him.

I don't answer him, and the face-off is about to happen, so we get into position.

But it's almost as if I can feel Oskar's stare on me for the rest of the game, and not just in a hockey way. In a "you have a secret, and I want to find it out" way.

Or now that I've accepted my sexuality, I get all the fun side effects. Like paranoia of being found out. Of someone knowing.

I'm completely useless on the ice because I'm distracted, but the good thing is, I'm not the only one who's sluggish.

As suspected at the beginning of the game, we walk away with the loss.

I would care if I didn't have bigger things on my mind. Like whether or not I invite Miles to drinks with Oskar.

CHAPTER TWENTY-TWO

MILES

Bilson snaps his towel on my ass as he walks past me.

"Didn't hurt," I say, even as the fucker stings like a bitch.

He lowers his voice over the echoey noise of our team-mates' conversations. "Forgot your ass knows how to take a beating."

"I'll have to work harder next time. Can't have you forgetting a thing like that."

He disappears into the shower, and my smile drops off my face as I head for my cubby to get changed into my suit. Talking about things here is risky, but I've noticed Bilson hasn't been spy-level stealthy lately. Something's changed with him, and while I love seeing him more relaxed and confident, I also haven't asked him about it. The pit in my gut every time I think about it tells me I won't like the answers.

Even with the warning sirens going off in the back of my brain, I still slump on the bench and lean back to wait for him. My eyes fall closed, blocking out the chaos around me, which isn't the greatest idea because then I'm alone with my thoughts, and there isn't a single one I want to listen to.

Our loss was frustrating. Back-to-back fails like that hit me hardest because one game I can shake off; two in a row plain pisses me off. Anaheim were on their game tonight, but that doesn't excuse me from not following through on the job I have to do. Some days make me question if I even want this, if I'm committed to the NHL when Nashville is the only team for me, and this season, while not terrible, definitely isn't making me a goalie in demand.

Fingers roughly scruff through my damp hair, and my eyes flick open to find Bilson standing over me in a towel. His eyes are bright, and he looks good, considering we just got beat.

He moves to his own cubby, but a flash of him stepping close, leaning in, lips hovering enticingly close to mine, floods my brain, and I quickly look away to where Finch is tugging his pants up his thighs.

They're good thighs. Thick. Topped by a hockey butt. Finch also isn't totally annoying, but when I look at him and try to imagine letting him fuck me, I shudder.

Maybe I'm going off dick?

But like Bilson can hear my thoughts, he drops his towel as he grabs his boxers, and my face goes so rapidly hot I swear I'm about to pass out. So, still interested, apparently.

I didn't realize the body attached to my walking strap-on made that much of a difference. But being friends first makes sense, I guess. Trust and whatever. I'm friends with Finch, but I don't exactly want to hang out with him all the time or show up at his house at midnight just because I can't sleep.

That's the kind of shit besties do.

And fuck, apparently.

It's a good thing neither of us is gay and it means nothing. No chance of Bilson falling for me or me getting too attached.

Something uncomfortable prods at my mind, but I go on ignoring that too.

"Ready to go?" I ask once Bilson is dressed.

Even though I kept my eyes firmly forward from the second he got naked, being this close to him has me horny and ready to climb into his bed.

"Ah, actually ..."

My head snaps his way, but Bilson isn't looking at me. He *is* looking awkward though, and I'm immediately panicked by what that could mean. Is he tired of me already?

"You're heading out?" I ask, forcing my voice to stay level. Then, before I can stop myself, I add, "Cool. I'll come too."

He shifts. "You might not want to be offering that."

"Why?" I pretend like the idea is only just now dawning on me and didn't the second he started acting weird. "Oh. Because you wanna hook up? That's cool. I'll come and kick the future potential Mrs. Bilson the fifth out. It's not like that wasn't our plan all along. Bros helping bros. Too much of a good thing can get boring, after all. Variety is important."

Acid burns in my stomach. Not over him hooking up, obviously, but because if I'm left babysitting his dumb ass, it means I won't be able to hook up as well. I'm not stupid enough to fall back on that threesome idea because I have no doubt if we tried it again, Lucia wouldn't be as forgiving. Bromance or no bromance.

And maybe I wouldn't like seeing someone else get to use my sex toy.

You're not supposed to share those things, after all.

Bilson drops onto the bench next to me. "No future Bilsons. Just Oskar Voyjik."

The acid in my gut increases for a split second before I stop being a fucking idiot. "Ahhh, your queer bros group meetup?"

"Exactly."

"And I can't come because I'm not a member."

He doesn't answer at first, and when I glance over, he's rubbing his thick stubble. "It's not ... that. I want you to come, but I didn't think you ..." His dark eyes skim the room, taking in how full it is, and doesn't say any more.

He doesn't need to, though, because our mind-reading powers are still going strong.

He didn't think I'd want to come and have people speculate about me.

Knowing he even considered that reminds me of why we have this bromance. The media can play it up all they like; they'll never know what it's really like to be friends with someone like Cody Bilson. They can have our pregame rituals. I'll keep this.

"Why can't they have two honorary members?" I ask.

"I'm not going to stop you coming, but you don't have to put yourself in that position."

As much as I want to say screw it and go anyway, he's telling me to think it through. To try to imagine what it will be like if rumors get back to my parents. The Collective meetups are well-known across the teams and even with NHL fans, but outside of that? Does anyone actually care about what they do and, by extension, me?

Nothing came of Bilson and me catching up with Aleks that one time ... but they are ex-teammates, so that's probably different. Plus, the dog-napping might have overshadowed any speculation.

I don't think going out for a couple of drinks is going to draw that sort of attention.

"Answer me something really quick: would you prefer to have solo time with your friend? I don't want to smother you or whatever, so if you don't want me to come, that's cool. Just say so." I mean it this time too. If he's not planning to sleep with someone else, he can do what he likes.

Bilson's crooked smile crosses his face, but he's quiet when he says, "Rook, making you come is top of my priorities tonight."

My dick likes the sound of that.

Bilson laughs at me, but what-the-fuck-ever. It's no secret by this point how much fun we have, so why would I play games by trying to brush it off?

"Can't wait to spend the night having Voyjik rub his win in our faces."

"Oh, good. You know what he's like already. I was preparing to give you the heads-up."

"I think everyone in the league knows about Oskar Voyjik's big mouth."

We pack up our stuff and grab our gear bags, preparing to head out to the team bus, but the second we step out of the locker room, there's Voyjik.

He's across the hall, leaning against the wall with his arms crossed. His dark blond hair is still wet from the shower, and he's wearing reflector sunglasses and a shit-eating grin.

"Good game tonight," he calls after Stoll, who flips him off.

Oskar starts a slow clap. "Wow. That really got one over on me. Pity you waited until *after* we left the ice."

Bilson walks right up to him, shaking his head. "I am surprised daily that you don't receive multiple punches to the face."

"Even if I did, I'd *still* be prettier than you."

I don't know about prettier. Voyjik took a skate to the face two seasons ago, and while the scar that runs from his cheek to his eye has healed really well, the skin around it is pinched and uneven in places.

I'm ninety percent sure he would have been offered plastic surgery to help fix it—he's known as one of the hottest men in the league—which means the scar stayed because he wanted it to stay.

Not that I can blame him. It gives him an edge.

"At least CB isn't wearing sunglasses inside," I point out. "Do you actively try to be as douchebaggy as possible?"

"Standing up for your man? How bromantic of you."

Discomfort shifts through me, but Bilson brushes it off. "If your personality was as pretty as your face, maybe you could have friends too."

"Personality?" Oskar repeats like the word tastes bad. "Who would bother with one of those?"

"Yeah, I'm going to need a drink to deal with you," Bilson says.

"You know, I get that a lot."

Bilson throws me a quick look. "You don't care if Rook tags along, do you?"

"It's not an official QC thing, so who the hell cares? I mostly wanted to catch up to gloat. It's not as fun talking about how awesome I am with my team. All I get is 'blah blah teamwork' before they tune me out."

As much as Voyjik might have dominated on the ice tonight, I think I actually like him. Dammit.

While he and Bilson shoot the shit, I use the moment to take him in. He's one of the few proudly out players, and unlike most of them who keep that side of themselves private, I don't think anyone missed Voyjik's infamous CCTV threesome. Now that he's settled down with his boyfriend, he still has no issues with public displays of affection. I swear he makes sure his boyfriend is at every event possible, and I distinctly remember them at last year's award show, where neither of them could keep their hands to themselves.

Oskar Voyjik and I live very different lives.

Even if Bilson and I weren't fucking around and I had a girlfriend, I'd keep things on the down-low because the last thing I want is indecent photos of me out there for my parents to see.

"Coming, Rook?" Voyjik asks, and Bilson backhands his chest.

"Don't steal my nickname."

"Oohhh, coming between the bromance?" Oskar laughs. "Tonight is going to be fun."

CHAPTER TWENTY-THREE

BILSON

"You're killing it this season," Oskar says to Miles. "Those three back-to-back shutouts made us crap bricks to go up against you."

Miles shrugs, his eyes sad. "Turns out you didn't need to worry. I haven't exactly been living up to my potential lately."

"Nah, fuck that," Oskar says. "That's the game. You win some, you lose some. You can't let that get in your head, or you'll find yourself in a slump. But for your first season as a starting goalie, you really are killing it. Take the compliment. I don't give them often."

"It's true. He doesn't. Unless it's to himself."

Miles still looks uncertain, but he nods. "Thanks."

"Get a few seasons under your belt, and we might need to poach you to the West Coast."

I point the lip of my beer bottle toward Miles. "No."

"You know Nashville has my heart," Miles says.

I turn to Oskar. "Get this. Miles actually likes his parents."

"Hey, I like my parents too …" Oskar hesitates. "Mainly because they live overseas."

I laugh. "Seeing my parents once every summer is my limit. And luckily, they're generally too busy to see me, so I don't always get that."

Oskar whistles. "And people say I have daddy abandonment issues. The three divorces make sense now."

Miles corrects him before I can. "It's four, actually."

"You got married *again*? What is wrong with you?" Oskar yells, catching the attention of everyone at the bar.

"Shhh. You know Hadley."

Oskar's brow furrows. "Oh, right. Wait, I thought she was number three?"

"You're probably forgetting Brea. She lasted a whopping forty-two days."

"How have you not given up yet?"

"Oh, I have." My gaze flicks to Miles, who immediately averts his eyes and sips his drink.

"It also explains your shitty wrist shots tonight. Carpal tunnel?"

I have to admit it's kind of thrilling having this secret, but at the same time, I want to embrace my new identity, which still doesn't have a label. But that doesn't matter to me. Not being confused is freeing in itself.

Oskar narrows his eyes. "Wait ..."

Miles jumps up. "I'm going to go get another round for us all." He couldn't move faster if he tried.

As much as I want to be able to tell Oskar I've started batting for his team, I don't want to put Miles in any situation where he's uncomfortable. Sure, I could tell him only about me, but that will come with follow-up questions like who I'm hooking up with. Knowing Oskar, it would also include questions like how many times we've done it, what positions, and if I've become acquainted with my prostate yet. Which I haven't. I'm not sure if I want to. Thought about it? A little. Mainly when Miles is begging for me to fuck him harder and hit that spot inside him. But with prep, cleanup, and the not-so-great things about anal, I generally stop myself from thinking about it too deeply. The only deep thoughts I've had are about being balls-deep inside of Miles.

"That was weird," Oskar says, staring after Miles.

Maybe it was a mistake bringing him here. He's obviously dealing with his own confusion over what's happening between us, but it's harder for him. He has people to disappoint. I'm used to disappointing people.

Oskar's still staring after Miles.

"He's a goalie. It would be weird if he wasn't weird."

"Fair point."

—

We only stay for one more drink before I can tell Miles is getting antsy, so I make an excuse for us to leave. Need to rest up and whatever. Which is a lie because we're finally on our way home tomorrow for three days off from games. But we are exhausted. This road trip has sucked all around. You know, other than the times where Miles was … sucking. That has been a fun time.

We head straight to my room, and I'm choosing to believe he's in a rush to get inside because he's desperate for me to get inside him, but there's a niggling feeling at the back of my mind telling me it's more of his weird mood he's been in.

Or I could be reading into things.

I'm probably reading into things.

It's possible that because there's no chance of a future here, I'm focusing on imaginary issues I can be neurotic about.

Seriously, what is wrong with my brain?

The answer to that question doesn't matter when we're behind closed doors and Miles pins me up against the wall.

His hands go for my pants, popping the top button and unzipping my fly. I reach for his to do the same, but he swats my hand away.

"So you can undress me, but I can't undress you?" I laugh because I don't really mean it, and I think it comes out lightly, but maybe I'm wrong because he pulls back. Looks at me. Frowns.

"I ..." His voice cracks. "I know I usually like when you take control of me, and you are so good at it." He closes the gap between us. "But tonight, I need ... I need ..."

Instinctually, I cup his face. "What do you need?"

His gaze drops to my lips, and I want him to take what he wants. I want it too. But he needs to take this step.

"I'll give you anything."

"Your mouth," he begs. "I need your mouth."

I don't know who moves first. Maybe we both surge forward until our mouths meet. Either way, the second our lips touch, I regret not having done this before.

When he parts his lips and licks inside my mouth, his stubble scraping against mine, it's more intimate and turns me on like fucking crazy.

I grip him close and then turn us so we can switch positions, and I have him pinned against the door, but we continue to kiss, drinking each other in.

As much as I want inside him or for him to blow me again, I actually want to take a step back from that and explore his mouth. Explore his body.

I want to touch him. Touch his cock. I haven't been game enough until now. I guess that part of me that was still in denial—thinking that letting a man blow me or using a man's ass without touching his cock is just sex and doesn't count—is all in now.

But what to do first? There's so much I want to explore. So many things I could do. If only I could pluck up the courage to make the first move.

With shaking hands, I hook my thumbs in the sides of his already undone pants and drag them down his legs. He lets me undress him this time, but I think it's because he's too entranced with our tongues intertwined to even notice I'm getting him naked.

I pull back to take his shirt off next, and he's so compliant it's as if he's already forgotten he wanted to be in control of this. He said he needed more, and the second I gave it to him, he melted back into who he truly is. Someone who loves giving up control.

It makes sense. On the ice, he has to be on all the time. He can't take his eyes off that puck. Unlike the rest of us who take shifts, he's out there for the whole game. In control. Switched on.

Miles tries to pull me back to him, but I pause before we go back to kissing, and I lose my train of thought in his mouth.

My voice is raspy, my lips dry. I want to take the plunge and sink to my knees, but the reality is I have no idea what I'm doing. "You said you wanted my mouth? What if I gave it to you ... here." I swallow my nerves and wrap my hand around his cock. The sensation is kind of weird because I've touched my own dick a million times. Touching someone else's ... it's almost like I'm expecting to be able to feel it but can't. It's different than when I used that sex toy on him. It's flesh on flesh. Warm skin against my palm.

It's like stepping on a broken escalator, expecting it to move and then getting disoriented when it doesn't.

I can't say it's a bad thing. Just disorientating.

Miles sucks in a sharp breath. "Please, yes. Fuck."

I lick my lips, trying to prepare for what happens next. I'm not scared of having another man's cock in my mouth, but I am worried I'll be bad at blowjobs. I want to make Miles feel good.

Whether it's that his lips are now too irresistible or I'm stalling for time—it could be either—I lean in for one more kiss before I drop to my knees.

Not wanting to jump right in, when I sink down, I kiss my way down his chest, his abs, his amazingly cut V.

"Why are you teasing me?" he whines.

I can't tell him it's because I'm trying to build up the courage to put my mouth on him because I don't want him to think he's pressuring me into this.

I'm excited for it. It's just the pressure … so much pressure.

To find the courage, I channel the energy I have on the ice when we're one goal down and only have a minute left on the clock. The "let's get this done" attitude.

Right before I lower my head, I glance up at him.

Miles's lips are parted, his eyes hooded, and I'm reminded of why we're doing this. That look on his face, the awe and need in his eyes … I want him to come alive.

I don't take my eyes off him as I lick over his tip. His lip trembles, and he has to bite it to make it stop. It spurs me on.

My tongue swirls around his head, and then I lick my way down his shaft.

His breath is shaky, and I've decided I love sucking cock, even though, technically, I haven't even sucked on it yet. But that's about to change.

I close my mouth over him and work my way down his hard length, going slow so I can work out where my limit is. On my way back up, I suck hard, and Miles's hand flies into my hair and pulls me off.

"Shit, did I do something wrong?"

He pulls me up to my feet. "Not at all. But nope, nope, nope, I've decided we're not going to do that."

"Why?" My lips quirk.

"Because I'm going to come way too quickly that way."

"What do you want instead?"

"Your hand," he breathes. "I want you to touch me."

I step back. "Only if you touch me too."

We shed the rest of my clothes and then come back together, hard cock against hard cock.

He reaches for me first, his long fingers wrapping around me. I shudder in his arms and slump forward, my forehead on his, and allow myself a few seconds of pure bliss. Then I take a grip of his cock too.

We start slow, getting a feel for each other, stroking in tandem.

Our breaths are heavy. My eyes threaten to close, but I don't let them because the blissed-out expression on Miles's face is too good to look away from.

The smallest moan falls from his lips, and I surge forward to swallow it down.

Kissing him isn't like kissing anyone else. I can't pinpoint why, but I like the way he explores my mouth. Savors me.

Miles begins stroking harder. Faster. I match his pace, and my hips get in on the action too. Our mouths wrench apart.

We're both so close. I can tell by the way he's panting that he's teetering on the edge as much as I am.

When I start to spill over, Miles tenses and grunts his release. I don't slow my strokes, coaxing him through his orgasm and prolonging my own. The mess between us is warm and wet, but I don't care about the cleanup.

We try to catch our breaths, foreheads resting against each other while we come down from our highs.

After my brain stops melting, I let out a laugh. "That was a fun new game."

CHAPTER TWENTY-FOUR

MILES

I wave after Bilson's car as he leaves my place, taking Killer with him.

"You know," Mom says, leaning closer, "I caught your dad looking up Chinese Cresteds last night."

"Don't tell me he wants to buy one."

"No." Her voice is resigned. "To make sure he was brushing the ears right."

"Is there a way you can brush them wrong?"

"Beats me. How was your trip?"

"It hurts you didn't watch me on TV and know that it was shit."

"I saw, but I mean outside of hockey."

That's the last thing I want to be talking about, especially with her. As much as I want to fight it, there's a rift building between us that she doesn't even know exists.

Because I can't ignore those feelings trying to get my attention anymore. The way I ached to kiss Bilson was the strongest emotion I've ever had.

I turn away from her. "I don't exactly get a lot of downtime, Mom." And that's all she'll get from me.

I head back toward my place, needing silence and hating it at the same time. It should have been easy to bullshit Mom about how great the team is and blah, blah,

blah, but all I can think about is Bilson. I haven't been able to stop since I left his room last night, only this time, I went wishing I could stay.

I'm no idiot—well, I *am* an idiot, a playful, ridiculous, goofy one—but I'm not stupid. This thing has been building in me for a while, and maybe if I'd acknowledged the hold he had on me from the start, I could have stopped things from progressing.

Is it possible there was a small part of me that didn't want to?

This obsessive need to always be around him sucks, but I like how close we are. I like the butterflies that took over when we kissed. That *kiss*. His hard, scratchy mouth and strong tongue. The way he gained control again as soon as I braved up and told him what I wanted.

We're a complete match in the bedroom. I crave sex with him like I've never craved anything. If only that's all it was.

Three days off. Three days that I should be using to get my thoughts straightened out, but I already miss the fucker. My plan to give us both a bit of breathing room isn't going to be easy.

I need someone to talk to about it. To get some outside perspective. My parents are solidly out, and my siblings aren't much better. There's no way I'm talking to my team, and I clearly can't go to Bilson about all of this. My frat buddies group chat would be a good option, but this feels personal, and a chat with that many people in it is as impersonal as it gets.

There is one brother I can call though. He knows what it's like to fall for one of his closest friends. For his teammate. His frat brother. And Robbie's a listener. That's not to say he hasn't got a big mouth because he does, but he's good at reading people, and whenever we talk, I know he cares.

I unlock my place and stumble inside, falling face down on my bed with a groan. The problem with talking is that I need to get the words out.

I'm still not so sure I can. Or that I even know what I want.

Instead of channeling whatever this anxious mess is, I put all my energy into trying to be as confident as Robdog. I mean, damn, as soon as the guy got curious, he went around the house asking if he could touch our dicks.

Good on him for asking first, but he really doesn't care what people think about him.

Besides, worst case, I can just call and catch up. We don't need to have the most terrifying conversation of my life.

The phone connects, and I'm scared he won't pick up, but only a few seconds later, a deep "Miles fucking Olsen, our newest Sigma superstar" comes down the line.

I switch the phone to speaker before dropping it on the bed. "Hey, Robdoggie."

"What are you up to? How's the NHL treating you, brother?"

We spend a few minutes talking hockey and my season, which helps to settle the nerves in my gut.

"We catch every game," Robbie says. "Brando and I have your schedule printed out and stuck on the fridge. He tried to do a shared calendar in our phones, but fuck, they're annoying. We're so proud of you. The NHL, dude, it's your dream. That and doing it from Nashville."

The bittersweet memory of being in the house, of talking to my brothers about being homesick, right on the verge of dropping out and moving back to Nashville ... but they wouldn't let me. They kept boosting me up and supporting me through it.

"What was it like when you hooked up with Brandon?" I ask so fast I don't have time to rethink.

I've clearly caught him off guard. "Horrible."

That's not the answer I'm expecting. "*What?*"

"Yeah. I proposed last night and everything. The asshole had the audacity to say yes."

"Holy shit." Happiness explodes in my chest for them. "Congratulations. How isn't this all through the group chat?"

"Dooms and Zeke are coming up for Brosgiving. We want to tell them in person, so keep it to yourself."

"Of course, man, I'm so happy for you."

Then he says the last thing I'm expecting. "And when you and this teammate you're fucking get engaged, I'll be happy for you too."

"I never said I want to marry the guy."

He chuckles, and I realize my mistake. "But there is a teammate?"

"Ah ... I mean. I—I don't ..."

"I love you, Miles." The sincerity in his tone helps me breathe again. "You don't have to talk about anything, and if this guy is closeted, I definitely don't want his name. How are you feeling about it all?"

I huff. "We're doing bromotions?"

"Nah, this is real talk. Just because I embraced dick like it was my day job doesn't mean it's the same for everyone. Want to talk about it?"

"I think that's why I called."

"You mean you didn't want to talk about how awesome my life is? That doesn't sound right."

The good thing about Robbie is he can always make the worrying not sound so bad. "We can come back to that."

"So how long have you known you were queer? Or is this a first time for you?"

"It's a first, and I … I'm struggling with the whole label thing."

"Why?"

The answer to that is one of the things I'm struggling with. "I'm not really sure. The things I'm doing are very, very not straight, and I love it, but letting go of that label is hard. And I have no clue why because it's just a word."

"We all grow up differently. Being straight was something you connected with. Being bi is something Brando and I bonded over. Have you talked to this guy about it?"

"Nope. We got into this with very clear rules that there would be no feelings involved. We're super close; I can talk to him about anything … except this."

"Worried about where it will leave you both?"

"Yep."

Robbie hums. "It's hard without the full details, but is it possible he could be going through the same thing?"

The memory of our kiss burns in my mind. "It's possible. But I'm chickenshit because I don't know what I want to get out of it. If he doesn't feel the same, all this ends, and that'd kill me. If he does, that might be worse because I'm not in a position to offer him anything."

"Bro, there are *so* many different types of relationships. You're getting ahead of yourself. Maybe all he wants is to keep going the way you're going. Maybe he's feeling the same as you and wants to keep it on the down-low. Maybe he likes you enough to be a secret, and maybe he doesn't."

I don't have an answer for that.

Robbie keeps talking. "I'm just saying the poor guy deserves to know if the deal has changed. He consented to no-strings fucking from what it sounds like, so if that's changed, you have to say something."

I hate that someone who once tried to drunkenly swan dive off our staircase is making this much sense.

"One question, and I want you to answer quickly. Take out all the other nonsense. When you think about him, and sex, and being together, how does it make you feel?"

And I'm glad he said to answer quickly, before all the other stuff could hit my mind, because I settle into the emotion that immediately hits. "Good. He makes me feel happy."

"And that's probably the most you that you've sounded all call."

"Fuck."

"Yep."

"If he was a woman, this would be so much simpler."

Robbie laughs. "Yeah, but he wouldn't be the person you're falling for, dumbass. Do you *want* him to be a woman?"

It's terrifying how easily and truthfully I can answer that. "No. I actually really don't."

"Cool." A comfortable silence falls. "It would have been so much easier to go through all this in a house of queer dudes. Trust you to be a late bloomer. You're telling me that none of us did it for you? Not even Rooster?"

"Rooster?" He couldn't have picked a worse example. "He's way too sweet."

"Ah, Miles likes a bit of an asshole, huh? A bad boy? Brando has a bad-boy kink too, obviously—that's why he's with me."

Brandon shouts something in the background that I miss.

But I can guess. Robbie is the furthest thing from a bad boy. More like a golden retriever who's always knocking into things at full speed and leaving a trail of destruction behind him.

"No bad boys for me either," I say. "Clearly, the only reason I wasn't interested in you."

"It's okay. We all have our faults. You gonna be good now?"

"I think so. Still have no clue how I'll handle this conversation, but you're right. We can't hook up again until it happens. I don't want him to think I've betrayed him or whatever."

"Unless he's an unreasonable dickweed, there's no way he'll think that."

Bilson is definitely not a dickweed, so that gives me some hope. Even if he's not interested in me as anything more than a hole to stick it in, I don't see him being an asshole about this.

Somehow, that only makes it worse.

"How do I do this?" I ask myself more than Robbie.

"Easy," Robbie says. "You face it head-on like a Sigma. And know you have all your brothers behind you."

CHAPTER TWENTY-FIVE

BILSON

It's a rare three days off where we don't have a game, practice, or any charity events to show up to—we only have to get our weights and cardio in to keep our bodies warm for our next game day—and I figured it would be the perfect opportunity to come as many times as possible.

But Miles has gone radio silent, isn't replying to my texts, and I'd like to think it's because he's spending time with his folks, but I'm not one hundred percent on that.

I think he's avoiding me, and I can't help wondering if it's because we kissed.

While I loved it and regretted not doing it sooner, I get the impression it was too far for him. Maybe it's made his denial harder to ignore, and if that's the case, I should give him space.

A revelation hits me. I want to see Miles, but I can acknowledge his feelings and need for space. Is this ... what growth feels like? Am I all cured of my neglect issues? Are dicks so magical they can fix all my emotional baggage?

As clear as day, my therapist's voice enters my head and says, "And you think Miles is the one in denial?"

Ugh. Okay, so fine. I still have those issues and probably always will, but this is at least what I'd like to call a breakthrough.

But it also means that I can't do what I want, which is get in my car, drive over to his place, and kidnap him.

It's only now that I'm realizing I don't have any other friends in Nashville. The team is great, and I've felt welcomed, and we gel on a professional level, but neither Miles nor I have made an effort to be real friends with any of them. Maybe it's time that changed. Dennan and Aleks back in Seattle became more than teammates. They were my friends—my Seattle family, if you will—and I haven't even tried to have that here because I've been too distracted by Miles's ass. Or his mouth. His hands ...

And there I go again, tempting myself to get in the car and drive over to see him.

Nope, nope, nope.

So I take out my phone and scroll through my contacts and click on the first teammate's name I see: Adin Finch.

Me:
Is the team doing anything tonight? I'm BORED.

Finch:
Shouldn't you be relaxing and doing nothing because you don't have kids to chase around? Please give me your life! I would kill to be bored.

Me:
Just clarifying here, you're not threatening to kill your children, are you?

Finch:

Okay, no. They're exhausting, but I love those little monsters. You should see what Stoll or Jorgensen is up to.

Me:

You could always come out with us so you get a break from the kids?

Finch:

And have my wife fry my balls so I stop creating spawns of Satan? We have a deal. Anytime I get more than one day off during the season, I'm on diaper duty.

Me:

Again, clarifying … your kid's diapers, right?

Finch:

… What is wrong with you?

Me:

I told you. I'm BORED. Don't blame me for my brain thinking inappropriate things when I don't have anything to occupy it.

> **Finch:**
> I'm starting to see why you and Miles get along so well. Ask him to go out with you.

Ergh. Hitting me where it hurts.

> **Me:**
> I think he's having family time too. Though, I really hope his parents don't change his diapers. Do you know anyone who's a full grown-up who is close with their parents? Do you think they're in a cult? Do we have to save his soul?

> **Finch:**
> I showed my wife your messages. She thinks I need to save your soul. So, where are we going? I'll message the other guys and we'll go for drinks.

Yes, I win.

> **Me:**
> You pick a place. I haven't been out much yet.

> **Finch:**
> You've been here since September. What have you been doing?

I know Miles is the wrong answer, even if it's the right one.

> **Me:**
> Being lazy.

> **Finch:**
> Meet us at a bar called The Ranch. It's all country and very Southern.

Sounds like a great homophobic time.

But I forget that no one knows about me, not even Miles. I haven't told him I've realized that having sex with a man has never been a big deal to me. I joked about doing it to join the Collective for real, but maybe that wasn't completely joking when the words were genuine. Not that they'd ever make me do it, but if they said I had to, I would've. That's not straight-thinking behavior.

Ever since I was younger, I've always had the whole marriage and kids equals complete life. Having that woman next to me, being "the man" of the family, and providing.

It's taken me until now to realize how bullshit that whole societal expectation is. I was never happy doing that, which is why when any of my wives brought up the topic of kids, I'd say I wasn't ready. Because deep down, I thought if I wasn't happy in my marriage, no way would bringing a kid into the world fix it. I had visions of becoming distant like my parents, and being a hockey player and always on the road, it would be easy to neglect them.

It's not until this very moment that I realize … I don't want children. Why have kids when I won't be able to spend time with them? Why would I bring them into a world where I would do to them what my parents did to me?

I'm just full of revelations this week.

Being a well-rounded person is depressing.

So fuck it. I will go out with the team, ignore the ass-backward Bible Belt view of people like me, and forget about real life for a bit.

Me:
See you there.

Okay, the Ranch isn't as bad as I thought it was going to be. There isn't even one single Confederate flag in here.

There's line dancing in the bar, a mechanical bull toward the back, and beyond the restaurant is a corridor that leads to a battle-axe-throwing place next door. It's like a playground for adults.

When I arrive, Finch and Stoll are already there, and it's not long after I get in that more guys filter through the doors.

I'm in the middle of ordering drinks for those who are here when more come through, so I end up ordering pitchers of beer to take back to the table. Or tables, now that it's filling up.

I want to ask if anyone thought to invite Miles, but I'm giving him space. Space, space, space. It would probably be nice for him to bond with the team though.

When I get back to the guys and put the pitchers down, I ask, "Did anyone invite Rook?"

Finch pulls back. "You didn't?"

"Yeah," Jorgensen says. "We figured out of any of us, you would. We're actually surprised you didn't arrive together."

"We're not tied to each other." Lies. I can see why he's ignoring my texts.

"I got you," Stoll says. "He said he'd come later after he's had dinner with Mommy and Daddy."

My lips turn up. That's such a Miles answer. I kind of love that he has no shame in his closeness with his parents like some guys might. But at the same time, that love for them is what's holding him back, and that kind of sucks.

"So," Finch says, "this entertaining your squirrel brain enough?"

"Definitely. I don't know what to do first. Axe throwing, line dancing, or the mechanical bull."

Finch rubs his chin. "If I were you, I'd do the ax throwing first since you can't do it if you're drunk—who would have thought drunk dudes and sharp objects could be dangerous? Actually, you and ax throwing might be dangerous in general, so maybe skip that one. You should ride the mechanical bull after you're drunk so you can't feel anything when you hit the mats. Ask me how I know how much that fucking hurts. So—"

"Line dancing it is. Who wants to come out there with me to make fools of ourselves?"

Half the guys decide to follow me, and apparently, our lack of grace on the ice also carries over onto the dance floor.

At least we can laugh at ourselves. The rest of the world will, too, when Stoll films it and sends it to the team's social media manager.

Good ol' wholesome team shenanigans? It's a viral magnet. "Look! The giant men who fight on the ice also line dance!"

We're only at the bar for about an hour when Miles breezes in.

He's so cute with his blond hair sticking out underneath his beanie, his large puffer jacket making him look twice as wide as he normally is.

He makes his way over to us and ditches them immediately.

I pour him a drink into one of the extra glasses and slide it over. He doesn't even look at me as he mutters, "Thanks," and takes a drink.

See, he is ignoring me, he does want space, and I've ruined a good thing by kissing him. Though, in my defense, it was him who asked me to. Maybe it was a test, and I failed.

I'm torn between wanting to talk to him about it and wanting to continue to give him the breathing room he needs.

I stand. "Fuck it. I think I've had enough beer to numb my ass when I fall from that thing. Who's with me?"

Stoll jumps up, taking out his phone. "Oh, this is so going up on the team page too."

Somehow, falling off a mechanical bull and embarrassing myself on the internet is preferable to talking to Miles and having him end things.

Look at that. I can't even have a casual fling without smothering them to the point of pulling away.

Needy, neglected Cody strikes again.

CHAPTER TWENTY-SIX

MILES

I'm a fucking idiot. I'm screwing things up. Since when does being around Bilson make me *nervous*? Like, heart-pounding, palm-sweaty nervous.

"You're not going?" Jorgensen asks, nodding the way Bilson went. I want to. I'm buzzing to follow him like a lost dog, but he came out tonight and invited the whole team except for me.

Ouch.

I'm getting the message loud and clear, CB.

Didn't stop you from showing up though, the snide voice in my head says.

This sucks. I need to do what Robbie said and talk it out, but the three texts he sent today made me realize how I won't be okay to lose this friendship. I typed out a thousand and one bullshit responses and couldn't send any of them because, dumbass or not, this isn't a conversation I can't put in a text message.

Oh, btw, man, totally might be falling for you, but it's not like I can do anything about it anyway, so let's keep fucking on the down-low and change nothing. K?

That's about as useless as tits on a bull.

"Earth to Rook." Jorgensen waves his hand in front of my face.

"Don't fucking call me that." I don't mean to snap, but apparently, my whole personality goes out the window when I'm angsting like a teen girl at a boy band concert.

Jorgensen's bushy eyebrows are at his hairline.

"Sorry, dude." I scramble for an excuse. "Superstitious."

"Whoa. Didn't know."

"You're okay."

At least that's an excuse that should shut them up from using that name, even if I'm lying through my teeth. I hate that it's become something I associate with Bilson while also loving it at the same time.

"He's up."

At first, I'm not following until Jorgensen and a few others jump up and head in the direction of the mechanical bull.

Do not go over there. Do not go over—

Oh, look, my feet aren't listening.

Is it possible to be pussy-whipped when the person you're acting silly over doesn't actually have a pussy? What's the equivalent? Cock busted?

I hate myself as I push my way through my teammates to get to the front as Bilson mounts the fake bull. I try not to notice how good he looks up there. How those sexy hips move in time with the bucking machine. Until we talk, both our cocks are staying firmly in our pants, but hot damn, the man is making my resolve difficult.

I drain my beer glass dry, trying and failing to fulfill my thirsty ass.

Like the universe is taking it easy on me, whoever is controlling the bull suddenly jacks it up. Bilson goes from powerful and in control to one of those flailing arm inflatable thingies businesses use to get attention. He flings to one side, rights himself, and then, with one big buck, flips off the back and smacks face down on the padding.

The team catcalls him, and I laugh as Bilson gives us a thumbs-up but doesn't move.

"Oh, city boy got his ass handed to him," Stoll says.

"Motherfucker, you've never left Nashville."

"Like you have."

I've got aunts and uncles with properties all over the state, spent a lot of vacations on the back of a horse, and one of the family things we did when I was younger and not being run between games and training was go to rodeos. This won't be my first time on the back of a bull.

"I'm up next," I say before anyone else can jump in. I climb up onto the padding and help Bilson to his feet, those pain-in-the-ass nerves rearing me up as soon as we clasp hands.

"Not too bad for an old guy, right?" He's joking, but it feels forced.

I want to ask him why he didn't invite me. Why I was the one left out. If Stoll hadn't given me the heads-up, would they all be here having fun without me? That hurts.

But now isn't the place, so I just wink and say, "Let me show you how a young buck does it."

Am I a professional at this? Nope. But I should be competent enough to show up the uncoordinated thrusting of my teammates.

What most people don't realize is that you need to sit as close to your hand as possible. It helps keep your center of gravity so when the beast is going wild under you, you have more control.

It starts off slow like the others, but I'm prepared for when it kicks up a notch. My arms strain with my grip as I try to anticipate the next move, the next kick or turn.

I'm thrown around, and it's harder than I remember, but I just want to hold on longer than the others. Maybe just long enough to impress Bilson.

The wilder it gets, the more I put my whole body into it. I'm sweating, grip locked on, thighs tense, and right when I can feel I'm getting out of my depth, I throw my head back and let out a "*yee-haw*" to be as much of a cocky shit as Bilson claims I am.

I land on my side a second later, *thwack* of the padding under me echoing in my ears. The catcalls and jeers of my team slowly sink in, and even though I'm panting, I force myself to jump up and bow, then make my way back to the team, arms raised like a championship fighter.

I'm overly aware of Bilson's eyes on me, but I try to pretend like I haven't noticed when it's all I can goddamn think about.

And when he catches up with me, team distracted watching someone else have a go, and leans down to my ear, his words send a shiver down my spine.

"I suddenly understand why cowgirl is your favorite position."

I swallow roughly. "It's the tits, man. I like the way they bounce."

His hum is gravelly. "Bet your cock bounces just the same."

Fuck.

And now I'm hard.

I *cannot* be hard around him. No, Cobra. Bad boy. There is no sexy times until we both know where we stand.

Taking advantage of the team's distraction, I grab his sleeve and drag him through the bar and down the corridor that leads to the axe throwing. It's all black and dimly lit, making it the perfect place to do this where he won't be able to see my face. This late in the night, people are a few drinks in, so the area isn't busy.

Before he can say anything, I cross my arms and go first. "Why didn't you invite me tonight?"

"Ah …" His handsome face falls, and he pulls his gaze from me to the wall. My heart is doing that stupid racing thing, and I wish it would shut up for a moment so I can get through this.

"Good answer," I add dryly.

"You're pissy with me?"

"You left me out, dude. Kinda hard not to be hurt when your best friend doesn't want you around."

"You haven't written back to any of my texts. I thought you wanted space. I've been really horrible about giving people space in the past, so I'm, you know, trying to pay attention to things like that."

Oh, wow. I thought he was being an asshole and wanted distance from me, but nope. My silence has been making him question all the same things. So, with the weight of Stone and Seddy in my pocket for courage, I finally do what I need to.

I can barely breathe when I say, "I'll never want space from you."

He holds my gaze, something shifting behind his eyes, and I know this is where I need to make a joke if I want to back out. To pretend this isn't happening and go on living in my denial bubble.

But I can't do that to him. Can't let him think this is something it's not.

I don't think I can do that to *me* either.

He steps closer, so close we're almost touching, and it's a goddamn mindfuck how much I crave this. Us. But even if I'm letting him see that, it's not like it changes anything with me. I can ache for him all I like, the simple fact is that it can't be more than this.

"Don't worry," I whisper, voice hoarse. "I'm not proposing or anything."

"Miles ..." His large hand lifts, but a second before he can cup my face, he pulls away. Steps back and straightens.

Disappointment hits me, but then a couple rounds the corner, headed for the bar area. We're both silent as they pass.

"What *are* you saying?" There are no teasing smiles or soft eyes as he looks at me. Nothing to give me any insight into his thoughts.

"I know we said that hooking up was a safe way to make sure you didn't fall for someone again, but we kinda, uh, forgot about me." I swallow. "I've never fallen for anyone, so I assumed I was immune." I look him straight in the eyes. "I'm not."

"Shit."

"I'm sorry. I had no idea whether to say anything or not, but my frat brother pointed out that it wasn't fair to keep sleeping with you if you didn't know."

A soft look crosses his face. "Your frat brother is smart, which isn't a phrase I ever thought I'd say. But I mean 'shit' as in ... now you've said all that, all I really want to do is kiss you."

I groan, low and deep in my throat. That kiss is something I haven't been able to stop thinking about, and now that it's on the table, it's so fucking tempting.

"Yeah ... but we can't. Here."

"Sounds like we need to leave, then." He makes me laugh, and I wish I could go along with it, but this next part is too important.

"You wanna let me in on how you're feeling?"

"Sorry, I thought that part was obvious." His face goes serious. "Yes."

"Yes, what?"

"Just yes."

I punch his shoulder. "That tells me nothing, you dick."

"What, like, 'news flash: I emote too' tells me so much."

"You know what I meant."

"I do." The affection in his eyes sends my nerves out of control. "And I still mean yes. Yes, as in, that's my answer to anything that happens between us from here on. I know you're worried about your parents, and I'm not going to push you to talk about labels if it's not something you want to do. We can be as public or as private as you like. I don't care. I just know I'm having too much fun with whatever is happening here, and yes, I'm feeling some things too, but for the first time in maybe ever, I … I'm happy to see where things go. To let you lead."

I pretend to scowl, but holy fuck, he's never said anything more perfect. "You mean I don't get to be the next Mr. Bilson?"

"Rook Bilson *does* have a nice ring to it …" Then he drops to one knee.

I burst into laughter and haul him to his feet. Bilson falls against the wall beside me, shoulder pressed to mine, chuckling along with me while he watches my face.

"Fuck," I sigh, letting out all the tension I've been holding on to for the past twenty-four hours. "I was so scared to tell you all that."

"We can tell each other anything, remember?"

"Yeah, somehow, I assumed we drew lines at stupid crushes."

"I wanna know about allll your stupid crushes—wait. Let's just stick to the one."

I contemplate how far I can tease him with that. My nerves have shifted, less making me want to puke and more lightness at the knowledge that this incredible, handsome, broad-shouldered, sweet man beside me sees something in me too.

"Miles?"

I turn my head so we're looking at each other. "Hmm?"

"We need to go."

"You don't wanna hang out with the team some more?"

"Nope. I want to take you home and get a front-row seat to those moves back there."

A shiver runs through me. "Now? Let's go."

"And then you're going to stay the night."

My mouth goes dry. It's exactly what I wanted the last time we were together, but admitting that makes me feel vulnerable. What the hell do we do? Fuck each other stupid, then ... snuggle? With *Bilson*?

I'm usually the big spoon, but I can't deny the thought of him surrounding me isn't horrible. Just hard to imagine. Sex is one thing; affection is worlds different.

But this is what I signed up for. This is what it means if we're going to continue this but with feelings.

"Okay."

"Good." He pushes off the wall. "But there's one thing I want to do first."

CHAPTER TWENTY-SEVEN

BILSON

My first instinct was to take Miles out somewhere, but no sooner do we get in my car and leave the Ranch than I realize I have no idea where to take him or what to do. I'm still not familiar with Nashville.

"Where are we going?" he asks.

"I have no idea."

Miles whines. "Then can we go back to your place already?"

"No."

"Why not?"

Because I'm going to do this right. "I figured we should go somewhere together. Like a date."

His eyes widen.

"Like non-PDA date. Nothing has really changed between us—this still has to be a secret, and you're not comfortable coming out—but that doesn't mean we have to continue to pretend this is only sex. We both want more without being able to have a whole lot more, so let me give you a proper date."

I'm not sure how he's going to react. He looks like he's trying to decide between kissing me or punching me.

"It doesn't have to mean anything more than what it is. I just want to show you that I'm on the same page as you."

"Oh, that's not what I'm worried about."

"Then what are you worried about?" Whatever concern he has, I'll fix it. I'll show him he has nothing to worry about.

"What if one date turns into two, and then you're proposing on the third?" His face slowly morphs into a smirk.

"You fucking little shit. For that, you can pick the place we're going."

"Sure. Has nothing to do with you not having any idea where to take me."

"Nothing at all."

Miles nods toward the windshield. "Take a left up here."

He directs me where to go, and we end up round and round a road leading up a hill.

"Where are we?" I ask when he tells me to park on the side of the hill.

"Love Circle."

"Why does that sound dirty but sweet at the same time?"

"We used to call it Love Circle Jerk in high school."

"That would be more fun. Is that what we're doing here?"

"It has a good view. It's supposed to be romantic or whatever."

"You mean *bromantic*? Because that's the story we're sticking with."

Even though he sends me a smile, there's disappointment in his eyes. "Yeah. We're sticking with that. If you're sure you're okay with it?"

I purse my lips. "If I really think about it, I almost prefer keeping us quiet. I'm embarrassed, but maybe not for the same reason that you are."

"I'm not embarrassed. If I thought for a moment my parents would be cool with it, I probably wouldn't hesitate. Though I wouldn't mind being more established in the league before I did. Okay, so I'd have things holding me back, but it wouldn't be embarrassment about who I am."

"I just mean that I've been married four times. I'm known for fucking up relationships. Even if I were still dating women, keeping things on the down-low sounds like heaven to me because I wouldn't be constantly watched waiting for the next failed relationship to hit the hockey gossip sites."

Miles seems to droop in his chair. "It sucks that we're both in a situation where it's easier to keep it quiet."

"It does, but at least we're in agreement." I flick my gaze to his. "Okay, show me your Love Circle. See, it is dirty."

We share a laugh and climb out of the car, but as he leads me to the small hill that overlooks the city, we pass these fenced-off squares.

"What's in there? Is that where the circle jerk happens?"

Miles snorts. "Sure. If you like getting electrocuted while coming. It's all electrical stuff in there. Like power exchanges or whatever they're called."

"So, what you're saying is, we could really make some sparks fly in there?"

This time, he shakes his head.

"We could be fire."

"You're going to be making electricity jokes for the whole date, aren't you?" he grumbles.

"Not at all. No jokes. I promise."

He narrows his gaze at me because I'm sure he knows what's coming.

"Can't promise not to pun the shit out of it though."

"Of course you think there's a difference there."

I nudge him with my shoulder. "Show me where the best view is."

He lowers his voice. "If I was going to show you the best view, we'd be at your house, and we'd be naked, but I guess I can show you the best view in Nashville."

I match his tone. "That would still be you naked in my house."

"*Of* Nashville, then."

We walk to a clearing, and the view is amazing, but I'm too distracted straining my ears trying to figure out what the fuck that moaning sound is. It's like a grunt mixed with some weird kind of mewling. Like an animal attack. It's close but still far enough in the dark for me not to see.

"Is that ... some kind of bear eating a kitten? Does Nashville have bears?"

Miles covers my mouth with his hand. "It's called Love Circle for a reason. Let the horny teenagers get it on." He releases me.

"Those are sex noises?" Wow. "Why does it sound like he's eating her?"

"He probably is."

Public sex. Weird. Sure, Oskar's known for that kind of thing, but I dunno. I wouldn't feel comfortable asking anyone to do that. Mainly because if it got out, I wouldn't be the one mocked. It would be them.

Though, with Miles, it's a whole other story, and I wouldn't do it to either of us.

"So, do we pretend like we can't hear it and keep watching the city lights?"

"Yup."

"Gotta tell ya, you sure know how to make this bromance special. A great view. Sex soundtrack. The threat of being electrocuted. This is the best date ever."

"Let's move away from the sex noises and sit over there so we can have real date talk." He points.

I'd rather take the sex noises and uncomfortableness, thanks. Mainly because I hate date talk. All the boring *tell me your whole life story* type things. But then I realize I basically already know all that stuff about Miles. So, really, what else could he tell me?

We sit on the grass on the hill, and while it takes away most of the view of the city due to the trees in front of us, I don't really care. Miles is a better view anyway, even if it is dark in this corner of the park.

"If you never got drafted, what did you want to do with your life?" he asks.

"Well, shit. I haven't really thought about it." When I think back to when I was a teenager, all I remember is not wanting to be corporate assholes like my parents.

"I reckon I would've made a good chef," Miles says.

"Can you even cook?"

"I'm a good Southern boy. Of course I can cook."

"Then why the fuck are we out here and you're not making me a good ol' home-cooked meal?"

He smiles. "Maybe another time. You thought about yours yet?"

I shrug. "I dunno. For me, it was hockey or college to begin that climb up a corporate ladder. I was so adamant

I didn't want that life, it's what fueled me to be the best I could be at hockey."

"That's a lot of pressure."

"Eh. It got me where I am, and I love what I do. I wouldn't change it for the world."

"I might," he says softly. Almost like he's ashamed.

"What do you mean?"

"I chose to play hockey because as the youngest child of four, I needed to make my parents proud somehow. And because hockey is the most expensive sport to play, of course my parents were willing to pay for it to make up for being the forgotten child."

"I thought middle children were supposed to be the forgotten ones?"

"True. Forgotten probably isn't the right word. The oldest is the one parents are the hardest on. The middle ones were forgotten. And the youngest is always spoiled, but only because by that point, the parents get over their helicopter phase and don't even blink at you playing with knives."

"So your parents put the knives on your shoes instead?"

"Yup. And bought me pet rocks and let me name inanimate objects like Annette."

"Oh, thank God you admit that Annette is an inanimate object. I was seriously beginning to worry that she answers back."

"What do you mean? She totally answers back. But I'm not delusional enough to think she's a living, breathing thing. She's a goalpost, CB. I'm not that weird."

I disagree, but not going to lie, I love how weird he is. So do his parents. I'm sure of it.

I turn to face him. "Question. If your parents can embrace all your weird, do you really think they wouldn't accept you for the teeny-tiny part of you that is your sexuality? It's not like that's all you are. You're a hockey player, a wannabe chef apparently, you have amazing respect for your parents, for your family … You're on almost a million dollars a year and could move out, but you choose to live in the separate apartment on your parents' property. I feel like they would love you no matter what."

He doesn't answer for a really long time, and I worry I've offended him or he might think I'm not okay with our arrangement, even though I am. I almost take it back, but he replies as I open my mouth.

"There's a chance they would accept me. But … what if they don't? What if they tell me that being bi isn't real or if I'm bi, then I could choose to be with a woman? What if—"

"Okay, I get it. I don't understand it because I know for a fact my parents wouldn't care if I came out. That would imply they cared about anything that I did. But I do understand not wanting to let people down. It's hard for me not to feel that way with every broken relationship I've had. That I've disappointed them. That I wasn't enough for them."

Sitting out here in the dark, where people are around but obviously distracted making bear attack noises, Miles inches his hand closer to mine and brushes his finger against my pinky.

"If it makes you feel any better, you haven't disappointed me yet. Only surprised me."

"Surprised how?"

"By how you allow me to be myself. Accept the real me. The way you encourage my weirdness and even the way you make puns."

I grin. "Are you saying ... I was a shock to your system? Get it? Shock? Like electric shock?"

He groans. "I take it all back. You're terrible."

"Terribly electrifying? Do I light your fire? Send sparks down your spine? Burn you up?"

"Are you done yet?"

I lean in close. "When it comes to you, I'm nowhere near done."

CHAPTER TWENTY-EIGHT

MILES

I'm aching for him to kiss me. Just to close the distance and give me the connection I'm craving. He's close enough, large body right beside mine, nerves skating through my gut at the thought of him reaching over and touching me.

I'm not used to this. To the anticipation. And not for sex—for ... more. Whatever that more is, I can feel it. The heart tickles and gut churning and the way I keep needing to swallow, over and over, just by him being right by me.

"I think we should go," I tell him, voice sounding like churned gravel.

"Should we?" Bilson looks smug as hell, and he calls me cocky. "Not enjoying our date?"

"I am, way too much. Which is why we need to leave."

"I'm not going to argue with that logic." He jumps up and brushes off the back of his pants, making my gaze drop to his ass. It pops out, big and round. That same desperate need to get him naked is there like always, but it's less about wanting to be pounded and more about wanting to touch, to have nothing but skin between us.

Bilson holds a hand out to me. "I thought you were in a hurry."

"Just admiring the view." I let him haul me to my feet and accidentally on purpose fall against him. I give his dick a sneaky squeeze before stepping back, thrilled to find it half-hard. "Apparently, so were you."

"You always have that effect on me. I need to find a way to make a third leg an advantage on the ice."

"Pop a little skate on him and teach him to hold your body weight."

"That was a disturbing image I never knew I didn't need until now."

I laugh, wanting to grab his hand. The chance of someone seeing us in the dark is slim, but you never know who's around. I wait until we climb into his car, then slide my hand over his meaty thigh. I love how possessive it feels, and then, when his hand covers mine a moment later, I love how possessed it makes me feel.

Bilson drives one-handed as much as he can, only letting go occasionally to use the turn signal. I relax into my seat, trying to picture this, us, and getting to have this every day.

Do you really think they wouldn't accept you for the teeny-tiny part of you that is your sexuality?

Bilson's question is stuck in my head. It's one I've been avoiding because the second I start thinking about it, the second I even try to consider telling them, hope sneaks in. That stupid little voice telling me, "But maybe …"

The thing is, I know there's a chance it might go okay because I know that they love me. I know that when my parents say unconditional that they really think they mean it.

But if it doesn't go well, it's not just a story that will become funny in a few years' time. I'll lose them. I don't think I can risk that.

So this can't be forever because Bilson might be okay with being on the down-low for now, but it's a temporary solution. That hurts, more than it probably should, to be honest.

"You've gone quiet," he says.

I crack a smile, not about to let all those thoughts out. "Trying to figure out what position I want you to destroy my hole in tonight."

"Tonight's my choice."

"Isn't every time?"

"Nope. Because I've never been inside you the way I really want to."

There go those nerves again. "What happened to me riding you?"

"We'll start there. Give me a bit of a show, then I'm going to lay you on your back and show you what real sex is."

My cheeks heat, and he's not even talking dirty. "Isn't all sex real sex?"

The way he looks at me, like he's in on a secret, tells me that maybe I'm wrong about that.

We pull up back at his place, Bilson driving right into the garage and closing the door behind his car, and the second we have privacy, he leans over the console and tugs me to him.

His lips cover mine, warm and strong, tongue licking into my mouth before he pulls back again. "Fuck me, I've been dying to do that."

"Then why'd you stop?"

"Because I want to do it again, but naked."

He jumps out of the car, and I'm quick to follow, both of us stopping to give Killer some love before we lock him away and head for the bedroom.

"You know," I say to Bilson's back, "if we're going to be sexing a lot here, we really need to make it up to Killer. Our poor baby is going to be in that laundry room constantly if I get to have you as much as I want."

"That can be tomorrow's plan ..." He bunches his hand in the front of my shirt and drags me into the room. At first, I think he's going to kiss me, but he shoves me backward onto the bed instead. I hit it with a soft thump, loving being manhandled as Bilson stands over me and undoes my pants. He strips them off in one smooth motion, and my briefs follow a second later. Then I get the most mouthwatering show as he unbuttons his shirt and pushes down his jeans.

The head of his cock pushes against his yellow boxers, leaving a large damp stain in the cotton. I know what it tastes like, feels like, looks like, and still, I want more.

My legs inch open, and he laughs, giving himself a quick tug.

"You are such a cock slut."

I spread my legs wider as I struggle to get my buttons undone. "Now say that again as you rail me."

Bilson finally pushes down his underwear and straightens, completely naked. My mouth floods with saliva at the sight, and it's hard to know whether I want him in my mouth or my ass more. If God was a real bro, he would have gifted Bilson with two so I didn't have to choose at all.

"No railing tonight."

My head drops back on the mattress. "You're supposed to love me."

"Ha. I don't think I said that. Shockingly." He walks forward until he's standing at the edge of the bed. "But don't worry. You're going to enjoy every second of what I do to you."

Before I can ask what he's planning, he grabs my ankles and yanks me to the side of the bed. I go easily, like I weigh nothing, and my cock loves the feeling, especially as he drops to his knees.

"I like where this is going," I say.

Bilson slings my legs over his broad shoulders, then turns his head and presses a kiss to the side of my knee. "Just relax, close your eyes, and let me make you feel good."

My balls ache at his words, but I do exactly what he said and melt into the mattress.

"Perfect. Keep doing what you're told, and I'll spoil you by feeding your needy ass my cock."

Ah, fuck. My eyes slam closed, and I cover them with my hands. I want to sob I'm so turned on. Bilson knows exactly what to say to get me going, and the fact he can do it with so few words makes everything so much more heightened.

His lips find my leg again. And again. A trail of soft, sweet kisses that are making my heart beat out of my chest the closer he gets to my groin. I can't stand the anticipation. Can't stand how close he is to where I want him. My hips buck off the bed, and before I can say a word, Bilson's large hand finds my ass. Hard.

The *thwack* echoes in my ears, and I bite back a groan of pain and pleasure.

"You're gonna make me come before you've done a damn thing."

His exhale gusts over my balls. "No coming. Not until I'm buried inside you."

I want to demand he hurries up, but then Bilson's tongue bypasses my cock and flicks over my hole. All words desert me. All I can do is make random sounds like I'm practicing my syllables as Bilson's tongue drives me wild. He licks and sucks, nipping my skin gently, making my whole body vibrate. His thumb joins in, rubbing and pressing at my hole until he's able to push inside. It's the most incredible tease. A hint of what I want, reminding me how good it feels to be stretched open but not getting me all the way there.

Once his thumb is moving easily in and out, Bilson's tongue takes over. He eats me out like a starved man while his hand loosely circles my swollen cock and keeps me on edge. Fingertips brush my tip and skim the nerves along my length.

I have to grit my teeth to hold back. To be good. To not come until he's filling me. It might be his rule, but I want it as badly as he does.

Bilson's mouth moves hungrily over me, tongue fucking my tender hole, and by the way his shoulder is moving, I'm pretty sure he's jerking himself off too. There's nothing hotter than knowing he's turned on by doing these things to me.

The growl he lets out vibrates through me as he stands suddenly, throwing my legs from his shoulders as he stalks to his nightstand. He pulls out a condom and tears the packet open with his teeth while I lie there watching him roll it down his magnificent cock.

"Fair warning, whatever position you're in when I climb on the bed is the one I'm going to fuck you in."

It's tempting to flip over onto my front, ass in the air, and let him go to town on me, but I don't. I hesitate,

216

curious, wondering what Bilson loves so much about missionary.

So instead of suggesting I ride him like we'd planned, I throw off my shirt and move up the bed until my head is on the pillow. He walks toward the bed, dark gaze roaming approvingly over my body. There's something almost affectionate in his expression that I've never seen once during sex before.

He climbs over the top of me, pulls my legs around his waist, but doesn't push right in. Instead, he brushes a kiss over my lips.

"Good choice."

I run my fingers through his hair. "You gonna convert me to the church of missionary?"

"Yup." He runs the smooth head of his dick over my hole. "Where you'll pray on your back while worshiping my cock."

"Show me."

He presses forward, and while I'm not as stretched as I normally would be to take him, I love it. Love the way he's going slowly, giving me time to adjust, just the hint of a burn before pure pleasure washes it away.

His face hovers over mine, and watching the expressions play over it as he fills me is my new favorite thing. "There's nothing like being inside you." He kisses my jaw. "Nothing."

Fuck me, I feel the same. I love sex. Love when it's cheap and easy and fun. But this? Being close physically, watching each other, taking our time, and letting ourselves feel, it's a whole lot of soft emotion that I'm not used to.

I kiss Bilson's nose because it's the closest thing to me, and for some reason, that makes him smile. Makes his eyes go all creased in the corners.

His hips meet my ass, and we both let out a deep exhale.

"This is what I needed," he murmurs, and as he says the words, I know exactly what he means.

"I think I did too."

He rolls his hips, starting slow and smooth while I move with him, rocking against his body and finding a rhythm that makes us both feel good.

I still want that easy and fun sex, but I want this too.

The thing about being with Bilson is that I get to have both.

Sure, we might be touching each other gently, like I'm in awe of him, but I have zero doubt in my mind that if tomorrow I bend over and ask him to spit on me that he'll do it.

I'm starting to learn that the only preference Bilson has in the bedroom is to make sure his partners feel good. That's why he loves this position. That's why he's taken so easily to the dirty talk when it's not something he's tried before. That's why he had no hesitation in being with me, even though I'm a man. What makes Bilson feel good is knowing his partner feels good.

And somehow, I'm the one he wants to share that with.

His ex-wives must have been high because being the focus of his full attention like this? Knowing that I can touch him and kiss him and hang out with him whenever I want? That we can fuck and then shoot the shit with the team? Win some games together? This has to be what people mean when they talk about heaven because life couldn't get any better than this.

I bring his mouth to mine, giving in to my need to have him overwhelm me completely. To own my body and fill my brain until he's the only one I can focus on.

I move against him faster, and Bilson immediately gives me what I want. His thrusts pick up, harder, deeper, pushing me up the bed and then dragging me back toward him again. My cockhead keeps rubbing precum against his abs, giving my length all the friction it needs, and as we kiss, Bilson's teeth clack against mine, tongue greedily drinking me in, one hand gripping the bed beside me while the other kneads my ass cheek.

Every pass of his dick over my prostate sends me higher, makes my balls ache with the need to get off. Goddamn, I'm close.

"You love my cock, don't you, baby?"

He's trying to kill me. I can't answer.

"Tell me." His lips press to my ear, making his voice louder and deeper than before. "Use my name."

"Need your cock, Bil—"

He cuts me off. "That's not my name."

My eyes flick up to meet his as I work out what he wants. "I love the way you fuck me, Cody."

Bilson's long moan is everything. His forehead meets mine, and he angles my hips forward, breaching me deeper. Harder. Panting breaths falling against my skin, bruising fingers gripping my ass. He's lighting me up from the inside out, and I get what he means.

Holding him to me like this, fucking but with feelings, this is a whole new way to experience sex, and it's raw and vulnerable but feels exactly right. With him. "I need to come."

His free hand is gentle as it cups my face. "Do it. I want to hear you fall apart."

I shiver, balls pulling tight.

"I want to see my pretty little slut come on my cock."

Nrgh. My dick explodes between us, pulsing with each spurt as it spills mess over both our abs.

Bilson's mouth slams down over mine, and his kiss is the high I need as he pounds his way to the finish line. He stiffens over the top of me, mouth breaking from mine as he comes.

His heavy body collapses on top of me, too boneless to hold himself up, and we lie there, for the first time ever not having to hurry up and run out.

I kiss his cheek and hold him close, breathing in the smell of sweat and sex between us.

Something in my heart just … settles.

CHAPTER TWENTY-NINE

BILSON

I struggle to keep up with Miles and Killer. I swear they're as energetic as each other, and Killer loves running with Miles. So do I.

That is, until I realize Miles's definition of a light run and mine are completely different.

Sweat drips down my forehead, and my muscles ache. Why is running so much harder than skating? It also doesn't get you where you need to go as fast. Miles seems just as fast on his feet as he is on blades.

I have to stop and raise my hand as I bend at the waist. "Wait up. Got a stitch."

Miles stops, but Killer doesn't. He wants to keep going and cries when the leash pulls tight. For a little prince, he has some damn energy. He's Miles's twin.

Miles keeps jogging on the spot. "Stitch? How old are you, old man?"

"I . . ." I heave. "Hate." Heave again. "Running. Put me on a bike, on a stair climber. Anything. Just don't make me run. And let's not forget we have practice this afternoon for our game tomorrow. I can't be exhausted before we even hit the ice."

"Aww, let's get you home so you can have your 4:00 p.m. dinner, get your walking cane, and head to the practice rink." He pats my shoulder, but when he sees my glare, he takes off in the direction of my place.

"You better fucking run." I contemplate chasing him, but I know I'll lose, so I wander back at my own pace.

When I reach the house, Miles is on the stoop of the porch with Killer panting happily beside him.

"I was about to send out a search party. Worried you'd fallen and broken a hip."

I can't help but smile. "You'll pay for that. And all the old jokes you've been making."

"Did you see the last press conference I had to do after the game? I was very complimentary of your age, thank you very much."

"You said you were surprised how fast I was given my *advanced age*."

"Still a compliment."

"Why do I put up with you? Honestly."

"I think it's my ass."

I huff. "Probably. You heading home before practice, or are we driving in together?"

He'll head home. He always does.

But he surprises me when he says, "We may as well go in together. By the time I get home, shower, change ..." He stands. "It'll be much easier to shower here and go."

"Easier, yes. Quicker? No." I step closer to him. "Because if you think you're getting in my shower alone, you're sorely mistaken."

"Don't threaten me with a good time."

We rush inside, and Miles gets the shower going while I refresh Killer's water bowl. By the time I'm closing the bathroom door behind me, Miles is naked in my shower, and his skin is lathered with foamy soap.

After our date, things have been more open between us. Before, when we were trying to pass it off as just sex, there were certain things I was conscious of doing, like looking at him too long or touching him in an affectionate way instead of sexual.

Back then, it was all about physical touch to get him off. Now …

I strip out of my clothes and step in behind him. I know he wants sex, and yeah, I'll get him off before we're done, but before that, I want to touch.

Kiss.

Explore.

I lean in and kiss a trail up his neck while I wrap my arm around his waist. He tries to push my hand toward his cock, but I chuckle against his skin. "Patience."

"Fuck patience."

"Hands on the wall. You're not allowed to move an inch until you've come."

Even though he whines in complaint, I know he loves it when I take control. Though with how torturously slow I plan to be, he's probably going to hate it this time. This isn't about getting off. This is about exploring a whole new side of our … brolationship.

One where I don't have to think or hold back.

So I ignore Miles's impatient whines and take what I want. Inch by inch, I explore his back with my mouth and his front with my hands. I pinch his nipples, caress his abs, and only when I've had my fill do I wrap my fingers around his hard cock and jerk him off until he comes.

I love the way he shudders in my arms and leans back against me with his head on my shoulder. His whole body trembles, and the gasp that comes out of his mouth makes my cock leak onto the skin at the base of his spine. But as impatient as he was to get off, I want to keep doing what I'm doing now: easing him through his orgasm and loving the feel of him against me.

Miles has other ideas. As soon as he's recovered, he drops his hands from the wall, spins, and falls to his knees.

I come embarrassingly fast down his throat, and when he stands back up, I anticipate the onslaught of mockery over being so old that I come faster than a teenager, but it doesn't happen.

Miles just stands, turns us to push me against the wall of the shower, blankets my body with his, and then seals his mouth over mine.

The kiss is slow but passionate. He presses in close, hums into my mouth, but everything about it is gentle. Almost like a thank-you.

"Ready to head to practice?" he asks against my lips.

Ugh. No. "I want to stay like this."

He pulls back. "Now, there's a way to get the team talking."

"Fine. I guess we'll get dressed and wear clothes to practice and whatever."

Our shared orgasms and the easiness between us put us both in good moods, but I can tell something's on Miles's mind when we get to the arena. There's a complete shift from his usual frat boy energy to ... this uptight aura about him.

"You okay, or are you worried about your game?"

We've had a string of losses and some wins, and I know the losses get to him more than they should, but that comes with the amount of experience he has. One day, he'll stop blaming himself for every shot that goes past him, but it's probably not going to happen during his first full rookie season.

"Nah. It's just a practice. It's fine."

Before I can ask more questions, he gets out of the car and doesn't wait for me to catch up.

Maybe he's regretting choosing to arrive together. I'd understand if that was it, maybe be a little disappointed, but I didn't expect him to ride with me in the first place.

He does, however, hold the players' door open for me, so there's that.

Once we're in the back halls of the practice rink, Miles practically runs away from me. At first, I think he's being a bit ridiculous. We're friends. We can walk side by side, but then when he starts talking to Stoll, I realize it's not about us as a couple at all but him being a tormenting little shithead.

"So, I made CB go for a run this morning to warm up, and he practically collapsed. I thought being a first-line winger, he'd have to be fit. Are we sure he doesn't use his stick like a walking cane on the ice?"

Stoll throws his head back and laughs while Miles winks at me over his shoulder.

I'd threaten him and say he'll pay for that, but I've used that threat countless times today already, and the worst I did was make him wait longer than usual for me to make him come.

I barge past them, giving both of them the finger as I do. When I enter the locker room, I give everyone the heads-up. "Don't listen to anything the rookie says. He lies."

While they get dressed and Miles, of course, tells everyone how old I am, I decide to fuck with him and the team.

I head for the training rooms, where one of our team trainers is organizing supplies in his cabinets.

"What's up, Cody?" Dustin says. "Got an injury you want me to work on? Tight muscles?"

"I'm good. I just had an idea to mess with the guys. You got one of those walking stick things for when we injure ourselves and need assistance?"

He hesitates. "I do, but I'm scared to ask what you're going to do with it."

"I want to use it as my hockey stick during practice."

"If anyone asks, you snuck in and got it yourself." He pulls one out of the buckets of crutches, canes, and other assistance items.

"Yes, sir." I make sure to leave it outside the training room and only collect it once I'm dressed. Which I do very slowly so I can be the last one on the ice.

People in the area are allowed to come watch us practice because we have it at a public rink, so I have no doubt photos of me playing with a cane will get out. And when reporters ask? I'm going to tell them it's because Miles Olsen called me old.

He thinks he can out-smart-ass me?

Good luck, Rook.

CHAPTER THIRTY

MILES

"Trouble in the bromance," I read aloud while Bilson listens from where he's wrestling Killer on his living room floor. "Such a clickbait title."

"Keep going."

I know that since whatever it says amuses him, I'm going to be rolling my eyes. He's already got the dad humor down pat. It probably kicks in naturally at a certain age.

"'At Nashville training yesterday, spectators had to look twice when Cody Bilson took to the ice—not with a hockey stick but a walking stick. When asked if the change in equipment signaled a retirement announcement in the future, Cody Bilson pointed at goalie Miles Olsen.

"'The rookie likes to run his mouth over how old I am. Just wanting to prove to him that experience counts—'" I glance up at him in surprise. "Excuse me, but who's been teaching who moves?"

He playfully rolls Killer over onto his back. "Keep reading."

I sigh and turn back. "'And that I can score on him just as hard, even in my old age.'"

My laugh is unhinged. "They *published* that?"

"I'm telling you, we could be fucking center ice, and they'd still be all, 'Aww, that's a bromantic pregame ritual.' I really don't think we have anything to worry about with the media, maybe not even with the team. People expect to see us together; they're used to us goofing around and being playful. None of that has changed—really, the only new thing is what we do in the bedroom, and I'm not inviting the media in here to watch."

I clamp my mouth shut. That basically answers my question of whether he noticed the blips in my mood lately. He thinks I'm being paranoid about getting caught.

The thing is, he's right that no one would notice a change in us if everything continues the way it has. He's *not* right that sex is the only new development.

My chest aches as I remember wanting to hold his hand as we walked into training yesterday. How I had to put distance between us so I wouldn't focus on being a sulky little shit and getting into both of our heads.

I know I should be happy. I'm getting everything I want. My dream career, in my dream city, and a relationship that goes beyond anything I ever pictured for myself.

When I thought ahead about having a wife, I always pictured someone cute and bossy. Pictured kids. A nice house. Very suburbia, and I don't even know where that image came from. My parents are ridiculous a lot of the time; my siblings are lovable assholes to each other.

Sure, we have a nice house now, but when I was younger, things were in shambles with us all sharing rooms until we moved.

So, where the hell did this smiling, picture-perfect image come from?

And why, when I think of it now, does it seem kinda disturbing?

My gaze flicks back to Bilson, and that familiar cartwheel flips over in my chest.

When I look at *him* and picture a future, all I see is us. Happily teasing each other after orgasms. Grumbly and exhausted, sitting next to each other on the team bus after a game. Holding hands while we drink beers at the bar with the team.

Houses and kids and all that other stuff is optional.

It's killing me how much I want that future.

And it hurts that I don't know how to make it possible.

Bilson clears his throat, and I notice his concern too late. "Let's get Killer to your parents so we're not hurrying to pack this time."

"Oh. You're coming too?"

His lips tighten. "I've come with you every other time. Has something changed?"

Yeah, that was before I started to hate them a little bit. Other than stupid teenage tantrums, I've never fought with my parents, never had anything come between us. I love them.

But I don't think that's enough anymore.

Because every day I spend with Bilson is making me more and more sure that he's my person. It's stupid and reckless and motherfucking terrifying, but it's becoming less a question of *how* I hold it all in and more a question of *if* I can keep this up.

He steps forward and runs his hands over my shoulders. "Is everything okay?"

"Of course." I flash him a grin. "Sorry, just being stupid."

"You sure?"

As quickly as that bad mood set in, he dispels it by just being him. "I can't take away your opportunity to kiss

Killer goodbye. Or your chance to get more baby Miles stories."

"They're my favorite part."

"Of course they are. Baby Miles was awesome." I whistle to Killer and start to head for the door when Bilson stops me.

"Don't forget our other babies." He picks Seddy and Stone up from the table and tosses them to me. "We've got games to win, and we can't do it without them."

See? He's perfect.

Bilson drives us to my place, and if I thought I'd be on edge with him around my parents ... I was not prepared for what I'd find when we drove up the driveway. Three other cars, which means my brothers and sister are here.

"Ah, fuck."

"What is it?"

"You're about to get the full Olsen experience," I mutter, climbing out of the car.

And when the first thing from Victoria's mouth as I walk in is, "Oooh, walk of shame, huh?" my fears are confirmed.

My family sucks.

"I was out with a friend, asshole."

"Mom says you've been out with friends a lot lately." Victoria can't keep the curiosity out of her tone.

"That's enough," Mom says, sweeping me up in a hug. "I never said that, baby."

"Aww, widdle Miles the widdle baby is all growing up," Philip adds.

I flip my oldest brother off over my mom's shoulder.

"Mom, Miles is sticking his finger up at us," Victoria sings.

Mark walks out of the kitchen, swigging from his beer bottle, and pauses when he spots Bilson. "Who's this?"

I pull away from Mom. "My teammate," I answer.

Dad whistles from where he's sitting on the couch, and Killer runs over and bounds into his lap. They scuffle for a moment before Dad wraps his arms around him, and for some reason, seeing that ... it kills me.

"Is that a rat?" Mark laughs.

"I know your IQ suffers, but surely you can spot a dog when you see it," I say.

"There's no way that thing is a dog." Philip goes to join Dad as Mom ushers Bilson inside.

"We're putting on a lunch. You'll stay, won't you?"

Bilson sends a questioning look my way. "I don't want to intrude—"

"Don't try to be polite. We want you here. I love when my babies bring friends home."

"Cody Bilson, right?" Mark asks, holding out his hand. "You look different without all the gear on."

Before Mom can drag me into the living room with the others, Victoria pulls me back. She's wearing that superior big-sister look that she always gets when she's hounding me over something.

"Out with it," I say.

"Who is she?"

My look couldn't tell her to fuck off any more clearly.

"Come on, weirdo. I want to know."

"Why?"

"Because I'm sick of being the only girl in the family, and let's face it, neither of those buttheads are finding a girlfriend anytime soon."

Everything she says makes me feel sick. "There is no girl. Sorry to disappoint."

"Come on. Mom says you haven't slept at home all week, and you've only had the one away game. We're not idiots."

"If your conclusion to that is that I've suddenly got a girlfriend, then yeah, you are." I'm trying to keep my voice down, trying not to take my frustration out on her when there's no way she could know any different, but it's a struggle.

"Then where have you been?"

I could go the standard line of *none of your business*, but it's pretty obvious who I turned up here with, and I hate lying. "Hanging out with Bilson," I say as casually as I can. "I just end up crashing there. He has a spare room, and it's better than being twenty-four and living with my parents."

She frowns. "I thought you liked living here?"

"Yeah, well, sometimes people change."

I walk off before she can say anything else to push me into talking about things I don't want to talk about, but when I join the others, I'm not so sure this is better.

"He was the younger brother," Mark explains. "It was our duty to do it."

"Do what?" I ask.

Bilson looks over, eyes shining with amusement. "They were telling me how they put your hand in water and got you to wet the bed at one of your sleepovers. Think it'll work on the road?"

Gah, I still hate them for that. "And I'll tell the team what I told my friends: why bother getting out of bed for it when you can have extra warmth and deal with it in the morning?"

Bilson's whole face screws up. "There will be no wetting the bed when I'm around. Fucking hell."

My gut tightens at the implication of that sentence, but thankfully, it goes right over Philip's head.

"Have you met his rocks yet?"

"Seddy and Stone? Of course. I love them as much as he loves Killer."

"Oh no," Mark gasps. "There's two of them. Help!"

Philip shoves him. "He's had them since he was, like, ten? There was Rocky too, but we lost him."

Mark groans. "Remember how Mom and Dad made us search for that stupid thing for a week?"

"It was your brother's pet," Dad says. "No different than when we gave your goldfish a funeral."

"It was a rock," Philip reminds him.

Mark points toward Dad. "You guys are the reason he grew up so weird. No other parents would have encouraged that."

"No other parents had a goalie for a son. We worked with what we had."

"And loved him anyway," Mom adds.

Philip uses that segue to talk hockey stats with Bilson while Mark teases me relentlessly about my goalie ticks. Dad and Killer are having a moment, and as Mom brings in snacks to set on the table, my gaze zeroes in on how she sets her hand on Bilson's shoulder as she asks if he needs something to drink.

He fits in so well with my family. I hate it.

Because they think he's my friend, and he's so much more than that. It's right there, the urge to tell them, to set things straight.

But I picture the hush that would fall over the room after telling them Bilson's my boyfriend. Picture Mom dropping the glass of water she's just filled. Picture the shock on Philip's face and the disappointment on Victoria's.

I can't do it.

Because while I hate it, seeing him with them is something I can't ruin. He looks so fucking happy, and if I pretend for a second that he's here as my boyfriend, it makes me so fucking happy as well.

I want it. So bad.

Why does this have to be so hard?

CHAPTER THIRTY-ONE

BILSON

With the randomness that is the NHL schedule, this is our first game against a Collective team since our run-in with Oskar Voyjik in Anaheim. Vegas is a force to be reckoned with, but I'm not so focused on the upcoming fight on the ice.

I'm distracted by the notion we'll be playing against Tripp and Dex Mitchell, who are basically the put-together version of Miles and me.

Goalie and forward. Best friends who became more. Though, they're married, and Miles and I are ... floundering.

Or, more specifically, I think Miles is floundering. I don't want to be a complication for him, and I don't want to come between him and his family. Just spending lunch with them before we left, they're the type of family I craved growing up. They're supportive, even if they snark each other out. But I could tell Miles was uncomfortable with me being there.

He didn't even want me to go with him to drop off Killer this time.

I want to ask Tripp and Dex how they handled their relationship, the coming out, and the pressure on them to do it or not do it. I remember seeing the articles, the news hitting the hockey world, but my thoughts about it extended to "Good for them" and then focused on my own crumbling marriage at the time.

Asking them how they navigated their situation would be a betrayal to Miles, though, because it's impossible to ask them without giving away I'm in a relationship with a man. Even without naming names, it's not like it would be difficult to work out who said man is.

But I don't know how to help Miles when he's obviously struggling, and talking to people who have been through the same or at least a similar thing might make it easier to deal with.

Because it sucks seeing him this way.

It's around this point of a relationship, when the insecurity kicks in, that I'd propose prematurely and make things worse, but I can't do that here, so I've got no ideas on how to fix it.

Who knew being in a same-sex relationship would cure me of my need to fix everything with a ring. This might take real work.

In the downtime between arriving at the arena and before having to dress for the game, I approach Miles, who's at his cubby talking to his rocks. The others are either in their own conversations or kicking a soccer ball around to fill the time, and it might not be the best moment to bring this up with him, but I don't want to spring it on him after the game either.

"Were you coming out after the game with the Mitchell Brothers?"

Miles glances around the locker room in a panic before realizing no one is listening. "Is it only weird to me that they're husbands but still referred to as brothers?"

"Don't yuck other people's yum. Maybe they're into brocest."

Miles finally cracks a smile, but I'm scared I'm about to wipe it off his face. I pull him closer toward his cubby, keeping my voice low.

"I was thinking … and you can say no, but … I want to tell them."

"You want to come out?" he whispers.

"Not to everyone. Just … to them." I make sure everyone's still not paying attention. "They know exactly what it's like to be in our positions, and … I thought maybe I wouldn't feel so alone if someone knew. Only those two people. And I'll only tell them about me. You don't have to be there. I—"

"It's your sexuality. Do what you want with it."

He sounds so sincere about that too.

"I don't have to."

Miles fidgets with Seddy. "I didn't mean for that to sound snappy. Sorry. It is your choice. Just … leave me out of it."

"I was going to."

"Suit up!" Coach's booming voice echoes around the locker room. "We've got warm-ups."

Miles's reaction is the exact reason I want to talk to Tripp and Dex, but now I'm thinking I should let it go.

I'm distracted as we hit the ice for warm-ups. Am on autopilot when the anthem is being sung, and when the puck drops, I'm completely spaced out.

Fuck, not a great start.

The team as a whole starts off on the back foot, and we spend our entire first shift in the defensive zone. Luckily for me and the rest of the guys on my line, Miles is on point and doesn't let any shots past him.

When I get back to the team box and have a chance to watch him at work, he's so damn focused. Vegas comes out of the gate swinging, and by six minutes into the first period, they've already had five shots on goal. They're thirsty for it.

But Miles shoots them down.

I finally pull my shit together, and the next time I'm on the ice, Finch, Jorgensen, and I manage to spend most of our shift in our offensive zone, trying to put one away.

Tripp Mitchell is a fucking wall, and he doesn't even look like he's working that hard at shutting us out. I'd hate him if he wasn't so damn impressive.

The thing is, though, Tripp has the best stats of all the goalies in the league and has for the last couple of seasons. Minus one of them where their whole team was a disaster, but I won't count that. And here's Miles Olsen, rookie fresh out of the farm, and he's keeping up with Tripp Mitchell.

It's an amazing game for him, and every time I'm on that bench, when I should be watching the puck, I'm watching *him*.

It's almost embarrassing how proud I am of him for having the game of his career right now.

The game goes back and forth. We all take our shifts, and I think nearly every damn player on the ice at one point has a chance to put the biscuit in the basket. But do we? Nope. Because Tripp and Miles don't let us.

They have the home crowd advantage, so even though their boos are loud when Miles makes the millions of saves, it only seems to encourage Miles more.

I can't stop smiling at him.

Throughout the first and second period, both teams get so close to scoring but never manage to do it.

The crowd is getting frustrated, and so are we. Because us scorers are playing an amazing game. Defense is intercepting and blocking. Offense is getting in that zone and firing, shooting our shots. But the stubborn-headed goalies don't want to be the first to let one in.

"This is a game of pure will at this point," I say to Finch as the third period gets underway and still nothing changes in scores.

"I don't think I've seen anything like it."

"We owe it to Miles to get out there and put one away. If we lose after this, he's gonna be pissed."

"That's all good and well, but if we can't put one away for the team, what makes you think doing it for Miles is going to make any of our shots more accurate?"

"Just set it up for me. I'll light up that lamp."

On the first try, the puck rebounds off Tripp's pads, and even though I get the puck back and shoot again, he's impenetrable. Damn him.

We pull a lucky-as-fuck penalty, one the crowd obviously boos at, and maybe, just maybe, they have a right this time, but I'm going to take every advantage I can get.

Which is why, before the face-off, I skate by Tripp. "Hey, Human Tripp. We going for drinks after this? I need to tell you about my big bi-awakening and how much I love dick now."

I don't even give him a chance to respond before I'm taking my spot opposite Tripp's husband.

"Hey, Dex." I lower my voice. "Turns out I'm bi."

The puck drops, and Dex swings but completely misses. I pass to Finch, who passes right back.

Vegas is a man down, Dex and Tripp are distracted, and that's how I win us the game.

Boom. Right through the five-hole.

Maybe I should weaponize this bisexuality thing to my advantage more often.

—

Tripp and Dex beat me to the players' exit, where they told me to meet them. I hold my hands wide. "Human Tripp. Dexter."

"That was a dirty trick, Bilson," Dex says.

"Is it even true?" Tripp asks.

I rub Tripp's hair. "You make me miss Dog Tripp. He and Killer loved each other."

Tripp swats my hand away. "So you are just milking this honorary Queer Collective membership thing, then."

I look back toward the closed door where our team-mates will be spilling out at any moment. Some have already left, but I know Miles isn't one of them.

"Oh, shit," Tripp says. "You were serious."

"But I'd prefer the team not to—"

Tripp immediately wraps his arm around my shoulders. "Let's go drink."

I let out a breath and follow them to their car.

Now that I've told them and it's out there, I don't even know what I want to ask them. There are those millions of questions about how they handled their situation, but I'm still trying to figure out how to ask without giving away Miles.

They don't pry on the way to the bar, just continue to tell me how dirty I played tonight.

"Someone had to get the first goal out of the way. It was taking too long, and your home crowd was getting bored."

"It was satisfying when they booed you for scoring," Tripp says.

"Don't they know that fuels us even more?"

"Your rookie goaltender was on fire tonight," Dex says.

"He was. It came at a good time, too, because he's been in a minor slump. He probably did it to impress you." I lean forward and tap Tripp's shoulder.

Thankfully, we pull up to the bar, and the conversation about Miles drops. I'm self-conscious about bringing him up or even talking about him, in case it's obvious I'm practically obsessed with the man.

The other time I caught up with Tripp and Dex with the Collective was last season with Aleks, and it was the same bar. Low-key, not too many fans around. Perfect for this conversation.

Tripp orders on his phone and then turns to me. "Okay. Details."

I glance between Dex and him, wring my hands together, and try to find the words.

Tripp smiles. "You look exactly like this one did when he was trying to figure all this stuff out."

"That's … reassuring?"

A waiter brings over our drinks, placing three beers in front of us.

"I get it," Dex says once we're alone again. "It was so confusing. Doubly so because I was having those feelings for my best friend."

I go to open my mouth and agree but stop myself in time. Miles and I have a very public friendship, so I can't be admitting I'm in the exact situation. Miles and I might not have been friends for as long as Tripp and Dex were before stuff happened, but we had that bond all the same.

"You don't have to talk if you don't want to," Tripp says.

"I know I couldn't really talk because I didn't know how," Dex says.

I cock my head. "Isn't that you on an average day?"

Tripp laughs.

Dex turns to his husband. "You're supposed to be nice to me and not laugh when people point out I'm a dumbass."

"Oh, honey. That's not why you can't talk. You can't talk to reporters because they're shitheads who like to confuse you by using stats and big words."

Dex's brow furrows. "Somehow, that doesn't make me feel any better."

Dex and Tripp are couple goals, and sitting here with them, seeing how far they've come ... I want that with Miles. But we have obstacles. Obstacles I'm not sure we can overcome.

I understand him not wanting to say anything to his family, but he didn't even want to be here for me to tell Tripp and Dex about myself.

I can feel it happening—getting ahead of myself. I want to skip to the happily ever after with Miles, whatever a happily ever after with him would be, but he's not there.

He might never get there.

And that's my current reality.

I'm out here by myself.

A tall presence looms over us, and I think the waiter is back, but I never saw Tripp or Dex order another round.

When I look up, I have to do a double take. Because there stands Miles, looking like he's about to throw up, but he's here.

I'm not so alone after all.

CHAPTER THIRTY-TWO

MILES

I'm terrified, but surprisingly, this feels right. Seeing Bilson leave tonight, knowing what he was coming here to do—alone—left a slimy, unsettled feeling behind.

I might not be able to give him PDAs and a proper relationship, but I can at least get my shit together enough to give him support. Tripp Mitchell is the sweetheart of the league, and Dex is his golden retriever; they both also know too well what it's like being in a relationship in the public eye.

If there's anyone I *could* trust, it should be these two.

I'm not sure I'm there yet, but I am in this goddamn bar, so that's something.

"Anyone going to order me a drink?" I ask around the lump of nerves in my throat. "I *am* the incredibly good-looking goalie who out-saved the Vegas master."

Dex points at Bilson and goes to say something, but Tripp sets his hand on him and talks first.

"You did amazing. You should be proud."

That burst of happiness lights up in my chest as I drop down next to Bilson, who cracks up laughing.

"You are such a praise whore, look at you."

I don't even try to hide the way I'm smiling. "I guess that'll be Tripp buying me a drink, then. Don't worry,

Dex. I'm sure the hero worship will wear off your husband soon."

Dex scowls at me, but this is good. This is what I need. To focus on being a cocky idiot and not ... everything else. While I'm teasing, Tripp actually does order me a drink, but when he's done, he glances at Bilson, and I miss what the look means, but Bilson nods.

"Ah, yeah, Rook knows. He's the only one."

Tripp smiles at me. "I take it you're supportive?"

If you call sleeping with him every night and wanting to crawl up on his lap supportive, then yes. "Of course."

"Sorry, sometimes guys can be ... weird. Dex and I had to deal with an asshole on our team when it all came out. Me being gay was one thing, but apparently, two of us in a relationship was too much for his tiny brain to handle."

"They were homophobic?" My gut twists, trying to imagine that coming from one of my teammates.

"Oh, yeah." Dex crosses his arms over the table. "Tried to hide it behind defending my ex, but it was obvious why he was being a dick."

"I thought the league had rules about that?"

The three of them laugh at me—or maybe it's for themselves. It's hard to tell, but it doesn't sound mean. Tripp's the first to talk. "They ... try. Some franchises are better than others. But when you get a bunch of people from all varying backgrounds together, there are bound to be some assholes in the mix."

"Great." I send a concerned look Bilson's way and find him already watching me. "You sure this is what you want?"

His hand flexes like he wants to reach for me, but he holds back. I hate it. "Yeah. Surprisingly, that doesn't scare me as much as losing ... ah, myself. I like this new side of me. A lot." He looks back over at the Mitchell brothers. "I don't know how public I want to go because there's a lot to consider there. But I do want people I can talk to about it."

Dex smirks. "You haven't said what 'it' is yet."

"I technically did during the game."

"That could have been fake-out smack talk, for all I know."

"I'm bisexual."

That's the first time I've heard Bilson say it out loud. Seeing him own it, state it like it's nothing, has the urge to cry sneaking up on me. Not tears of support—tears of anger, for myself and because I don't get to have that too.

I shove it all back because this moment isn't about me. *It could be though.*

A round of drinks appears at the table, and I quickly scoop up my beer and gulp half of it down.

As soon as the server is gone, Tripp says, "Congrats, man. It's a big thing to acknowledge about yourself, and I know we only focused on the negative just before, but there were a lot of positives too."

"Like what?" I ask before I can stop myself.

They share a lovesick look between themselves. "Most people weren't surprised we were together, which was a relief for me. I didn't want them questioning Dex and getting in his head. Our sisters were super supportive, most of our team cared more about our losing streak than who we were going home with, the media backed off by the end of the season, we have the Queer Collective, and those guys are invaluable to us, but ... the biggest positive—"

"Is you," Dex cuts in quickly. "Ha! I said it first. I'm the romantic one."

"Sure you are, babe."

"Trippy's my person. When you find that, you can deal with everything. *Everything*. It doesn't matter what comes for you because you always have that person at your side. I'd never had that with any of my exes, but I always had that with Tripp. Even before we got married. Even before my brain woke up. Everything was different with us, and when it clicked, I knew this was forever. Sure, staying married was probably a stupid choice for anyone else—we were still new and whatever—but it didn't matter to me. I could *feel* he was forever. I didn't need time. I didn't need to adjust. All that stuff people say to get in your head is bullshit. You just know, you know? And I've never regretted a day with Tripp in my life."

Tripp drops his head against Dex's shoulder. "Fine. Okay. You get to be the romantic one. You're going to kill me."

Dex punches the air. "That's how it's done."

But while they joke, everything Dex said was like he plucked my thoughts from my brain. I don't dare look at Bilson because if he's looking at me, I won't be able to not touch him.

It's only been a few months, but that moment of it all clicking for Dex? It's happening for me. Right now. I've said before that I've never felt anything like this with anyone, and I'm starting to worry that I never will again.

If Bilson is my person, can I really let that go? Risk it? Even if he's not ... do I want to?

All of this ending, not being able to call him mine, it sends this panicky wrongness through me.

And if I can't let him go, I'm going to have to start thinking about the unthinkable. Are we strong enough to get through anything like the Mitchell brothers are?

Dex lifts his glass. "To Bilson, the newest QC member."

Before I can toast with him, Tripp tugs his arm down. "He's not a member yet. Ezra will kill you if it's not done properly."

"I thought he was an honorary member?" I ask.

"We've told him a thousand times that's not a real thing."

"Damn, I was hoping to get in on that."

I'm not sure what makes me say the words because the second they're out, Dex's focus snaps to me. "You? Honorary?"

"He's been a huge support," Bilson says quickly. "My best friend on the team."

"Yeah, we've heard all about your bromance." Tripp grins my way. "Having someone you're close with is a huge deal. Especially your rookie year."

"You know, *I* was Tripp's best friend on the team," Dex says, clearly starting to put together what his husband hasn't.

"Don't make it weird." Tripp shoves Dex. "It wasn't the case for you, but straight men can be supportive too, you know."

"Exactly." Bilson tries to steer the conversation away. "There are some other guys on the team who I know won't be a problem. Maybe down the line, I'll tell them, but for now—"

The second Bilson redirects the others, it hits me that I don't *want* him to redirect them. I wanted them to guess and to force me to say the words, and Dex was so damn close, but we didn't get there. Disappointment hammers down on me.

I want to be free too.

I want everything the men across from me have.

It might come at the cost of my family, but ... *what if it doesn't?*

The need I have for that to be true is overpowering.

I'm not brave enough for much, but before I can stop myself, I move my chair closer to Bilson's and set my hand on the table so ours are side by side.

Then I link my pinky over his.

Bilson's immediately tightens around me, cutting off what he was saying as his head flies my way. There's a deep question in his eyes, and even though the urge to puke rolls over me, I give him the cockiest smile I can manage.

"Can't be outdone by a dinosaur. I thought I was meant to be the progressive one in this relationship."

"Miles ..." He drops his voice and quickly glances around. "What are you doing?"

"Exactly what the fuck I want." I turn and look Dex dead in the eyes. "Thank you."

"Ah, for what?"

"Putting into words everything I've been struggling with."

His whole face lights up. "I've been known to be smart sometimes."

"I dunno, man, between now and that press conference I saw you in, it seems to me like you're smart when it counts. Who cares about the rest of the time?"

"Sorry, Trippy, I think I've found a new best friend."

I bark a laugh that's less amusement and more this overwhelming ball of relief.

Tripp doesn't look as happy as his husband though. "I take it, ah, *this* is one of the things you have to consider about going public?" he asks Bilson.

"It's one part, but the other is that my relationships have been so public in the past that I don't want to have to see all those catty posts and comments about how long until we get hitched or ... or—"

"You've dated the entire population of women, so now you're turning to men?" I supply helpfully.

Bilson glares at me. "You'll be paying for that later."

Oh, damn, I hope so. "I love when you say that."

Tripp directs his next question my way. "And you? Do you want to keep it quiet?"

"Yes. I want to hope for the best with my family, but I just can't see them reacting well. And even on the off chance they come through for me, I don't see how it won't change things."

"Miles is really close with them," Bilson adds. "It's not something I want to come between."

"As long as you're both on the same page. I'm not going to lie and say everything will be easy, but you both have to keep talking and make sure you're comfortable with where you're at. I was nervous—so fucking nervous—to come out when I was younger. To my parents, my team, I remember throwing up right before I did it. But they surprised me. I hope it's the same for you."

"*If* I tell them."

Bilson's hold on me tightens, and I know it's in support. That if I keep us secret forever, he'll understand. So I correct myself.

"When." I suck in a breath. "*When* I tell them."

"What?" Bilson's knee knocks against mine. "Hey. You don't have to. I get why you're holding back, and if I had a family like yours, I'd probably be hesitant too. Don't do it for me."

"I'm not." I meet his eyes, and the affection looking back at me makes me fall that bit more. "The more I think about it, the more I question how great they are. It's easy to love someone when they're who you want them to be, but the fact I'm unsure how they'll react, that I think there's a chance they might value my sexuality over my happiness ... that's not okay."

"If you lose them—"

"That'll be their choice. I didn't think that was ever something I could risk, but then Dex said all that stuff about having your person, and ... I think that's what you are for me. We might not be forever like they are, I have no idea, but I do know that for this one moment, you'll be there, and you'll make sure I get through it. No matter what."

Bilson turns to the others. "And with that, we've gotta go. If I don't get Miles somewhere I can kiss him in the next minute or two, I'm worried I'll do it right here in the bar."

My heart soars, and when Bilson lets go of me and stands, I hurry to follow him.

"I'm happy for you," Tripp says. "But don't rush into anything. I almost did that with divorcing Dex, and if he hadn't been so stubborn, things might not have turned out the way they did."

I look from him to his husband and back again, trying to imagine a world where they aren't together. "Nah, there's no way. I read all about your story on the ride here, and no matter what way things happened, you were always going to end up here."

"Dex wouldn't be Dex without Human Tripp," Bilson agrees.

"Quit calling me that."

"Sorry, man, I didn't know you before the dog. So he gets name rights."

Tripp sighs. "I'm going to kill Aleks."

"Good for you." Bilson slaps his shoulder. "Miles, we're down to thirty seconds. Don't mean to freak you out, babe, but you better run."

CHAPTER THIRTY-THREE

BILSON

We barely made it back to my hotel room without touching each other, and the second we got behind closed doors, we were naked and coming. It was the dirtiest, quickest, hottest hand job of my life.

But even better than that is the way we are now: wrapped around each other, skin on skin, face-to-face, and breathing one another in.

We're sated, still trying to recover, but it's the quiet in my brain that really does it for me. There's no buzzing doubt, no voice in my head telling me I have to hold on to him any way I can so he doesn't run away.

The thing is, out of all my relationships, Miles has the most reason to leave. Sure, he came out to Tripp and Dex, and he says he wants to come out to his family, but I would totally understand it if he changed his mind. Or if, when he came out, they disapproved of me so much that he ended it so he could still make them proud.

It's easy to say, "If they don't love me for me, then that's their issue," but if my parents had even shown me a scrap of love growing up that wasn't in the form of money, I'm not so sure I wouldn't do everything I could to keep getting that affection. That support.

I just happened to try to find it in all the wrong places.

Miles finally seems like the right person for that, but I might not be his.

So in a way, I'm scared of him following through, too, because it could be the end of us.

"I guess I should get back to my own room soon," he murmurs, half-asleep. "Roommate and whatnot."

"Poor Rook. Still having to share a room. You can stay here. Just tell everyone you hooked up. It's technically not a lie."

Miles's eyes crack open. "Is that what you want me to tell everyone, or are you saying that because you think it's what I want to hear?"

I cup his face. "You've *just* decided that you want to come out. It doesn't have to be all at once, and I don't want to push you into something you're not ready for. Hell, I don't even know if I'm ready for the world to know about me. I wanted to tell Tripp and Dex so I had someone outside of you to ask for advice."

"Advice on me?"

"For starters. Plus myself. Like all those swirling thoughts about how long I've been this way, why I didn't work it out sooner, and why sex with a teammate was so easy for me to transition into."

Miles snuggles in closer, burying his head in the nook of my shoulder. "I think I knew back in college." He says it so quietly, like he's ashamed that he's known all this time but has been ignoring it.

"It doesn't matter how you worked it out or when or when you were able to admit it to yourself."

"I know that, but ... when my frat brothers started coupling up with guys, I was curious enough to ask a friend of mine to peg me. If that isn't a big *I like cock* flashing neon sign, I don't know what is."

I shake my head. "Nah. You don't have to be gay to like certain sexual acts. Like you said, you had a girl get you off that way."

"But I know it's not straight to think of your queer frat bros while you're being fucked by a woman."

I hesitate. "Okay, I'll give you that one, but I'm just saying enjoying anal can be a straight dude thing too. If God didn't want us to put things up there, he wouldn't have made the prostate a cum trigger."

Miles bursts out laughing, his soft breath on my skin and the sound of happiness warming my gut. "Are you saying you've had some self-exploration? Some sexploration with your own ass?"

"No, but I did do some, umm, internet research on it."

"When?" He pulls back to look at my face.

I bite my lip. "Possibly after the first time you and I had sex? Because I wanted to make sure it was good for you, and I did it right? If there is a right way to have anal. I swear some sites made it seem like finding the prostate is as hard as finding a woman's clit."

His warm smile lights me up inside. "You definitely have no trouble finding it."

"Good." I kiss the tip of his nose. "Stay the night. Tell the team you hooked up, don't tell them anything, it's up to you. They're all so oblivious they probably won't even notice."

"You're right."

"Of course I am." I hope.

—

Luckily, our teammates are just as oblivious as we hoped they'd be, and for the whole three-game road trip, they don't even notice that Miles and I are sharing a room. The other rookie, Viktor, hasn't said anything, and why would he? He gets his room to himself now. No one would question why.

I start to think we could really do this—have a relationship on the DL. Who knows, maybe they are all noticing but staying out of what's not their fucking business?

That's probably wishful thinking, but I like where we're at. I like sleeping in the same bed, waking up together, and then playing hockey, even if we lose.

Which we did on our third game, but I blame it on us all being tired and having to play back-to-back against Arizona after Vegas.

But now that we're on the plane on the flight home, I sense a shift in Miles. It was there before we left for Vegas, and it's there now. This coldness that I can't help thinking is my fault.

Logically, I know it's about his parents, but if it weren't for me, he wouldn't even have to question them. Or at least right now. Maybe never? If I hadn't signed with Nashville and been so desperately hopeless when it came to the opposite sex, Miles and I wouldn't have hooked up, he wouldn't be questioning his love for his parents, and I'd ... I'd probably be married to the very next woman I'd slept with after my breakup with Rina.

I'd be miserable, but at least he'd be blissfully unaware of himself. Though, is that better or worse?

For me, accepting myself hasn't been difficult because I have no one I could disappoint.

"Question," I say randomly.

He glances up from his phone. His hair is in his face, and I want to reach over and push it back, but I don't.

"If the world was about to end, would you rather know about it so you could say goodbye to everyone you loved or be oblivious so when it happens, it's over with quickly?"

He blinks at me. "Should you really be asking this on a plane?"

I chuckle. "Never mind. I was ... thinking that some things are better left unknown, even to those who it's happening to."

Miles's brow furrows, and he's so damn cute when he's confused. I can't pinpoint when I started thinking of him in that way. Cute. Hot. Attractive outside of the social norms. Only that now we're deep in this, everything he does is endearing to me.

His heart must be protected at all costs, and if he comes out to his family, there's a really good chance it'll break. I don't want to be responsible for that.

"Are you high?" he asks.

I wish. "About thirty thousand feet high, yes."

He's derisive as he says, "Stop being weird. That's my job."

I smile, but then he goes back to his phone, and I go back to my overthinking.

When we touch down, we climb into my car so I can drop him off home and pick up Killer from Miles's parents.

"You're not planning on telling them today, are you?" I ask. I shouldn't because it's not my decision, but I need to know if I have to prepare to be kicked out of there for corrupting their little boy.

"Nah. Not today. I ... I don't know when I'll take that leap."

"Sorry, I didn't mean for that to sound like I'm pressuring. I'm actually the opposite. I'm worried I forced your hand with Dex and Tripp, and I don't want that to happen with your parents too."

He reaches over and puts his hand on my thigh. "I followed you to the bar because I wanted to do it. I wasn't thinking you were pressuring me. I was jealous that you had the guts. If and when I come out to my parents, it will be my decision. I promise."

I cover his hand with mine. "Good. Because I don't want to be the source of that kind of stress. You don't need it. Hell, with it being your first full rookie year, something complicated with me is the last thing you need."

"You might be the last thing I need, but you're the first thing I want when I wake up in the morning."

"That might actually be the most romantic thing anyone's ever said to me."

"No wonder you have four ex-wives, then."

"And then you finish with that. Pointing out all my failures."

"Nah, if I was going to point out your failures, I'd also mention that you've played professional hockey for years and still don't have a Stanley Cup."

"I think that's what I love most about you. We can be having a serious moment, and then you make me laugh."

"L ... love?" he croaks.

I wave him off. "You know what I mean." My voice is just as crackly though. Because even though the context of the L-word wasn't a confession of undying love, I do know I feel more for Miles than I ever have for anyone else.

With the others, I thought I was in love. I thought I knew what love felt like. With Miles ... I'm sure of it.

And it scares me to death.

CHAPTER THIRTY-FOUR

MILES

Bilson loves me.

He says he didn't mean it, but I saw his face. He can't lie to me.

My heart feels about seventy billion sizes too big for my chest as I climb out of his car back home. Bilson jumps right out and heads for the house, but I'm ... possibly stroking out, maybe, because I can't get my feet to move.

He loves me.

I've never had someone love me before. Only my family, who kind of have to, but I'm questioning how much they actually mean it. How far that love for me goes.

Whereas Bilson? He knows it all. Every dusty corner of who I am, and he loves me anyway.

He's already at the front door before I remember to follow. I'm like a puppy trailing after his owner, but honestly, it's not wrong. I'd beg for my man.

Mine.

I still can't figure out how the hell his exes let him go. But bad luck to them.

Because he's mine now.

I can hear Mom and Dad talking to him as I push through the front door to join them. Mom's saying something about Killer while he attacks Bilson with kisses, and Dad's laughing at them both while he watches.

I watch too.

The way his eyes are all squinted happily as he leans back, trying to avoid Killer's tongue. His brown hair is a mess, shirt pulled tight over the back I love to grip when he's on top of me, mouth moving with words that wash over me completely.

It's like they're all talking through water.

Bilson loves me, and the ache in my chest at seeing them together, wanting it to be real, almost has me doubling over. My hand slips into my pocket to wrap around Stone and Seddy.

"So proud of you boys ..." Mom says. "And Annette too, of course."

"Bilson's my boyfriend."

The haze snaps, and I look around, trying to figure out where those words came from, but the three shocked faces that swing my way make it clear they came from me.

"Oh, fuck." It sinks in what I've just said. "Oh, *fuck*."

But the knowledge that it's out there doesn't fill me with the dread I'm expecting. Instead ... relief. I'm so relieved my head goes light.

"Miles." Bilson approaches and wraps his arms around me, and I'm not sure if he meant to steady me or to hug me, but I bury my face in his neck anyway. Anything to avoid looking at my parents.

I don't look up as I force all the feelings out of me. "So I'm bi, and I think I have known for a while, but I've never given myself time to think of it as an option because the last thing I ever wanted to do was disappoint you. Or make you love me less. But then I met Bilson, and there was no way to stop myself from falling for him, and now that I know what it's like to be loved without bullshit expectations, it's made it pretty damn clear that I can't change who I am. You're the ones who have to change your mindset. If you want me in your life and if you love me how I've always thought you did, you need to figure it out fast. I'm not straight. I've never been straight. And I know that queer people scare you or make you uncomfortable or whatever the hell the Bible teaches, but please. *Please* try to remember you love me, a real person you made, more than some imaginary dude in the sky."

Bilson's arms squeeze me tight as he whispers, "I'm so proud of you."

My soul lights up at the words, even though the silence that follows them makes me feel sick.

When I can't handle it anymore, I grit my teeth, step back, and turn to face them.

There are tears running down Mom's cheeks, and Dad's face is buried in his hands.

That can't be fucking good.

"God dammit," Dad mutters.

I brace for what's coming.

"Miles, I ... We thought we failed as parents when you became a goalie, but this is ... this is ..."

"Not something I chose," I snap, and Bilson's hand settles on my lower back.

"What?" Dad frowns at me. "You didn't fail us. We failed you."

I turn to Mom.

"I'm so sorry," she chokes out. "I ... I don't know what to say."

"We had a ... a feeling," Dad says. "Thought something was different about your friendship."

"We hoped we were reading too much into it."

"Hoped?" My voice cracks.

"No, not hoped. More ..." She looks to Dad for help.

"Didn't wanna assume," he says. "We both figured you would have come to us and we were being silly."

"But we did some reading," Mom adds quickly, slowly sounding more like herself. "There isn't anyone we could have talked to about it, and we wanted to know things, just in case. You were always talking about those fraternity brothers of yours, honey, and then Cody ... I couldn't shake the feeling."

"You ... you knew?"

Bilson steps closer, and having him here to anchor me, having his familiar scent and presence right by my side, gives me that burst of confidence I need.

"Why didn't you say anything? Growing up ... the things you used to say ... all that 'hate the sin, love the sinner' bullshit? What happened to that?"

"We love you," Dad says simply.

"It isn't that easy. I'm with a man. You'll have to tell people, people at your church, that your son has a boyfriend. I'm not going to hide it. I want a chance to have a real relationship, same as anyone else. And you can't tell me you love me and support me now, then get all embarrassed when people are talking about me. Because you know they will."

"We know," Mom says and shares a look with Dad. "We've had a lot of talks about it. Done a lot of reading. I'm not going to lie and say it was easy to unlearn everything we've always believed, because it's not. But let me make one thing clear: we will never, ever be embarrassed by you. When you're a parent who loves their kid, it really is that easy."

I have to bury my teeth into my lip to hold back tears.

"God," Dad scoffs. "We embraced you being a weirdo a long time ago, and if anything, you having a boyfriend is a lot less concerning than you talking to inanimate objects."

The laugh that hiccups from me is pure relief.

"I dunno," Bilson says, finally joining in. "The way he thinks they answer back has to take the cake."

I shake him off me. "I didn't say they *talked* back. I can just feel what they'd say if they could."

Bilson lets out two short whistles as he circles his finger by his ear.

Dad clearly agrees. "Good luck handling that one."

But I'm more than happy for them to tease me because it means … it means …

Fuck.

I actually did it.

And it hasn't blown up in my face.

Mom is still crying, so I move closer to pull her into a hug. "I love you so much," she sobs.

"I'm not going to lie, I'm still waiting for you guys to wake up out of this trance and change your minds."

"I'm so sorry you were worried."

"Me too."

"Just be patient with us. Please. We've both still got a lot of learning to do." She lets me go and dries her eyes. "Are you both going to stay for lunch?"

"Are we welcome?"

"Always."

"Yeah," Dad says, patting Killer. "We love Cody."

The happiness on Bilson's face lights up the goddamn room.

"Me too," I say softly.

Our eyes meet, hold for a moment, and then he clears his throat and turns to my folks. "Do you mind if we take Killer for a walk first?"

"Not at all."

He whistles to our baby and all but drags me from the room and out the front door.

"Where did you want to—*oomph*."

My back slams into the wall as Bilson covers my body with his.

His lips meet mine, tongue surging forward into my mouth while I grip the front of his jacket. We kiss until my lips feel bruised, and I drown in the sound of the satisfied groan he lets out.

"You love me?" he asks, pulling away to kiss along my jaw.

"Did you really think your stammering in the car hid what you said? You don't let that word drop and cover it up with the whole 'you know … platonically but with fucking kind of love, not love love.' Idiot."

"Hey, I hid it well."

"Not at all. But it's okay. Because I love you too, and I'm not going anywhere."

His smile is weary. "Lots of people have said that to me before."

I scowl, about to tell him that's not romantic *or* bromantic, when he continues.

"But I think that's the first time I've ever believed it. I've had four different people promise their lives to me, and none of them made me feel as secure as you do."

"Good. And I should probably let you know that no one else will ever promise themselves to you again. Just so we're clear. You're mine."

One corner of his lips hitches up. "Did I hear you say boyfriend earlier?"

"Sure did, bro."

"I liked it."

"I know. I might be a slut for your cock, but you're a slut for affection. For being wanted. I know how to keep my man happy."

He grabs the backs of my thighs and hauls me off my feet. "And I know how to keep *my* man happy, even without my dick."

"Oh, yeah?"

"Yeah. Starting with telling you that I think you're incredible."

Ah, shit, he's right. That does feel good.

"And brave—on the ice, but especially back in there. You always blow me away with who you are, Rook. You can't be surprised I fell ass over tit in love with you."

"Yeah, but you fall ass over tit a lot."

Something serious crosses his face. "It's because I've had all those relationships that I can say confidently that I don't. This is a first for me. I'm not trying to minimize that I *did* really like those women, but it wasn't love. It was … desperation. That's why it never worked. You don't make me feel so insecure that I keep pushing to be a better partner so I end up smothering you. You just want me. I've never had that."

"And while that's all I ever want from you, I'm a bit of an attention whore too. I don't think it's possible for you to smother me."

Killer yaps loudly, startling us out of our moment.

"All right, all right, we're coming," I tell him.

Bilson takes my hand as we follow Killer, darting off toward the trees. I'm still struggling to believe we get to do this. Just because.

"How are you feeling?" he asks.

"Happy. Annoyed. Scared they'll change their minds."

"You know I'm here."

"That's the only thing that got me through it." I only wish they'd been more careful with their opinions; then maybe I never would have been worried. I glance over at him. "Are you okay I told them?"

"Of course. It wasn't something I had an opinion on either way, so long as you were making the choice for you."

"And ... what next?"

He squeezes my hand. "Coming out publicly, you mean?"

"Yeah. Is that something you want to do?"

"I–I don't want to hide us, but I really don't want all the attention that goes along with our relationship. Some of our teammates have been through multiple girlfriends this season, sometimes at the same time, and no one looked twice. It won't be like that for us."

I get exactly where he's coming from. "Then let's do neither."

"What do you mean?"

"We don't have to come out, but we don't have to hide us either. It's like you said, people believe the bromance because it's what they want to believe. I'm sure there'll be questions when we're seen holding hands or whatever, but we don't have to confirm shit."

"Damn, I'm smart sometimes."

I pull him to a stop so I can kiss his scruffy cheek. "Thank you."

"You're welcome, but also, why?"

"For giving me everything."

CHAPTER THIRTY-FIVE

BILSON

We figure the first thing we should do is give Lucia a heads-up. Who knows? Maybe she'll murder us, and the word of us being together won't come out at all.

After our next practice, we head for the PR department.

Since coming out to his parents, Miles is like a new person. He has a spring in his step, and he slaps my ass in the locker room without caring if anyone calls it out, which they don't because, you know, jock rules: touching other people's butts is okay as long as it has to do with sports.

He seems ... free.

And I love seeing him with this newfound freedom. While also kind of dreading it because I'm sure I'm going to fuck us up somehow.

I have relationship PTSD.

I wasn't lying when I told him it's different with him—I don't have that same need I've had in the past where I worry about holding on to him—but I can't help wondering how long that's going to last. What happens when there's insecurity or jealousy or we fight?

He says he can't see a time where my affection could be annoying, but he's also never seen the extent of my neediness when I'm peak Bilson.

When we get to Lucia's door, I pull on Miles's hand. "Just double-checking you're okay with taking this step?"

"It's not like we're telling everyone. Wait … are you still okay with this?"

I nod but swallow hard.

"We don't have to if you're unsure."

"Nah. I'm all good." Again, for now. Doing this isn't going to change anything. Not really. It's the next step that might make me break.

Miles knocks, and as soon as Lucia answers, he turns on his boyish charm. "I have bad news for you, Chia."

She slumps. "What have you two done now?"

"Nothing. Everything. Nothing bad, I mean." Miles loses some of his confidence. "It's that your and my impending marriage is off."

"Oh no," she deadpans. "How will I cope? Please, tell me why we could never be?"

"I'm a taken man now."

She glances between me and Miles, and she slumps. "You two didn't run off and get married, did you?"

"Why do I feel like that's directed at you?" Miles asks me.

"She went with the odds?"

"So who is the lucky la—" She stops herself from finishing *lady* and side-eyes me. "Person?"

I raise my hand. "That would be me, but we're not married. We're … together."

To her credit, she doesn't even flinch or act shocked. "Good to know. What's your game plan here? Do you have one? Want to release a statement, a press conf—"

"No," we both say at the same time.

"We kind of want to keep it quiet," I say.

"Not because we're ashamed," Miles adds, almost panicking. "We're not. I'd have sex with Cody on the ice if he'd let me."

"What he means is we don't really want to deal with the pressure of having the media, our teammates, and the whole circus that goes along with it, but if it comes out, or this one says he's not going to come out and then blurts it all over the place like he did with his parents …" I point at Miles. "Then we wanted to tell you first so you know how to deal with it if it happens."

She holds her heart. "Aww, I love when idiots fall in love and have the sense to give me notice before I find out by reading it online. Your old PR manager was wrong, Cody. You're not impulsive and annoying at all."

"I take offense," I protest.

"Do you though?"

"I'm not annoying. I'm delightful."

"I notice you didn't say you weren't impulsive," Lucia says.

"I've been married four times, became a free agent so I'd stop running into them, and then had sex with a teammate because we couldn't find a woman who wanted to be the meat in our sandwich. I think if I were to argue the impulsive thing, you'd send me for a psych evaluation."

"Fair point," Lucia says. "I'll whip up a few different statements to keep on hand in case you can't rein in that impulsiveness. I also might suggest you tell your agents and give them the heads-up, but I don't see this becoming a problem with your contracts. Also make sure you tell someone if your teammates are dicks about it whenever you tell them. And ignore the rednecks in the stands who'll scream ignorant shit. You're welcome here."

Oh, look, my fake smile is back.

Miles takes my hand. "You okay?"

"Uh-huh," I say numbly. Because we're not telling anyone yet. It's still fine. It's all good. The only people who know are Lucia, Dex, and Tripp. That's all who need to know at this point.

Miles has to practically drag me out of the office because the weight of reality makes my feet feel like lead.

The thick fog of doubt and uncertainty, media scrutiny, and endless jokes about more failed marriages blankets me.

I squeeze Miles's hand and try to bring myself back from panic, but it claws at me, making me hold tighter and tighter.

"Fuck," Miles hisses and then backs me against the wall in the corridor. "What's wrong, what's happening, why do you look like you're about to pass out?"

"What if we're a mistake?" The words tumble from me.

His eyes turn sad, but he doesn't let it show for long. "You think we're a mistake suddenly?"

"No. Yes? I'm confused. It's real now."

"It hasn't been real for you?"

"It has, but ..." I shake my head. "When we thought we couldn't actually be together or have a proper future, the worry of you leaving me wasn't there because I knew you would do it. I didn't try to smother you to make you stay because you were never going to stay. You were always going to leave, and I was okay with that. But now ..."

"Now I actually want to be with you, and come out with you, and do this relationship for real ... you, what? Don't want it anymore?"

It makes absolutely no rational sense, and I know that, but I can't help it. This is me. This is what I do in relationships. "That's the problem. We have an actual chance. You could potentially be my endgame. I want it so much

270

that the thought of losing you, the thought of me being too much and making you walk away … what if I repeat the same mistakes? What if—"

Miles kisses me right here where anyone could see, but I don't push him away. Because when his mouth is on mine, the fear goes away. Nothing else exists.

He breaks his mouth from mine once I've calmed down a bit. "Cody." He sounds patient now, but really, how long is that going to last?

"Mmm?"

"I know you're a mess when it comes to relationships. You have baggage. Someone your age will always come with baggage." He smirks.

"Fuck you."

Now he's laughing. Of course.

"If you're unsure, talk to me," he says. "If you're feeling insecure, I'll be there to remind you that I'm here. That I'm yours."

"And when that fails and I get possessive and ask where you've been and why you weren't home on time and—"

Miles presses a finger against my lips. "Can I ask something, and I really want you to think about it. Don't say the first thing that comes to your head; truly think."

"Okay …"

"What changed between telling my parents and coming here to talk to Lucia?"

I press my lips together and really think. "Telling her made this serious."

"Come on. We've been serious since we met. Best friends who fuck. That's what we've been the whole time. It hasn't changed. The only difference is it won't be a secret anymore."

"What if I go and ruin it by proposing?"

"You won't need to worry about that."

"Why?"

"Because I'll say no. I, Miles Jonathon Olsen, solemnly swear to never let you walk down the aisle again. Ever."

"Then how will we know that we have our happily ever after?"

"Tell me. Have any of your marriage licenses been proof of your happiness?"

"No, but—"

"Happily ever after is what makes you happy. Not what society says will mean you're happy."

The lingering nerves finally leave me, and I take a deep breath. "I really hate that you have your shit together at your age. Shouldn't I be the one giving you life advice?"

"Maybe on what not to do?"

"You little punk."

"You love me this way though."

Yeah, I do.

CHAPTER THIRTY-SIX

MILES

So Bilson's total freak-out wasn't solved by a kiss—who knew? The thing is, with the weight of coming out to my family off my shoulders, I have all the time and energy for whatever he has to throw at me.

Worried about him questioning where I've been and who with? Joke's on him, because wherever I've been, he's likely to be there too.

Worried about him smothering me with love? My man's forgetting I'm needy as fuck. We're barely apart, and I know he's worried about that making me sick of him or whatever, but it's not going to happen.

He's my best friend because I love spending time with him.

He's my boyfriend because I love everything else.

It's freeing being able to sleep over at his place or in his room at away games, to show up for training and games together, and even go on dates, all without looking over my shoulder and worrying about who sees. We're team-mates in a bromance, so people expect to see us together, which means when we are, no one pays us attention.

That was Bilson's whole theory, but it seems he's forgotten.

He has baggage. I get it. I'll love him anyway and keep reminding him what a dumbass he's being.

"You invited us here for a game night and didn't get nachos? What is wrong with you?" Stoll grumbles, taking a slice of pizza.

Bilson tips his beer Stoll's way. "I don't get paid enough to feed all you animals anything but this."

"Animals?" Finch drops his mouth in shock, showing off the half-chewed food inside. "I have no idea what you mean."

"There are potato chips crushed into the carpet," I point out, perching on the arm of Bilson's chair. He stiffens, just like I knew he would, but sometimes I push how close I can get us before there's a Bilson-shaped hole in the wall.

He knows exactly what I'm doing, too. He calls me on it when we're fucking, and he won't let me come. Like that's some kind of punishment for making sure he knows I'm his. I won't scare easily.

It's gotten to the point I don't even think he knows what he's freaking out about anymore, but for all his talk of not wanting people to know about us, sometimes I think it'd be better for him if he ripped the Band-Aid off.

No hiding. No secrets. No anxiety over the future.

"It's about to start," Jorgensen says. "Who are we going for?"

"Not the Kiki brothers." Am I still bitter about how easily they score on me? You betcha. Those assholes are the only ones I can never get a read on, even when I know the exact play they're setting up for.

"Don't make me go for Buffalo," Stoll protests. "Little Dalton's attitude stinks."

"He had a killer rookie year though," I point out. "How many people in this room have a Stanley Cup ring?"

There are a few exchanged glances and some glares thrown my way.

Bilson picks up my hand. "Nothing here either. Does that mean he's a better rookie than you?"

I shrug, playing up my ego. "It's so hard to soar like an eagle when you're surrounded by turkeys."

There's boos and sneers right before a couch cushion belts me in the face.

"For that, I'm going for Colorado."

"Wow. I thought teams were supposed to back each other. But no. All it takes is a reminder that I'm better than everyone else—"

A second cushion hits me, harder this time.

"Hey," Bilson snaps. "Stop throwing shit at Rook."

"Thanks, CB."

"You almost hit me."

I sigh because it's so hard to get love these days.

"Are we watching or what?" Jorgensen calls over the top of everyone.

"Who wants to play a drinking game?" I ask. "We drink every time Connor plays the pass to Easton for the sniper shot. So predictable."

"Works on you every game though, doesn't it?" Finch says through more pizza.

I grumble, "Shut up," under my breath.

While we wait for the game to start, there's footage of the teams during warm-ups, and one of the first things I notice is the pride tape covering both of the Kiki brothers' sticks. My heart gives a kick, and Bilson shifts beside me. It's a pretty common thing for players to show their support, but I think this is the first time I've seen it since acknowledging who I am.

As much as I try to fight it, I soften toward those two— only a little. And only because we're not the ones up against them tonight.

The footage goes back to the commentators, who talk briefly about the pride tape before the screen switches again to the ice, where they're waiting for the puck drop.

It's an intense first period. Somehow, Buffalo keeps them from scoring, even with the Kiki brothers on the top of their game—I try not to feel bitter about that. I know the crowd always hates low-scoring games, but it's thrilling for me. Seeing the saves from both goalies, watching how they move and position themselves in the crease. It's like hockey porn.

Though I can't help but notice neither of them makes sure Annette is hydrated.

The team leave the ice, and the cable reporter pulls up Easton Kikishkin to interview. Connor immediately stops too, looming behind him like they aren't the same height.

"The pride tape in warm-ups was a nice surprise," the reporter says. "But with no points on the board, what would you say to the people who claim theme nights and symbolic gestures are more of a distraction than anything?"

Easton doesn't hold back. "I'd tell them that if a bit of tape was all that stood between me and the game of my life, maybe I don't deserve to be playing in the NHL."

"It's a mental game as well as physical though, isn't it?"

"Of course it is. Which is why, mentally, representing who I am only gives me more fire."

"Who ... wait." The reporter is clearly trying to piece together what Easton's said, the same way my teammates are. Quiet falls over the room.

Finch's head swivels between us all. "Did he just come out?"

"Think so."

"Are you a member of the LGBTQ community?" the reporter asks, stumbling over the question.

Connor slings his arm around Easton's shoulders. "My brother's sexuality isn't important here. Who he loves has zero impact on him being one of the best snipers in the game and one of the best people I know."

The interview ends, cutting to ads, and while the room is still quiet, I start laughing.

"Well, that was one way to do it."

"In the middle of a game too," Stoll points out. "Won't that psych him out?"

"Maybe it's a play," Finch suggests. "To get into Buffalo's head. Coming out is a big thing, isn't it? Does he think Ayri Quinn and Asher Dalton will take it easier on him because they're ... you know?"

"Queer," Jorgensen fills in. "You can say it."

"Sorry." Finch goes red. "I don't know any queer people. Don't want to say something wrong."

They start debating labels and locker room etiquette, and it occurs to me that Bilson hasn't said anything. He's got his phone out, scrolling down the screen.

"What's wrong?"

He glances up, and he doesn't look happy. "People are already talking about it."

"Little Kiki coming out?"

"Yeah, and ... there's a lot of good, but ..."

"Assholes can't help being assholes."

He glances around to make sure no one is listening before dropping his voice. "That could be us."

"Probably will be one day. But a stranger's opinion doesn't mean anything to me. You and my family have my back. That's all I need."

His teeth sink into his lip as he looks down at his phone again.

I reach down and cover the screen. "Stop looking."

Then he huffs a laugh. "Ezra just posted, 'Welcome, you queer-do.'"

"Sounds like him."

"Oh, wow."

"What?"

"The other Collective guys are posting too."

That makes me smile. "See? Little Kiki isn't alone. And we won't be either."

He glances up at me suddenly. "I want to do it."

"Support them? Go for it. Plenty of straight dudes are."

"No ... not just support. It's getting too much. I know we said down-low was better and it would be fun and freeing, but I don't feel free. I hate that I'm always worried about fucking up. About taking it too far and giving us away."

"Ah ... guys?"

We glance over at Finch. "Giving, umm, what away?"

By his tone, we clearly weren't as quiet as we thought we were. The game is back on, but none of us are paying attention.

I turn back to Bilson. "I'm down for anything, CB."

He exhales, looking like he's letting out every worry he's ever had. When he talks, it's so fast I think he's lost control of his mouth. "There's no bromance. We're dating. Me and Rook. All homo, butts and dicks and—"

I quickly cover his mouth to stop whatever *that* was. "What he means to say is our bromance is more of a romance with lots of love and hearts and stuff."

He shakes me off. "Yeah. That."

"Wait." Finch almost climbs over his seat. "Now *you* guys are coming out? Both of you?"

"Sure are."

"Holy shit. Can I say holy shit?"

"Say whatever you want, just don't be a homophobic dick."

Stoll laughs. "But apparently, you guys like dicks."

Jorgensen rubs his jaw. "You're sending mixed signals, Olsen."

Olsen. Not rookie.

Best. Day. Ever.

Bilson pulls me from the arm of the couch into his lap. "Let us clear it up, then: the only dicks we're interested in are each other's."

"I dunno, we haven't tried gay porn yet."

"Fine. The only dicks we're interested in are each other's *and* maybe the ones in pornos."

"We're all interested in the ones in pornos," Stoll says. "Doesn't make you special, dude."

"Maybe we're all a little homo, then."

"And little Kiki scored," Jorgensen says, pulling our attention back to the screen. Easton and Connor are hugging, like every goal, and the rest of the team are back or ass slapping like usual.

Bilson nudges me. "I'm going to post."

"Me too, then."

"You sure? It can just be about me. You don't have to."

"Are you okay with everyone knowing about us?"

His big arm tightens around me. "Definitely."

"Then post."

He sucks in a breath, and I watch as he shares the Easton quote the NHL page has shared, then types one-handed, *Welcome to the team.* Then he adds a rainbow emoji.

I kiss his cheek as he hits Post, then immediately click on it to share and add, *But keep your hands off Bilson, he's mine.*

Almost immediately, I have a comment from Stoll: *Maybe you should keep your hands off each other and just watch the damn game, already?*

I glance over at him as he sends me a wink. "We got you."

"Yeah, but seriously," Jorgensen says after commenting, *We love you guys, but come out quieter. I almost missed little Kiki's goal.* "If anyone messes with you, they'll have us to deal with."

"Thanks." I might not have been with the team for long, but they already have my back.

"We're a team. Watch our net and not your boyfriend, and everything will be okay with us."

"Deal."

Bilson takes both our phones and sets them on the floor beside us. "Nothing on there is going to make this day any better. Now I can stop worrying about blowing our cover and focus on worrying about screwing this up."

"And I'll focus on reminding you that's impossible."

He gives me a soft kiss. "You know, you basically gave me a promise ring the day we met."

"I did?"

He points to the friendship bracelet he's still wearing. *My guy, CB.* "It's how I knew. Almost immediately. You were kinda special. And ..." He shifts to pull something out of his pocket. "This is me, not proposing but wanting you to know you're kinda special too."

Bilson opens his fist to show off the friendship bracelet there. *CB♥Rook*.

"Aww ... baby ..." I hold out my arm.

He can't hold back his smugness as he ties it around my wrist. "Full disclosure, your mom stole these out of your room for me."

"Lucky I don't keep them in the drawer with my sex toys."

"In what world *would* you keep them there?"

I shrug. "I'm a goalie."

He glances over at where Stone and Seddy are sitting in their glass of beer. "At least I know our lives will be interesting."

"Always." I take his face in my hands. "Through all the smothering and the weirdness, you've promised yourself to me. No take backsies."

"No take backsies."

A cushion hits us both this time. "You're both very cute and whatever, but *dear God*, shut up."

I laugh and melt back against Bilson, surprisingly not sad when Colorado beat Buffalo 2 to 1. Because Dex was right, the little genius. All the other stuff doesn't matter.

I have Bilson, and he's my everything.

EPILOGUE

BILSON

The official Queer Collective Palooza this year is being held in Ezra and Anton's large Boston apartment.

Coming out midseason, even if it was in solidarity with someone Miles and I can't stand, might have not been the best idea because no matter what was going on with the game, we had interviews to face and questions to answer. Not only from the media but from Ezra Palaszczuk, self-appointed ringleader of the Collective.

The audacity for Miles and me to come out without consulting him first. The gall. The *gumption*.

We didn't hear the end of it the two times we played him throughout the rest of the season, and we're still not hearing the end of it now. He told us to be here at five but told everyone else six, just so he can drill us with all the questions he wants to know.

Like do we have a sex mentor and did we do enough research.

He's currently trying to offer to have us watch him and Anton have sex to make sure we're doing it right.

Miles leans in and whispers in my ear, "How can I be so scared yet turned on at the same time?"

I snort.

"Anything you'd like to share with the class?"

"Uhm, yeah. Does your boyfriend know you're offering to have us watch you have sex?"

"He does not," Anton says, entering the room at the exact right moment. "Is he still bitching you two out for not giving him the heads-up?"

"Yup," I say. "And making sure we're doing all the gay things correctly."

Anton just sighs, turns, and walks back out of the room.

"Fine, I won't be your sex mentor. Who's your queer mentor, then? I can help with that."

"Uh, well, I got pretty close to Aleks in Seattle," I say.

"I have a whole bunch of frat brothers who are queer."

"Why won't you need me for something?"

"Ignore him. He has issues," Anton yells from wherever he disappeared to.

Miles and I look at each other, and as if having a silent conversation, we both stand and then rush Ezra in a hug.

"We need all your advice," I say.

Miles nods. "All of it. How do two men have sex anyway? Whose penis goes inside whose?"

Ezra pulls back. "That all depends on who's cut and uncut. It won't work with two cut guys."

Miles stutters. "U-umm, what?"

I turn to him. "We're so not doing whatever the fuck he's talking about."

"Ah, yes! I can teach you something, even though you were being condescending and pretending to need me even though you don't. Gentlemen, take a seat, and let me introduce you to the wonderful world of docking."

Thank God Ezra's doorbell sounds.

"I'll get it," I say.

"No, let me." Miles and I practically run for the door, trying to push the other back to where I'm ninety percent sure Ezra was about to lose his pants.

I get to the door first, but as it flies open, Miles snarls at Easton Kikishkin standing there, all caramel-colored hair, pouty lips, and blue eyes.

I tap my boyfriend's ass. "Be nice."

"I am nice! I'm always nice. It's not my fault that my inner hockey player is jealous of Easton's talent. And I'm still angry at him for kicking us out of the first round of the playoffs."

Easton cracks a smile. "I want to say that it wasn't me but my entire team, but I'll take it. It was all my doing."

I step aside. "Come in. Ezra was taunting us over being baby bis and trying to give us sex tips. Come and join the chaos."

"I really hope you're joking," Easton says.

"Unfortunately, he's not, and if we have to endure it, so do you." Miles turns on his heel.

"Don't mind him. He was really hoping to pull an Asher Dalton and bring home the Cup his rookie year."

"Ugh. I think we all hate Little Dalton for that."

We head down the hall.

"You can talk, Little Kiki. You had a killer rookie season, too, last year."

"I'm middle Kiki. Little Kiki will be getting drafted this year."

"Oh, God, there's three of you. I hope Colorado doesn't get him too. I have a feeling the three of you on a team would be unstoppable."

"That's the plan, but I doubt it'll happen. Lachie will be top three pick easy. He's probably got the most talent out of all of us."

"Okay, now I'm going to hate him too."

Easton laughs.

We go into the living area, where Miles is back on the couch, but Ezra has disappeared. In his place at his built-in bar is Anton.

"Ez?" Anton calls out. "What are you doing?"

"Trying to peel the tip of a carrot for a demonstration!"

"Kikishkin is here."

"Does he want to learn about docking too?"

Easton's gaze flits between us like he's trying to figure out if Ezra is serious or not. "I'm, uh, all good on that front, thanks."

"For fuck's sake." Anton heads into their kitchen.

"Was he being for real?" Easton asks.

"We really hope not," I answer.

Anton and Ezra return, and Ezra's sulking.

"Apparently, I'm not allowed to make you uncomfortable with sex stuff. Not on your first official meeting or whatever." Ezra hangs his head.

"Damn. I'm really curious how the carrot turned out," Easton says.

Ezra's face lights up, and he looks at Anton with puppy dog eyes.

Anton puts his hands up. "It's Easton's choice. I was just saying don't scare them off with your enthusiasm."

Ezra turns to Easton. "Let's go. It's like a work of art."

"Of course you'd think a carrot in the shape of a dick is art," Anton calls after him and then brings us drinks and sits on the opposite couch from us. "Sorry about him. He's like an excitable puppy when new people join the Collective. He's determined to take over the entire NHL. One queer player for every team. Oh, which reminds me, when he asks one of you to trade so we can achieve that goal, tell him to fuck off. I give you permission."

"There's no way I'm leaving Nashville," Miles says.

"Ditto."

I know it's only been one season, but I love the team, where I live, but most of all, I love that Nashville is where my heart is. With Miles.

Do I still freak out about losing him? Not as much, but it's still there. That type of insecurity doesn't just go away, but I am getting better. And Miles is amazing at calling me on my crap and talking through my issues instead of trying to cover them up with grand gestures and relationship Band-Aids.

The doorbell rings again, and more Collective guys arrive. Ezra and Anton's place fills with queer hockey players, past and present, and before long, everyone is accounted for.

Drinks flow, and if I ever had any doubts about going public, this right here makes them all go away. The support system these guys are building for players like Miles and me. For Easton or anyone else in the league struggling with who they are. This is important.

They welcomed me even when they thought I was straight—hell, even when I thought I was straight—but now I see this whole Collective thing differently. Throughout the rest of the season, we'd had games against them as individuals. We'd smack-talk, then drink together like the best of friends. Being in the one room with them all, including the guys who have already retired, it's more than support. It's like we have our own little family.

Holy. Shit.

The thing I've been searching for in a partner has been what these guys have with each other. Family.

Sure, Miles is my everything, but he doesn't have to hold the burden of being the only one to make me happy. Support, platonic love, family ... This is the missing piece I never had with anyone else. It was too much pressure to put on one person, which is why I'd always drive them away.

But not Miles. He's adamant to stick around, despite my tendency to be smothering sometimes, because he might be the only person I've met who understands that my childhood neglect is a part of me.

His hand slips into mine. "What are you thinking about? You look kinda spaced out."

I squeeze his hand. "That you're perfect for me."

"Duh."

"And that even though our teammates tell us to get our lips off each other and our heads in the game, with these guys? I can do this whenever I want." I lean in and press my lips to his, and it leads to hoots and hollers from around us.

Aleks, my old teammate, pipes up. "You know, when you said you'd blow a guy to become a full-fledged Collective member, we didn't think you were serious."

"Funny, neither did I, but I'm glad I did it. Obviously." I pull Miles close.

"Though, technically, we bypassed all that stuff and went straight to anal. Advanced from the beginning."

Ezra turns to Anton. "So he can talk about sex, but I can't?"

Everyone lets out a "Yes" at the same time.

I grin.

Ezra flips us all the double bird and then jumps up on the cushion of his armchair. "While we have you all here—"

"You say that like you didn't send out mass email after mass email saying it was a mandatory meeting," Asher snarks.

"Yes, this amazing coincidence that was totally not planned and every detail worked out down to the minute is finally here. Anton and I have an announcement."

"You're getting married?" Dex asks.

"Bilson! How could you?" Aleks yells in my direction.

"What did I do?" I ask.

"Sorry. I heard married and got ahead of myself," Aleks says. "Continue, Ez."

Ezra continues. "We're not getting married—"

"Yet," Anton interrupts.

Ezra looks lovingly at his boyfriend, and I bet they'll be married by the end of next season.

"What I actually wanted to bring you all here for is now that we have New York"—he points to Ollie Strömberg, one of our retirees, and then to Caleb Sorensen, the other retired dude—"New Jersey, Montreal ..." He goes around pointing out all of the teams that have at least one queer dude on it. "We have enough."

"Enough queer guys?" Tripp asks. "Like, you want to cap the Collective?"

Ezra frowns. "What? Fuck no. I want more! We have to get a full set eventually."

"Coming to a sex toy store near you," Oskar calls out.

"My point is we have enough to play an all-queer LGBTQ charity event. Soren and Ollie can come out of retirement for one game. We can play three-on-three. We have two goalies now ..."

"My brother's best friend is a ref for the PWHL and queer if you need someone to ref it," Easton says.

"Brother's best friend?" Oskar asks. "Ever hit that?"

"No," Easton grumbles. "If I hit that, Connor would hit him even harder, though not in the fun way."

"Yeah, even I wouldn't be dumb enough to do that if I were single," Ezra says.

Westly and Asher Dalton look at each other and then back to Ezra with confused looks on their faces.

"Again. Look! I'm learning. But also, Connor Kikishkin is a hell of a lot scarier than West." Ezra turns to his best friend. "No offense."

"None taken. I never got the chance to play against Connor, but he's intimidating as hell."

Easton crosses his arms. "Hence the reason why I'm perpetually single. Everyone is scared of my brother. Connor would play for the charity game, too, if you ask him. He's not queer, but he supports me. Would be good to invite allies to play. Show that the gay isn't catching. Can't have that shit flying around the place."

"Ooh, the Dalton brothers versus the Kiki Brothers?" Ezra asks. "That would be amazing."

"Nah, fuck that," Asher says. "Little Kiki and me against the old fellas."

West gets Asher in a headlock.

Ezra jumps up and down like a kid, bouncing on the cushion. "This is awesome. Are we all in?"

I glance at Miles out the side of my eye, but he's already looking at me.

"If it's too much pressure to be that public," he says in a low voice.

"Not too public at all. It's a good idea. I want to be out there, next to you, proud to stand up for something bigger than me. Bigger than us. Do you think your parents would be okay with you displaying that much gayness publicly?"

"We'd be playing hockey, not fucking on the ice—wait." He turns to Ezra. "We won't be having a huge gay orgy on the ice, will we?"

"I wish," Oskar mutters.

"What is wrong with you?" Ezra asks.

"He's a goalie," Aleks says. "Cut him some slack."

"Hey! This isn't a weird goalie thing," Miles exclaims. "Before you all got here, he tried to give a docking demonstration. I've been too scared to even google it!"

Everyone laughs, but I lean in.

"Don't worry about it. I got you. I googled in the bathroom earlier. Let's just say it wouldn't work for us anyway." We're both cut.

Asher rubs his jaw. "I wish I could say this was a new low for Ezra, but sadly, this is just a new medium for him."

Anton agrees. "I should protest on my man's behalf, but I really can't. He peeled a carrot in the shape of an uncut dick."

Ezra holds up his hands like he's innocent. "I'm hilarious, and honestly, babe, I think it says more about you than me that you're in love with all this." He waves his hand over his body.

"Also something I can't protest," Anton mumbles.

Foster Grant, the latest Queer Collective member to take out the coveted Stanley Cup, stands with his phone in his hand. "While all of you are fighting, I've got an LGBTQ hockey charity on board for the game."

Right. The game.

"So we're in?" I ask Miles.

"I'm in with everything when it comes to you."

"Even—"

"Except marriage."

It might be weird that Miles never wanting to marry me makes me happy, but it's only because I know why. He'd rather face our relationship issues head-on, and he won't let me use marriage as a fix for an argument.

He wants me to know he's with me by choice and not for legal reasons.

He wants me just the way I am.

"Whatever gets thrown our way, we'll go through it together," he says.

"That's all I need to know." I kiss his nose, and then we turn to Ezra.

In unison, we say, "We're in."